To Every Season

To Every Season

A novel about the early Quakers in Piedmont North Carolina

Nancy Learned Haines

Pleasant Green Books Hillsborough, NC 2024

To Every Season

This is a work of fiction. Names, characters, organizations, events or locales
in this novel are either the product of the author's imagination or, if real,
are used fictitiously. Any resemblance to actual persons, living or dead, is
entirely coincidental.

ISBN (paperback) 978-0-9979848-1-1
ISBN (e-book) 978-0-9979848-2-8

Cover & Book Design by Melissa Bourbon
www.WriterSparkBookCovers.com

214 Pleasant Green Road
Hillsborough, NC 27278

nlhaines@gmail.com

A Note About Eighteenth-Century Quakers

In the eighteenth century, British citizens were expected to defer to individuals of authority or higher social rank, addressing them in the plural as "you," rather than the singular "thee" or "thou." Quakers, as a form of social and spiritual protest, refused to follow this practice. Their founder, George Fox, explained that when God spoke to him, "He forbade me to put off my hat to any, high or low; and I was required to *thee* and *thou* all men and women, without any respect to rich or poor, great or small." Naturally, Quakers used the plural "you" when talking to more than one person. By the time of this story, the more formal form "thou hast" was giving way to the use of "thee has," which I have chosen to use throughout.

The calendar used by Britain and its colonies changed in 1751, just as this story begins. Until this time, the new year began on March 25. At the end of December 1751, the first day of January 1752 became the start of the new year. I avoided this complication and confusion by pretending that the year began on January 1 from the beginning of the story.

The Quakers refused to call the months of the year or the days of the week by their "heathen" names, instead calling them by a number. When the Jacksons left Pennsylvania in the early spring of 1750, they were leaving in Third Month (March). What we call Sunday was, to them, First Day.

I have tried to be sensitive in referring to people of color and indigenous people. In modern times, some consider the use of the word "Negro" as socially unacceptable. I am leaving it as written in the eighteenth-century minutes of the meetings and in John Woolman's letter about Quakers and slavery, but I avoided using the term in dialogue and other references. Along the same vein, eighteenth-century people referred to the indigenous people as Indians, a term I use when my characters speak about tribal peoples. Many in the modern Occaneechi Saponi Tribal Nation prefer to be called Indians.

All Scripture quotations are from the 1769 edition of the King James Bible (King James Bible Online, 2023. www.kingjamesbibleonline.org.) I do not include specific chapter and verse citations when the quotation is in dialogue. Early Friends were so familiar with the scripture, they knew their fellow Quakers would know from whence their Bible references came and the context.

Most of the historical events are described as accurately as possible, although I shifted a few dates and locations for the sake of the story and a few times, I compressed events so that I can keep the focus on my main character, Mary Jackson. For more information, see the Historical Note at the end of the book.

To everything there is a season, and a time to every purpose under

    the heaven:

A time to be born, a time to die;

a time to plant, and a time to pluck up that which is planted;

A time to kill, and a time to heal;

a time to break down, and a time to build up;

A time to weep, and a time to laugh;

a time to mourn, and a time to dance;

A time to cast away stones, and a time to gather stones together;

a time to embrace, and a time to refrain from embracing;

A time to get, and a time to lose;

a time to keep, and a time to cast away;

A time to rend, and a time to sew;

a time to keep silence, and a time to speak;

A time to love, and a time to hate;

A time of war, and a time of peace.

Ecclesiastes 3:1-8

Prologue

19th of Sixth Month, 1771

Mary Jackson stared at the gallows, the broad brim of her bonnet hiding the tears streaming down her cheeks. The cruel structure had been hastily constructed during the past week on a small hill, just a few hundred yards from the county courthouse in Hillsborough, North Carolina. The governor's men had cleared away trees to give the spectators a better view of the punishment they would mete out. From where she stood with a few women from her Quaker meeting, Mary could also see the flowers blooming in the town square not far from the courthouse, but, for once, this sight failed to soothe her soul.

Six anxious men stood on the sidelines waiting to be hanged with militia men surrounding them to prevent their escape. Two of the men were Quakers—men who had been raised to be pacifist, to abhor violence, to find that of God in other people—but they had been disowned by their meeting for associating with the rebels who called themselves Regulators. In her heart, she knew they did not deserve to die; none of them did.

The previous year, a mob of Regulators had led a violent riot in Hillsborough, targeting abusive officials. The Regulators were angry at the political corruption and the loss of their lands and livelihoods to unscrupulous tax collectors. The provincial governor, William Tryon, used the riot as justification to send the militia toward the town. Thousands of farmers and merchants armed with muskets and pitchforks gathered a mile west of the camp of British encampment.

Led by a Quaker, Herman Husband, the leaders of the Regulators tried and tried again to negotiate a peaceful resolution. Fed up with the delays, in desperation, the rebels attacked. They fought valiantly against the better-armed and better-trained militia, but were defeated within two hours with many casualties among the Regulators.

The victorious militia had been brutal over the month since the battle, burning the farms of suspected rebels, arresting them and forcing them to sign loyalty oaths. Those who refused were thrown into makeshift prisons. Mary was despondent. These men who behaved so cruelly against the Regulators were not British soldiers from overseas; most were neighbors. How could she ever look them in the eye again? Although they supported Governor Tryon, they too were colonists; in far too many cases, brothers were fighting against brothers.

Mary hugged her arms around her waist. She had to set a good example. She had spent the past twenty years guiding the moral and spiritual life of the women and children in her Quaker community. She grieved that the women were unable to convince their menfolk to step back, to pay the taxes no matter how onerous, to render unto

Caesar the things which were Caesar's, no matter how unreasonable. And she did try; they all tried.

How did it come to this? she begged of her Creator. *Why did I and my dear Isaac not do more to prevent the rebellion?* She was selfishly relieved that her husband, by the grace of God, was not among the condemned; he had participated in only the early days of the protests. *"Our life in North Carolina started out so promising. How can I accept that our neighbors have come to such a brutal ending for standing up against corruption?*

Mary was determined not to let her courage fail her. She wanted to close her eyes, to walk away, but felt compelled be there. She struggled to witness each of the six hangings, fervently praying the entire time.

Finally, the feet of the last man lost purchase, his neck broken with a loud snap. A faint cheer arose from the townspeople who had opposed the rebellion, but the extent of the slaughter had been crushing for even them.

Isaac pushed through the crowd to reach Mary and sweep her into a comforting hug. No words were needed to express the horror of what they had witnessed. Nothing in their Quaker upbringings had prepared them for such a spectacle. He looked at his beloved wife and had no answer to still her tears. They both would be crying for a long time.

Mary looked up at Isaac. "We came here twenty years ago with such hopes. Why did we leave Pennsylvania for this God-forsaken place?"

"Mary, God did not forsake this place. Thee has been happy here. Our children have their own land to build homes for their families. Our grandchildren are thriving here in the Carolina sunshine. We are blessed, despite the cruelties inflicted by the governor's minions."

Mary reluctantly gave one last long look at the executed

men. She was loath to leave them alone, just dangling. Someone else would have to see to their broken bodies.

She wanted to believe that everything would be all right, though she knew it would be a long time before it was.

Chapter One

Twelfth month, 1749

Mary stared through the tracery of frost on the window pane at the falling snow on a day of the month her non-Quaker neighbors called December. Her husband sat beside her on the cushioned bench in front of the kitchen hearth in New Garden, Pennsylvania. She and Isaac were enjoying the hush that seemed to only come during a heavy snow with little wind. Even the children were playing quietly.

"Are we really going to do this?" she asked, her nervous excitement causing her Irish lilt to deepen and quicken. She spoke softly so as not to wake William, the toddler cradled on her lap. "We've lived here for ten years. Thee brought me to this house as thy bride. Our three children were born here. Can we leave? Should we?"

Mary and Isaac had been talking about moving to the Piedmont of North Carolina ever since Isaac and his brothers had traveled to that wilderness last year. The men had spent weeks wandering through the dense forests, and each had staked a claim in the lush valley along the Eno

River. Since their return, Mary and the children had asked Isaac over and over again to tell them about their new land. He happily described the golden sunsets over the wooded hills, the sparkling river and creeks flowing through the valley, and the surprisingly rich, bright orange-red earth, downplaying the difficulty of farming in the packed clay soil. Carolina was, he told them, an enchanting land of beauty and opportunity.

The couple had spent several months considering whether they really were ready to leave their home, their friends, and, especially, Mary's beloved twin sister. They talked about the dangers of such a long journey and the difficulties of traveling with their small children. They met with elders in their Quaker meeting for guidance. They made their decision, reconsidered it, made it again, and ultimately agreed that yes, they were going to undertake this adventure.

Today, Isaac knew his wife was as delighted as he was in anticipation but wanted just one more reassurance that this was the right path forward. He smiled, wrapped her shawl about her shoulders, and pulled her closer. He lightly kissed her forehead.

"Aye, Mary, my love," he said, "we're ready. We truly are. Quit trying to make the decision again. Our parents have all passed on. Most of our brothers and their families are going with us. There is nothing here to hold us. We may not know what is to come, but God will be with us. We're moving to North Carolina!"

Mary rose and carried the dozing toddler to his basket on the hearth, careful so as not to wake him. Then she grabbed Isaac in a big, happy hug. The older children, surprised, joined in. "We're moving to North Carolina!" they shouted. "We're truly going!"

. . .

Land was becoming scarce in eastern Pennsylvania. Isaac's older brother had inherited their father's property as was the custom, and Isaac didn't want to spend his life working for someone else, not even his brother. He wanted his own farm and land for his two sons and the sons that he hoped were yet to come.

King George II had granted Lord Granville large tracts of the Carolinas, and Granville was anxious to have the property settled and profitable. The Jacksons had seen advertisements describing the abundant, fertile lands available in the Piedmont of North Carolina. They were invited to stake a claim in the region in exchange for annual quitrents, which Isaac thought were quite reasonable.

Mary and Isaac had both grown up hearing the stories of their parents' decisions to emigrate from Ireland to help establish New Garden Friends Meeting in the Pennsylvania colony. Mary and Isaac also wanted the thrill, and maybe even the responsibility, of building a Quaker community in the New World, but deciding to leave their home was hard. They had grown up in the New Garden Meeting and were beloved by many of the elders. The members had witnessed their wedding and welcomed their children.

Still, sometimes the elders who controlled Quaker life in New Garden seemed driven by fear that the Society of Friends was changing, and they tried to impose the familiar ways of their ancestral meetings in the old country. Mary knew they cared for the souls of the younger members of the meeting and believed that strict adherence to the discipline of their faith would ensure salvation. Yet a few women seemed too willing to ask the meeting to censure or even disown members for making art or music, for skipping worship meetings, and for consorting with non-Quakers. Sometimes the atmosphere in the women's meeting was tense as the elders considered the behavior of youth in the meeting. Fortunately, Mary was not often the subject of their censure.

She especially disliked the rule against marrying non-Quakers. By the grace of God, she had fallen in love with a wonderful man in her own meeting, but what if her heart had chosen a man from another faith? How could the elders dictate that such love was against good order? She hoped her daughter, Hannah, would someday find a man as wonderful as Isaac and said a small prayer that her future son-in-law would also be a Quaker. But if Hannah chose otherwise, Mary vowed that she would love her daughter's beloved as another son.

Not that she disagreed with the rules and restrictions of the Society of Friends; she approved of them, at least most of them, with her whole heart. She had spent her life trying to live faithfully, and, by and large, she did. Perhaps in the Eno River community in North Carolina they could relax a few of the more oppressive admonitions. Mary especially hoped to be able to enjoy more music, even though many Quakers considered it frivolous and not in keeping with deep listening to God. She recalled, ruefully, her appearances before the discipline committee for pausing too often to listen to the hymns from the Anglican church and to the lively songs of the nearby German families. After all, she argued, didn't their founder George Fox say, "Sing and rejoice ye children of the day and the light for the Lord is at work?" Surely God was not offended by these expressions of joy. At one of these disciplinary meetings, Mary was surprised, and secretly pleased, when an older woman said, "Dear Mary Jackson, we sense that God is calling thee to great things in His service, and thee must not be distracted from the righteous path."

Mary and Isaac also looked forward to moving far away

from the encroaching city of Philadelphia and the political maneuverings of the colonial government. Now that William Penn was gone, the Quakers were losing their influence, and the new governors were breaking some of Penn's treaties with the Indians and advocating that a stronger militia be raised.

Some of their neighbors had urged Isaac to run for office. He was respected and thoughtful and, they said, would help counter the non-Quakers who were taking over the colony. But Isaac did not see himself as a politician. He needed to watch his crops grow; he needed to feel soil under his fingernails and carry mud on his boots. He did not have the patience or temperament for politicking and compromise. He was content to be a support for Mary in developing her ministry.

Isaac and Mary spent the winter months in frantic preparation for the move south. The wagon and pack mules could hold or carry only so much. They had to carefully select what to take, both for the months-long, arduous journey and for setting up their homestead. And they had to make room for their three growing children, who wriggled and sprawled and took up more space than their wee sizes should require. They sold off their excess furnishings and livestock, and offered their house to one of Isaac's distant cousins.

Nine-year-old Hannah watched all the bustling about and became sullen and withdrawn. She was scared. The boys at her school teased her about Indian attacks on the frontier, telling her how dangerous the wilderness was. When they saw that upset her, they began taunting her even more about being captured by vicious Indians and scalped in her sleep. She started having nightmares and crying when her parents talked of the move.

One night, when Hannah woke up screaming, Isaac went to her bedside and held her tightly. "My dear little Hannah. Thee should not be afraid. Friend William Penn made treaties with the natives, thee knows that. The Indians see that we're peaceable, and they are, too. We'll become friends with the Indians in North Carolina, just like here."

Hannah hiccupped and nodded. Her tears subsided to a few watery sniffles. She snuggled into her father's arms.

"Aye, what the wee boys are saying is worrisome to thee, but they are saying these things just to see thee upset. They think it's fun to make thee cry. I know it's hard, but try to ignore them. Tell them that the Indians have moved far away from our new home. Any Indians we meet in North Carolina are peaceful, just like the Lenape here in Pennsylvania. We will trade with them, and they will be our neighbors. Thee will see. My Hannah, I wouldn't ever put thee in danger. Thee is my precious wee daughter, and I love thee too much to let anyone harm even a hair on thy head."

Isaac kissed her soft curls and held her until her tears stopped. He laid her carefully in her bed when he heard her soft snores. He would talk to their teacher about the boys' behavior, he decided, and try to put a stop to their teasing.

As he climbed back under his own covers, he took Mary in his arms and said, "My love, we must be extra tender with Hannah. She worries so much, and the boys in her class tease her to make her cry."

Mary murmured softly and fell back asleep.

As he packed, Isaac was looking forward to breaking ground in North Carolina and establishing a thriving farm.

He looked longingly at his extensive supply of tools and implements. He wouldn't be able to take them all. He carefully selected the barest minimum, settling on his cast iron hoe, scythe, axe, and plow. He removed the handles, which took up space, and included several whittling knives, a plane, mallets, and some chisels for making handles and furniture. He also put in a long, sharp machete for hacking through brush and a two-person saw for felling big trees and cutting logs. The remainder would be given to his cousins who were staying in Pennsylvania. Other tools would have to be made or purchased when they were settled.

Mary asked Hannah to help her decide what they should take to their new home. Her daughter was a hard worker, jumping to do as her mother asked. They gathered bedding and food, cooking supplies, and other household goods. Mary, too, had to limit what they could take. Of course, she needed her kettle, a few kitchen utensils, tin plates, spoons, and a few cups. Isaac promised to carve wooden dishes and furniture as he found time. She looked around their home and packed her mother's pewter candlesticks and a precious wooden cardinal that Isaac had carved for her while they were courting. She placed the family Bible in a wooden box, then made it watertight with beeswax; she wanted it to be safe, and the box would keep it accessible during their journey.

Mary asked Hannah to select a few simple toys for her brothers. Hannah chose to pack her favorite dolly, the one her grandfather had carved for her, and the doll dresses her grandmother had made from fabric scraps. The girl took great pleasure in bossing around her two younger brothers, five-year-old Edward and the toddler, William; her harried mother much appreciated that the boys were not underfoot while she worked.

Moving day arrived all too soon. A light snow was falling, but this was expected in the last days of winter in early 1750. Mary and Isaac rose before the first light of morning. Isaac readied the wagon and the pack animals for the long journey, and finished loading the last of their supplies, household goods, and implements. Still, not everything they had hoped to take could fit. Mary shed a tear as she pulled out the cradle Isaac had carved when Hannah was born—all three of her children had lain in it, rocking gently to sleep. She needed to take her washtub, so she packed it with blankets for young William to use as a bed. Both Isaac and Mary reluctantly removed more items that they would have to do without. Once everything was efficiently packed, Mary bundled the still sleeping children in warm quilts and tucked them behind the wagon bench with a few of their favorite playthings. They wanted the children to stay asleep while they finished their last-minute preparations.

The day of leaving was a day of great sadness and greater excitement. Several of Isaac's brothers and sisters, along with their families, were traveling with them, and the caravan would meet the others along the way. They had been warned to travel in large groups because of the dangers of wild animals and natives who might be more aggressive than the Lenape Indians who had made peace with William Penn. The men would work together to repair broken wagons, clear overgrown trading paths, and hack through virgin forests. The women would share the responsibility for the children and domestic chores. They each had their own gifts to offer to their small community, and they would all be essential to its survival and spiritual well-being.

Then came the hard part—saying goodbye to their friends and the family members who chose to remain in Pennsylvania. Very early in the morning, they had called together their family and closest neighbors for an impromptu worship meeting. Several rose to say prayers for their journey. Mary wanted to leave her friends with an inspirational message, but the words did not come to her; she was trying too hard to sound important, rather than listening for God in the worship.

After ending the meeting, they woke the children for last hugs with aunts and uncles, and let them run around with their cousins to burn off some energy before being confined to the wagon.

Hannah spent almost an hour in the barn tearfully saying goodbye to her little brown pony, Acorn. She had learned to ride him when she was four, and she often ran to hug him when she was upset or lonely. She had begged her father to let her take Acorn to North Carolina, but there was only room for work animals. Knowing she was disappointed, Isaac offered her the job of caring for the horses and mules on the journey. She eagerly jumped at being given this important responsibility and had carefully packed a small trunk with brushes and combs and feed buckets. Hannah still wished she would be caring for Acorn as well as the pack animals.

Mary had an especially difficult time leaving her twin sister, Katherine. For the first time, they would be separated, as Katherine's husband had chosen to stay in Pennsylvania on his family's land. Mary's brother George and his wife said they would join Isaac and Mary in a few years, and Mary hoped he would be able to convince Katherine to come too.

After the extended, teary goodbyes, Mary gathered her three young children and lifted them back into the fully packed wagon. Isaac smiled as she tucked in their children. He climbed onto the wagon seat and gave Mary a reassuring hug. The time had come to get moving. Suddenly, Mary put her hand on his arm and told him to stop. She scrambled down and ran to hug Katherine tightly.

"Dear sister, how can I leave thee? We shared the same womb and have been together all our lives. Life without thee nearby is too dreadful to countenance."

The two women stood weeping with the realization they might never see each other again. After several minutes, Isaac climbed down and gently led his wife back to her place beside him on the wagon bench. A few more tears rolled down her cheeks, but she smiled bravely and waved at her sister, nieces, and nephews as they pulled out.

The caravan headed west, meeting up with others making the journey. The snow picked up a bit; fortunately, it was not too icy. Spring was on its way. The weather improved as they journeyed and became fairly pleasant.

In the first part of their journey, the roads were well-used. Women and young children usually rode in the wagons. The men and older children mostly walked the entire way, although they could crowd among the supplies in the wagon when necessary. Traveling was relatively comfortable, although things would be more difficult as they headed farther south.

The group frequently stopped to visit Quaker families along the way. These brief visits were welcome interludes, for both the travelers and the folks with whom they visited. They were able to sit together in worship, to share their stories, and to seek solace and joy in the spirit found in community. Other nights, they gathered in clearings by the rivers and creeks, eating fish and small game, and sleeping on quilts under the wagons. The children enjoyed splashing in the creeks and chasing their cousins and friends. What a grand adventure they had embarked on!

It took two weeks to arrive at Hopewell Meeting, the westernmost community of Friends in Virginia, not very far from the growing town of Winchester. The meeting had been established twenty years earlier by Quakers initially from Nottingham Friends Meeting, which was not far from New Garden. Isaac had arranged for their caravan to stay with area Friends for several weeks before undertaking the more arduous part of the journey south.

As they pulled into the yard of one of the houses near the meetinghouse, Mary spied her childhood friend Deborah Lupton. It had been a long time since they had last seen each other. As soon as she could stop the horses, she dropped the reins and jumped down. They raced together to hug and hopped up and down in excitement.

The children watched from the wagon and called to their father to help them climb down. Isaac nodded, but took his time getting the pack animals tied up to give the women a chance to renew their friendship before the children demanded their attention. When he walked over to the wagon and reached out his arms to Hannah and Edward, they were suddenly shy when they saw the large group of children racing over to meet the newcomers. Isaac set them on the ground and smiled as they ran to their mother to hide behind her skirts. Mary and Deborah laughed and stooped down to introduce the youngsters. Deborah's daughter grabbed Hannah's hand and dragged her over to a small group of girls who were eager to make a new friend. Edward was more hesitant, but he, too, eventually left his mother's side to play in the yard with a couple of boys. Mary set William on a quilt laid near some of the older women of the meeting.

Deborah and her oldest son helped Mary and Isaac unload things they would need for their stay at Hopewell. Other men and women joined them, greedy for news of the families and friends they had left behind. Mary was happy to hand over the packets of letters she had been asked to carry from Pennsylvania.

Mary enjoyed her time catching up with the women as they watched the children running around the yard near the meetinghouse cemetery. She knew some of them from when they themselves were children, playing together at yearly gatherings, and, later, flirting with young men from each other's extended families. This visit among these Friends was a welcome respite. Mary found comfort in the companionship of Friends who knew where she was coming from and had themselves moved from their homes in the east, just as Mary and Isaac were doing.

ON A WARM, sunny afternoon a few days later, Mary and Deborah reminisced as they mended torn linens. "Mary, does thee remember my brother Thomas?" Deborah asked, setting down her fabric and taking Mary's hand in hers.

Mary giggled. "Of course. Every time he saw me, he would stammer and look at the ground."

"Aye, he was right smitten with thee, but thee only had eyes for thy Isaac."

"I recall him putting a worm down thy dress one First Day. Thee chased him and threatened to get back at him."

"I had some good ideas, too, until me Ma clapped her hands at us and put a stop to such frivolity."

The women laughed loudly. One of the elders on the other side of the yard looked at them and frowned. This caused them even more merriment. When they were finally able to be serious again, Mary asked, "How is Thomas? Does thee see him often?"

"Nay. Thomas has gone to the western frontier. He felt a calling to minister among the Indians, and the meeting agreed that his ministry is rightly ordered. He left months ago. I'm worried. The French and British armies are clashing over control of the lands west of the mountains. They are heading toward war. The French have enlisted the Indians and are turning them against the British. I don't think Thomas is safe."

Mary put a reassuring hand on Deborah's arm. "My dear friend, we will pray for his safety and for an end to this needless warring. But, tell me, is thy family safe here, in the Hopewell community?"

"We have made peace with the natives in this area. We can only hope that if there is a war over the border that it does not come here. For now, we're out of harm's way."

"Aye, we met up with some Indians several days before arriving here. They looked threatening. They were not Lenape, and we didn't know if William Penn included their tribe in his treaty. They silently watched from the trees as we passed. A few of the young men followed us for many miles, making rude noises. At least they seemed rude to us. We didn't know their language. Maybe they were just joking around, but we were scared and gathered the children into the wagons. Our men had hunting rifles, but they wouldn't use them against another person, no matter the threat. At least I hope so. I'm glad we didn't have to find out. The young Indians eventually got tired of taunting us and turned back."

Deborah shuddered and hugged her friend. "Enough of this depressing talk. I'm grateful that the Indians did thee no harm. For now, thee's here. Our children are playing together as we once did. And, I sense that the mid-day meal is ready. Up we go."

The meetinghouse was packed the next day. The members of the Hopewell community were excited to worship with their visitors. As Quakers, they were used to sitting for hours, listening to the still small voice of God within them, but many secretly hoped someone would stand and give a sermon or prayer to break the monotony. And, as God seemed always to lead the same men and a few women to preach, everyone looked forward to hearing ministry from their visitors; new voices were always welcome.

After a while, the meeting settled. Only a creak from someone shifting in a seat or an infant's quiet snoring broke the silence. Mary soon felt steeped in the presence of God. She hated to be the one to break such a deep worship, but she felt that God had given her a message to share. She lifted William, who had been sitting quietly on her lap, and handed him to Hannah. Mary rose and looked around nervously. She was not comfortable speaking in groups, even among friends and family, and had only occasionally risen to preach in New Garden Meeting. This was even harder, to be among so many Friends that she did not know well. Still, she felt God's urging. Her legs quivered, and she grabbed onto the bench in front of her to steady herself.

She cleared her throat and began to recite the Scripture that had been guiding her on their journey thus far. A few words into the passage, she hesitated; unbelievably, she had forgotten the very words that she had used every day in her prayers. She almost sat back down in hopes that the compulsion to speak would pass. Tentatively, she started again, and by reciting it quickly, she was able to get all the words out, "Be careful for nothing; but in everything by prayer and supplication with thanksgiving let thy requests be made known unto God. And the peace of God, which passeth all understanding, shall keep thy hearts and minds through Christ Jesus."

Her speaking slowed down, and her voice became

stronger as she became more assured. She fervently urged Friends to pray and ask God for his help. He wouldn't give them more than they could handle if they placed their concerns in God's hands. She concluded with a later passage from the same Scripture: "I can do all things through Christ which strengtheneth me."

She sat down, spent, picked up her young child and enveloped him in a hug, reassuring to her if not to him. Hannah smiled, awed that her mother had spoken such important words, and laid her head against her mother's arm. Mary was still a little shaky; she patted her daughter's head and settled back into worship with a soft sigh.

After the elders indicated the end of meeting, she rose with William sleepy in her arms and stretched her back. After riding in an uncomfortable wagon for many days, she was still not physically ready for these two hours of sitting on a hard meetinghouse bench. She sent Hannah and Edward out to play in the yard with the other children. As she neared the open door, a couple of the elders from the women's meeting at Hopewell stopped her.

Margaret Stabler said, "My dear Mary Jackson, thee was well-favored in the message God hast given thee. We think thee has a gift of ministry in thy hearing God's voice in the worship and sharing this gift with us, simply and clearly."

"Thank thee, Friend," Mary replied. "I dream of someday serving the Lord by traveling in the gospel ministry. But I have not yet been called to that work. For now, my young children demand my time and energy."

While they sojourned, Mary found many opportunities to sit with the Hopewell elders. She learned much from them and grew more confident in her fledgling desire for ministry. As much as she wished it, she was still quite uncertain whether God expected her to preach the gospel.

Mary confessed such to a group of women elders. "I accept that I'm not as holy and devout as other Quaker ministers. I oftentimes struggle with the disciplines imposed by the Society of Friends, and I occasionally—sometimes intentionally—violate some of the dictates." She added silently that she thought she felt sufficiently repentant when she danced in her kitchen or made a wish upon a star, even if she did not confess it to her meeting.

The other women didn't gasp or look shocked; a few even smiled.

Margaret said, "Mary, my dear Mary Jackson, God does not expect us to be perfect, only faithful."

Mary disliked not knowing what to do, but the women had convinced her that her job was to be open and to wait upon the Lord and, in time, the way forward would become clear.

Their friends urged them to stay. The Hopewell community had a well-established meeting and a small school for the children. There was still plenty of open space north and west of Winchester. Isaac, however, was looking forward to settling on the land he had claimed in North Carolina. Besides, he and Mary anticipated being the pioneers who would start their own community and Quaker meeting, just as their parents had done.

As the Jacksons were packing to leave, Margaret Stabler said, "Perhaps thee will confirm thy ministry of sharing God's word in the wilderness. Perhaps He has other plans for thee. Be open to answering God's call, however He may desire to use thee. Please write to us when thee can. We would love to hear about God's work in the Piedmont and, most definitely, news of thy delightful family. Thy presence among us has been a blessing. We ask the Lord to protect thee and thy family as thee goes on thy journey."

Margaret's words were a comfort to Mary as she and

Isaac finished their preparations and climbed into the packed wagon. Mary looked back as they left Winchester. As eager as she was to get to their new home, this was another sad good-bye, probably forever. She had been inspired and challenged by the women who urged her to listen for God to guide her in developing her gifts as a minister. She wouldn't let them–or God–down.

Chapter Two

1750

Spring slowly came to the valley in Virginia. The far-off mountains were tinged blue in the sunlight, creeks and rivers sparkled, and game was plentiful. Most of the trail was wide and well-packed, so the Jacksons and their companions made good time, traveling ten to twenty miles a day, usually stopping early enough to allow time to gather for grateful worship before supper.

About a week after leaving Hopewell, dark storm clouds rolled in. The air grew heavy, and thunder rumbled in the distance. Isaac, who had been walking, climbed into the wagon to take over the reins. Mary scrambled into the back to make sure everything was securely packed and to spread a heavy cloth covering for the children to shelter under.

Suddenly a streak of lightning flashed nearby. One of the pack mules, the one Hannah had named Curious, reared and broke his tether. He bolted in a panic, the bundles strapped to his back slipping and sliding. Mary heard a loud primal scream. The animal had fallen off a low ridge. Isaac and his brother ran to the fallen mule and spied his broken leg.

As Isaac retrieved his rifle from his pack, Hannah cried to him, "Da, don't shoot Curious. I'll take care of him. I'll help him get well. Please, Da, please."

Isaac picked up his daughter and hugged her. Then he set her in the wagon beside her mother. Mary wanted to cover her own ears to shut out the creature's pain and the sound of the gunshot when Isaac put him out of his misery, but she put her hands over her daughter's ears instead. Hannah whimpered and snuggled into her mother's side, inconsolable at the loss of one of the mules, but especially Curious, her favorite.

Hannah cried, "I could have saved him. I should have saved him."

Mary held the child until her sobs settled into quiet hiccups, handed Hannah her doll, and bundled her back under the shelter in the wagon.

The rains came down hard while the men were removing the bundles from the dead mule and repacking them on other mules and in the wagons. They talked among themselves and decided they could travel no farther until the storm let up. It was just too dangerous; the trail was slippery, and the fog and unrelenting rainfall made it difficult to see the path. When Isaac walked back to the wagon and told Mary, she was relieved. Her children were cold, wet, and scared. So was she. The children were upset that Curious was so wounded that he had to be killed. The death had unnerved all of them, and stopping would give them some time to recover.

They were getting wetter and wetter and needed to find a dry, or at least drier, place to settle for the night. Mary gave her children one last hug and called to one of her nieces to watch the younger children. She and Hannah climbed down from the wagon and ventured into the dense woods. Soon they spotted an outcropping with a jutting ledge that formed a canopy over a small clearing. They went back for Edward and William and helped them slide into the cave out of the hard rain. Some of the younger cousins joined them.

Isaac tied up the animals nearby and made sure they had water to drink and grass to munch. The horses and mules were not as bothered by the downpour as their people were. There was no dry tinder for a fire, so the travelers ate dried meat and stale crackers. Mary bedded the overtired children wrapped in damp blankets; she was thankful they fell sound asleep quickly. She and Isaac then lay down covering themselves as best they could. They were exhausted, without the energy for passion or talk or more than a quick prayer. They fell asleep warmly wrapped in each other's arms.

The weather was no better in the morning. Isaac and two of the other men went back out to check the trail. During the night they had been awakened by a loud crash, not far from their encampment. A large tree had fallen across the path, blocking it completely.

Edward and his cousin Josiah, Benjamin's son, wandered over, and he put his hand in his father's. "Da, can thee believe this? I'm a big boy and almost six years old. This tree is lying on its side, and it's much taller around than even I am!"

Isaac smiled down at his young son before setting to argue with his brothers about how to deal with the obstacle. Isaac directed the men to clear away the tree even though it would take them at least a day and a lot of hard work to open the path. Benjamin chafed at being told what to do by his older brother. He wanted to leave the tree as it fell and see if he could find another way around. He stomped off into the woods, returning almost an hour later before conceding that the tree had to be moved. The stress of the trip was starting to wear on all of them.

Isaac sent Edward and Josiah back to the wagon. On the way, they jostled between themselves to see who would announce this important message. The boys ran to their mothers, coming to an abrupt stop, panting. When he was able to catch his breath, Edward said, gulping air between words, "My Da, he says go back, back to the clearing. By the creek. The one we stayed at yesterday before it started raining so hard."

His cousin interrupted, "It's a long way back, but *my* Da says he wants us to have clean water to drink and wash in."

Mary sighed. It was a long way back, at least an hour of travel. The boys turned to run back to watch the men. Mary grabbed Edward by the back of the shirt and called after her nephew. "Boys, stay here. We need thy help to set up camp."

The little boys grumbled and looked with longing at the path to the fallen tree. Neither wanted to miss out on the excitement of seeing such a great tree cut apart. Besides, neither considered himself to be one of the "little" children who had to stay with their mothers.

Mary silently shook her head and pointed to the wagon. Edward was sullen as he climbed in, but he knew better than to disobey his mother.

That night Isaac and Mary sat by the fire, trying to talk quietly. The children, however, were becoming restless.

"Do a duck, Da. Quack like a duck," hollered Edward.

"Shh, thee doesn't have to shout," Isaac said with a smile. He enjoyed making animal sounds for his children. They thought it was funny and imitated him as best they could. Being able to call small game was a good skill to learn when they went hunting for food. And talking to their livestock could sometimes be a way to calm a skittery animal down. The girls especially liked to practice on the baby calves and an occasional foal, although sometimes they treated them as pets rather than working animals.

"What sound does a cow make?" he asked his young son.

"Moo, moo, moo," the boy said with a giggle.

They played this game for a little while longer until Mary said, "That's enough. Let's get settled on thy blankets under the cart."

The children protested that they were not sleepy and wanted to keep playing the game.

Mary shook her head. "Not tonight. Sit here for a few minutes and look at the stars. Aren't they beautiful? See, God and his angels are twinkling down on us."

The family sat quietly for a few minutes until little William started to fuss. "Well, children. It's time to say thy prayers and snuggle in for the night," Mary told them. She stood, brushed off her skirt, and picked up her youngest. The other two children followed reluctantly, but fell asleep quickly once their mother got them settled in.

When the sun came out the next day, Mary and Hannah spread the bedding and linens out on rocks to dry in the sun. They washed their mud-stained clothing and rinsed off in the creek. The younger children had a splendid time splashing in the water, even though the air and water were still quite cold. This was just another grand adventure to them.

The caravan lost five days of travel because of the storm and having to backtrack to the clearing. Everyone was anxious to continue their journey toward their new home, but they took an extra day after the rains stopped to dry out their bedding and drain the water from their wagon beds. The women used this time to supplement the provisions that the Friends in Hopewell had given them, scavenging for nuts, tubers, and early greens. Some of the boys in the group had success fishing. After everyone ate their fill, the women dried what was left over for later. Before finally leaving the clearing, they gathered in worship, asking God to bless the next leg of their journey.

Four days later, the travelers stopped again to regroup, gather more provisions, and rest before starting across the mountains. They had been told this would be the roughest part of the trip, along a crude route worn through a pass along the James River. Parts of it were still quite dangerous; more than once after they started, everyone had to get out of the wagons to walk while Isaac and his brothers led the horses and mules through the narrow, rocky parts. Hannah held Edward's hand tightly; the boy always wanted to run to the edge of the path to look down onto the river.

The group paused before a particularly harrowing stretch. The stormy weather that had been dogging them for the past week finally arrived with great fury. They struggled in the rain and dense fog; even during the day, visibility was low. The water in the river below them was turbulent and, in some places, overflowing the banks. The rocks were slippery, the path so steep and narrow that they were hesitant to continue until the weather cleared.

Not far ahead, they spied a place where the path opened up. The adults gathered as they pondered a way forward. The heavy spring rains, coupled with the melting snowpack from the mountains, made flash flooding a very real possibility, and even this clearing could one day be under water. Who among them knew when the weather would break? The way forward was precarious, but waiting could mean further delays of many weeks. They had to push forward despite the risks. Calling the children to join them, they settled in for a period of prayer and supplication. Isaac closed the impromptu meeting for worship with the prayer, "May God keep us safe and watch over us on our journey."

The men checked that the wagons and animals were securely packed. They decided to carry some of the bundles, to lighten the load on the mules. Most of the women and children, Mary included, chose to walk well behind the caravan, praying all the way. Isaac let his animals have their heads, doing his best to keep them on the path and away from the edges of the raging river. Although it was well worn and clearly defined, the path was, in places, far more treacherous than they anticipated. A few times an animal slipped, and the men rushed to its side, adjusting the packs and leading the animal to a safer part of the path. Several times, a mule stopped suddenly and balked at going forward. Isaac had to drag the animal while his brothers pushed from behind until the mule found its footing.

Mary had not been sure that the wagons would make it, but after many hours they had spotted a wooded area away from the dangers of the rising water. She breathed a long, loud sigh of relief when they paused to thank God for their safe deliverance. It was decided this was a good place to stop for a day or two to recover. Fortunately, none of the animals, or humans for that matter, were seriously injured although many of the men were bruised and scratched, and a few of the animals had wounds that needed tending.

Camp was set up in a sheltered cove. Isaac built a crude lean-to of branches and leaves; at least it provided a little respite from the constant rain. Everyone was cold, wet, exhausted, and hungry, and wished for the warmth of a fire. But the unrelenting rain meant the dead wood around them was too wet to set ablaze. In the shelter, Mary offered her children some dried fish and a few berries; they were too tired to eat more than a few bites. She, too, was bone-weary but needed to eat to keep up her strength. Still, before she could allow herself to rest, she set about treating the injuries of the men and the animals, almost depleting her small supply of healing herbs. Finally, she and Isaac were able to join their children in deep sleep.

Though the rain continued the next morning, the sky seemed to lighten in the distance. Hoping the day would turn drier, they packed up the makeshift camp and headed out. Eventually, they reached the well-traveled trading paths used by the Indians in the region and their way became a little easier.

The Jackson caravan still had weeks of hard going ahead of them, and mustering the energy to continue was a constant struggle. Even with the daily chores required by travel, there were long, boring stretches and not enough time for the children to run off all their pent-up energy. The wagon bench seemed impossibly hard at times.

One sunny morning, Mary quickly stopped the horses, threw down the reins, and leaped off the wagon. She vomited several times in the bushes.

Isaac had been walking with the pack horses and ran to the wagon. "Hannah, what is wrong with Mama?"

Hannah shrugged, but seeing the worried look on her father's face, she began to cry in earnest. Edward didn't know why she was crying, so he joined in. William, thankfully, stayed asleep in the washtub behind the wagon bench.

"Hannah, Edward, stay in the wagon." Isaac ran to Mary and touched her shoulder. "Is thee ill? Is it something thee ate?" He handed her a clean piece of cloth. Mary stood and wiped her mouth.

"Nay, Isaac, thee's a *wretched* man, for sure. It's bad enough that I ride on a hard wagon board with thy whiny children in the back! Sleeping on the hard ground! Eating whatever little we can forage. Nay, I'm again with child. And it's surely *thy* fault."

Isaac burst out laughing. He grabbed Mary and started to spin her around for a hug, when she pulled away to finish emptying her stomach. "Aye, my love, I take full responsibility. 'Tis my fault, it is." He swept her up in his arms and carried her to the wagon, set her on the dratted wagon bench, and motioned to their children. They rushed to hug their mother.

"I'm fine, dear ones," she said, "I'm sorry to give thee such a fright."

Isaac went around the wagon and clambered up to sit beside his wife. He snapped the reins and clucked to the horses.

Mary leaned against his shoulder gratefully. "I'm just so tired all the time. I'm happy, truly I am, but I'm oh so tired."

Isaac grinned. "I'm picturing a whole brood of young'uns, running about the house. Fair colleens with red hair and flashing green eyes like their ma, and brawny, brave lads like their da."

Mary laughed. "Oh, brawny and brave, is thee? Oh, my hero." She swooned in mock adulation.

They rode in happy silence for a while before Isaac said, "My love, does thee remember when our dear Hannah was born?"

Hannah perked up. She loved to hear her father tell the story of the day she was born. She enjoyed hearing about the days her ma and da met and when they said their marriage vows, but even more she liked when he told stories of when she was a babe. She stood behind the wagon bench and put her thin arms around her father's neck. "Da, tell me again about the porch," she said. "Please."

Isaac moved the reins to one hand and rubbed his chin thoughtfully and smiled. He patted his daughter's hand and gave Mary a little hug before continuing.

"Well, Hannah, I was sitting on the porch with my brothers. Thy uncles and I were whittling and telling each other outrageous stories, trying to outdo each other. Thy aunts were in the house with thy mother, waiting for thee to be born."

He paused. Hannah shook his shoulder. "Go on, Da, tell the rest."

"It was late afternoon, and we had run out of boasts. Soon thy aunt Susan came outside and told me that I had a lovely new daughter. I was so excited to meet thee, I tried to jump up. And I fell backwards off the railing! I was lying upside down in the bushes, and thy uncles laughed and laughed. They just stood there and did not even help me. It seemed that I struggled forever before I was able to right myself and get into the house. Thy mother was so beautiful lying there with a babe—thee—in her arms." Again, he paused.

"Hannah, my sweet, I took one look at thee and fell in love all over again. Thee was the fairest colleen in all the land. Yes, thee was indeed."

Edward bounced up. "What about me, was I fairest, too?"

Isaac grinned at his children. "Nay, Edward. When thee was born, thee was a squalling red creature, waving thy arms and squawking like a bantam strutting about the yard. But we loved thee anyway."

On a beautiful early summer morning, Mary glanced around to see if anyone was looking. Isaac was next to her on the wagon bench. Hannah and Edward were traveling in their uncle's wagon to play with their cousins. William was asleep in the washtub in the back. The other wagons in their large caravan were following at a distance. For now, anyway, she and Isaac were alone.

She clasped his free hand and held it in her lap. She leaned toward him, smiling and blew a kiss. She would have preferred to do more than blow a kiss, but they had found from past experience that the stiff brim of her bonnet made sneaking a quick kiss very difficult. They had managed to steal kisses in the past, but it usually involved lots of maneuvering and giggling. The other wagons were not as far away as she would have liked, and they were not willing to do something so undignified in front of the others.

"Mary, thee is the dream of my life," Isaac drawled, "my heart, my reason for living."

Mary guffawed. "Aye, go on with thee. Thee must have kissed the blarney stone as a wee lad, for thee's surely flattering this old woman."

Isaac looked at his wife and winked. Lord, he loved this woman—he knew he was taking the Lord's name, not in vain but in gratitude. At thirty years old, silver strands were starting to appear among the coppery curls peeking out from Mary's bonnet. There were lines on her face, though mostly from laughing. He reveled at how she recovered quickly from adversity and rarely held a grudge or spoke in anger. Fortunately for him, she was usually able to draw him out of his most dour moods. Her joy in life was infectious. Others in their family and community looked to her for guidance, support, and friendship. He knew he was blessed that they were joined together.

"Isaac," she asked, "have we crossed into Carolina? The children are restless, and I am truly sick and tired of sitting on this hard bench seat."

Isaac nodded in understanding. "I agree with thee. We have been on the road for almost three months. I'm frustrated by our slow progress. I wonder how we ever thought this journey would be an exciting adventure."

"Well, my husband, other than the storms and that wicked crossing over the mountains, our travels have been mostly tedious."

"I agree and certainly wouldn't call the mountain passage tedious. I didn't tell thee, but many times during the violent winds and rains, I feared for our lives. I prayed that I had not taken my family to thy death."

"Oh, Isaac, God was protecting us. We placed our decision to move our family to North Carolina in His hands. Thy worry was not thy burden to bear alone. Thee should have shared thy fears with me."

They rode quietly a few miles. Mary smiled at her husband and said, "I truly enjoyed our visits with the Quaker families we met along the way and getting to know a few who are distant relatives. Our stays with fellow Irish Friends were especially lovely. Isaac, they are living in the Light of the Lord, even in the wilderness. We must seek the same when we get to our new home."

Isaac smiled back. "Aye, they made us all welcome. The times we had to stop to make repairs to the wagons, when we had a broken axle or a thrown wheel, were thankfully minor. We even made it safely through the storms. Thee is right. God is protecting us."

"Have we crossed?" Mary asked again.

Isaac knew they were approaching another difficult part of the journey. There were no established roads into the Piedmont. The going would be rough over what narrow tracks had been worn through the woods. He reckoned they were still a day or two away from North Carolina, and then had three more days' travel until they arrived at their claim on the Eno River.

"Getting closer, my love. Just a few days more and we will be at our new homestead."

ONE CLOUDLESS, hot afternoon almost a week later, Isaac stopped the horses in a wide clearing. He beckoned for Mary and the children to get down from the wagon. Pointing into the distance, he said, "Mary, would thee look over to the left? See that silver streak shining in the sun? That's our river. That is the Eno. Our land is on the other side. We're almost home."

Mary let out a delightful laugh, leaped up, grabbed Hannah, and swung her around. William gurgled and reached out his arms to be held; he wanted to be swung in circles too. Young Edward whooped and raced around the wagon. The whole family hugged in joy. Home was in sight, the trip almost over.

"Let's make camp here, Mary. I know we want to get to our new home as soon as we can. But there are only a few places where we can safely cross the river, and I don't want to attempt it in the dark."

Mary nodded and hugged her husband one more time before starting to set up camp. Edward was sent to pick up sticks for the fire, while Hannah searched for edible greens to cook with the last of their salted meat.

Before bedtime, Hannah and Edward asked their father to tell them again about the new land they were moving to.

They loved hearing about the men who had bravely fought in the Indian wars between the Tuscarora and the British settlers thirty years earlier, and how they signed a peace treaty. Secretly, Edward wished he could fight in a war against the savage Indians. His mother constantly stressed to him that Quakers don't fight others. From the beginning, the Society of Friends had an admonition against using violence, his mother told him, stressing that the Light of Christ was in all people and asking, "So why would we harm any of God's children? William Penn," she reminded her son, "befriended the Lenni Lenape in Pennsylvania, and will do the same with the Indians who remained in their part of North Carolina.

"Maybe the Indian children will want to play with me," he told her. "I'm not scared. If they want to fight, I'll say no. I'll tell them we don't do that. I'll say, let's have fun and be friends." Yet somewhere deep inside, the idea of warring sounded exciting.

In the morning, the rising sun cast a rosy glow over the water in the distance. After a quick breakfast of mint tea and dried oat cakes, Mary gathered the bedding and cooking supplies and loaded the wagon. The rest of their caravan joined them as they all made their way to a shallow ford in the river. One wagon's wheel got stuck in the soft creek bed, but the men were soon able to free it. Finally, all the families made it across safely, waved their goodbyes, and headed in various directions to the plots the men had previously staked.

An hour later, Isaac pulled up the horses in a very small clearing. The woods were dense and the path through them was faint. "We will need to get out here and walk," he said.

Puzzled, Mary asked, "Isaac, how far? How will we get our wagon and our trunks to our new home?"

"We're almost on the land I staked out when I was here

with my brothers last year. But the shelter I built, a very small rough cabin, is still about a mile in. We will need to walk from here, and I'll hack a wider path later today."

He silently worried, *What if my claim has been taken over by someone else? My brothers and I made the long journey to Edenton on the coast to register our claims. But my land has been sitting empty for over a year.*

He knew that if he shared his concerns with her, his Mary would reassure him—she was always telling him that he worried too much—but he didn't want to dampen her excitement. His family was here with him, ready to start their new life. There was nothing he could do but go forward and share in their joy.

They set off, Mary carrying William and a small bag of food. Hannah and Edward each carried a few supplies. Isaac went ahead with his machete, chopping through the overgrown brush and making a narrow pathway for her and the children. They came to the area that he had cleared the year before, which was now becoming overgrown—a small problem but a good sign of the land's fertility.

Mary and Isaac stopped to look at their shelter. Isaac relaxed. His worrying had been for naught. The left rear corner had collapsed and part of the roof was missing, but to the Jacksons, the sight was beautiful. The travel was over. They had arrived at their new home. This was the land they would tame and cultivate and on which they would raise their children.

Mary set William down on a blanket Hannah had brought, and they went inside to see the condition of the crude cabin. Mary stood in the doorway and sighed deeply. It was obvious that a critter had moved into the back. A few birds were in the eaves, and the walls and ceiling were festooned with a complex of spider webs. *After all,* she thought, *the structure had sat empty for more than a year.* It was not built to last in any case, just be big enough and sturdy enough to mark their claim. It would take a lot of work, she knew, to make this a livable space until they built their house. A lot of work, but she and Isaac were used to hard work.

And they were *home*. She grabbed Hannah's and Edward's hands and spun them around, laughing and squealing. "We're home, children! *This* is thy new home!"

They drew Isaac into their circle and the festivities.

"Oh, Isaac. We will fill this shack with love. The babe I'm carrying will be born here. All our children will thrive in this wilderness. I am so happy." That happiness shone in her eyes and her smile.

Once they stopped and caught their breaths, Isaac headed back down the path. As he went, he chopped away more brush and small trees, and dragged branches deeper into the woods so he could move the mules and wagon closer to their claim.

Mary brushed her hands down the sides of her skirt. She went outside and found a flexible branch with leaves and handed it to her son. "Edward, take this and start sweeping down the spider webs. Thee needs to get them out of every nook and corner. Then we must gather wood to make a fire to fix our supper before thy father returns with our supplies. Oh, my son, isn't this a grand adventure?" With those words, Mary laughed and spun around, hugging herself. "Our new home!"

Chapter Three

In the morning, Isaac began in earnest to clear the land around the shack. This was an arduous job. He and his brothers would work together to cut down and move the larger trees on each other's land, but Isaac had to clear the brush and rocks by himself before he asked for their help.

He directed Edward to gather sticks and pieces of fallen logs to carry back for their mother's cooking fire. The little boy seemed more interested in chasing the small blue-tailed skinks and green anoles that were skittering around. Isaac smiled. The little lizards kept his son busy and out of the way. He let it go on for a little while, then told Edward to leave the wee creatures alone.

"Thy mother needs wood to make us supper. Get back to work, my son. Thee will have time to play with the little reptiles later. Besides, they need to get back to their own work, eating the insects that might harm thy mother's garden when she's able to plant vegetables for us."

Edward looked forward to the carrots and potatoes they used to eat before they went on this adventure to North Carolina, so he scurried to do his father's bidding.

Isaac cleared away heavy underbrush and marked some trees to cut later for cabin logs. Mary and Hannah worked at making the shelter into a home, temporary though it was. Planting a garden would have to wait a few more days, although it was already well into the growing season.

A WEEK later Mary and the children finally found time to clear the land for a simple vegetable garden. She planted seeds carried from her Pennsylvania garden that she knew would germinate quickly. Fortunately, winter would come later in this colony so much farther south; they needed the longer growing season since she was starting the planting so late.

On the third First Day since they arrived, Isaac invited his brothers and their families to join them in worship, the first formal Quaker meeting in their new land. More than fifteen adults gathered in the clearing while the children played quietly under the watchful eyes of their older cousins. Mary looked around in wonder and satisfaction before settling into the silence of the meeting. The messages were of gratitude for their safe passage and praise for God's blessings. Mary rose at the end of the meeting. "Friends, what a joyful celebration of our new life in the wilderness. Let's rise and break bread together. Our children have gathered wild greens and berries, and the men have caught some fish. Come! *This is the day which the Lord hath made; we will rejoice and be glad in it!*"

ONE EVENING, Isaac led Mary and the children to a small rise overlooking the narrow, winding river. He had cleared enough of the scrub trees and shrubs that they could see the view of the distant hills. He put his arm around Mary's waist, and she leaned into her husband. The children were wriggling and wanted to run and slide down the slope, but Isaac and Mary grasped their small hands firmly.

"This, Mary, this, dear children, is where I want to build our home," he said. "We can see the river from here and watch the sunlight play over the hills. Even better, over by those rocks," he pointed out, "is a clear, cold spring. 'Twill not be far from our new front door. I'll build thee a small spring house so thee will have a cool place to store food," he promised his wife with a smile.

"Oh, the children will be pleased. No more trekking down to the river and lugging water in buckets."

The family stood a long time, looking over the small river valley. Shortly before sunset, they turned toward home, walking hand in hand. It had been a glorious afternoon.

WHEN WINTER CAME, Mary and Isaac were grateful that the weather was not as harsh as in the Pennsylvania colony. On a cold but sunny day, Mary felt the pressure that let her know her baby was soon to be born. At dusk, she gasped from the pain.

"Isaac, my love, my time has come. Please drive the children to thy cousin Lydia's house. Then get thy sister-in-law Susanna to assist me in delivering thy new child."

Lydia herself was expecting a baby in four months, and she and Mary had agreed to watch over each other's children while their babes were being birthed. Isaac bundled the children in their warmest clothes, set the three of them in the wagon, and covered them with blankets. Thirty minutes later, Lydia helped him carry the children into the house and bed them near the fire.

Isaac's brother had staked a claim not far from their

cousin. He stopped by their shack and said to Susanna, "It's time, dear sister. Mary is calling for thee."

While Isaac was away, Mary was busy preparing for her confinement. She set a kettle of water on the fire, placed the cloths for the baby nearby to keep warm, and put her oldest bedding on the straw pallet they were using for a bed. Mary had birthed three other children, but in Pennsylvania she had a midwife in attendance, and her aunt and sister Katherine were also there. It was scary to be going through this alone.

Mary had been walking around as the pains came closer and closer together. Now, she knew, it was almost time. She was grateful when Susanna arrived, along with her twelve-year-old daughter, Miriam, and quickly took charge, hustling Mary onto the pallet.

Less than an hour later, Isaac heard a lusty cry. Miriam rushed outside to find him. "Uncle Isaac, thee has a fine new daughter. I watched her being born. I've never seen anything like it! Ma says it was an easy birth, but it looked hard to me. Mary moaned and cried out."

Isaac didn't want to hear of Mary's pain and suffering, but Miriam continued proudly to describe how she helped. Finally, Isaac cut her off and went into the shack to see his wife. Susanna handed him the baby wrapped in a warm cloth.

"Brother, here is thy daughter, the first child born in our new colony. This is a glorious day, to be sure."

Isaac knelt by the pallet, and together he and Mary held their daughter.

"Dearest Mary, I so wanted to build thee a snug house before our child was birthed. This shack is poor and humble."

"My husband, this shack is our home. Our savior was born in an even more humble place, crowded with animals and smelling of their muck. At least thee left our horse and mules outside." At that, Isaac laughed, and Mary went on. "Thy babe is a blessing to our family."

Isaac wanted their child to be named Mary out of love for his dear wife, which filled Mary with pleasure. However, William, still a toddler, struggled to pronounce Mary, and eventually the little sister became May to the family.

OVER THE WINTER, the shack they once considered cozy was drafty, smoky from the makeshift hearth, and uncomfortably crowded with three small children and an infant. In early spring, Isaac was finally able to start building their larger, sturdier house.

When Isaac's parents had emigrated to Pennsylvania from Ireland, they carried with them a small pamphlet, issued by William Penn, with detailed instructions on how to build a basic cabin in the American wilderness. Isaac had meticulously copied these instructions and brought them with him to the new land, knowing they would be too far away to rely on the advice of their older relatives.

He and Mary spent an afternoon laying out the boundaries of the house and gardens with sticks. The house would be twenty feet by eighteen, with one large room on the lower floor and a loft above for the children's sleeping space. Mary walked through the area several times, envisioning where they should place the fireplace and hearth for cooking. She wanted the front door and, maybe, in the future, a window to look out over this view. The house would face somewhat west, and she anticipated the great joy of standing in the doorway at her favorite time of the day, admiring the colors of the setting sun as it sank below the hills. They marked off boundaries for her kitchen garden close to the house. And she needed a root cellar for storing the vegetables they would get from their garden. She wanted shelves for the crocks of pickled vegetables and fermented fruits she planned to process when she had a better kitchen. Of course, she needed time to make the crocks and pottery jars from the rich clay on their land. Smiling, she thought, *Or, more likely, I need money to buy them from the traders who passed through the region.* Making pots was not one of the skills she had developed living in New Garden.

North Carolina was blessed with deep forests of strong trees, which made a sturdy log cabin for the Jacksons. Isaac and his brothers helped each other build their houses, and all used the same general plan. Working together they cut logs, and Isaac's older nephews and nieces stripped bark and cut off the branches with a hatchet. The men placed the logs horizontally upon each other and chinked the spaces with stones and wedges of wood. The women and older girls plastered over the logs with the mud and clay that was plentiful along the banks of the Eno River and the creeks. The roofs were covered with boards held in place by weight timbers. The door hung on straps of hide; Isaac intended to carve some wooden hinges over the winter. For the two windows on the front of the house he made sturdy shutters that could be opened for light or closed against the weather. He also built a strong ladder with wide steps against the wall so the children could safely clamber up to the sleeping loft.

At one end of the house, he and his brothers built a stone fireplace capable of holding several large logs. Since this would be used for cooking as well as heating, he contracted with a blacksmith, who had recently arrived, to forge a crane, andirons, and pot hooks on which to hang the heavy kettle Mary had brought from their home in New Garden.

They also made a temporary chimney on the side of the house, stacking and mortaring stones until they were about chest high; the upper part was made of hardwood logs and mud daub. Hannah laughed to see the way the top part of the chimney leaned away from the house.

Isaac laughed with her. "Aye, my Hannah, the chimney is a funny sight, but I'm not a stonemason. I fear if I tried to build a tall, straight stone chimney, the whole thing could tumble down. At least this way, the house will be safe from wayward sparks. We'll find a mason who can finish it and make us a fine, watertight chimney, one that does not look so odd."

Mary asked her husband, "Please, Isaac, add a wooden floor; I'm already so tired of the red clay dust from the dirt floor settling over everything inside."

"Mary, my love, I won't be able to give thee such a floor right now. We have no sawmill to plane the planks evenly. But others have shown me how to make a puddled floor. I'm assured that the clay in these parts can be packed in, smoothed out, and dried. Such a floor will be almost as hard as solid planks. It's the best we can do for now. I'll give thee what thee desires when I can, I promise."

"Oh, Isaac, the house is perfect as it is. Thee's right. I ask too much too soon. And thee did give me window openings—two of them, when I had hoped for one. And that will do splendidly!"

Looking over their new house, Mary and Isaac sighed contentedly.

The major part of the work was completed before cold weather settled in. Isaac still needed to build her a root cellar; he planned to nestle it into the hillside and line it with river rocks. He also promised her a well, so that she wouldn't have to carry water as far. Again, that would have to wait until experienced well diggers could be found to help him. In the meantime, Mary convinced him the nearby spring would do nicely.

When they moved in, Mary looked with pleasure at the pair of candlesticks on the rough oak mantel that Isaac had built into the stone fireplace. Her mother had brought them from Ireland in the 1720s, and Mary had packed them carefully for the trip to North Carolina. Their few tin dishes and cups were stacked neatly beside the candlesticks. Isaac and his brother carried in the bedstead and the wooden plank table and benches; Isaac had found time to build these simple pieces of furniture during their first winter, before they started construction on the house. Hannah helped her mother drag the children's bedding up to the loft. Building shelves, chairs, and other furniture could wait until winter came again.

On a sunny, warm day early in the following spring, Mary was digging out roots and rocks in the area for the herbs she wanted to plant next to her vegetable garden. As she worked, she daydreamed about the herbs she planned to dry. She could already smell them hanging in her rafters, lending a pleasant fragrance to the somewhat foul air in the closed, crowded house. She pictured herself, maybe someday, taking them to market for some money, which they sorely needed, although the closest was all the way down near Cane Creek. Someday, there would be one much closer, she predicted.

Suddenly a tangle of very young black snakes slithered out from a large rock as she moved it with her hoe. Mary jumped back, catching her heel in the hem of her long skirt. She lost her balance, waving her arms wildly and sat down hard in the vegetable garden, her legs splayed in front of her.

"Saint Patrick," she wailed, "patron of my homeland, I beseech thee, rid my garden of these writhing creatures who lurk in the undergrowth, as thee drove the serpents from Ireland!"

Dismayed, she saw the remnants of the young, tender bean plants now crushed and poking out around her. A whole section destroyed.

"My beans, all that hard work," she moaned. Then she started to laugh. "Nay, 'twas a great bean massacre! And me, a good Quaker, invoking a papist saint!"

I can't even blame the snakes, she realized. *They are the harmless kind, not the venomous ones with diamond-shaped heads we were warned about.*

"Never thee mind, Saint Patrick," she called out. "Leave them be. The creatures eat rodents that would damage my crops. At least the ones I don't massacre myself!" And she started laughing again.

She scrambled up, brushed down her skirt, and straightened her bonnet. She glanced around. No one else had seen her humiliation, nor her own private joke. Although, she thought, she would probably tell Isaac in the privacy of their bed tonight. He would enjoy a good laugh.

ONE DAY not long after their new house was completed, Isaac brought home a small, wriggling puppy. The children were ecstatic. Hannah remembered their old spaniel, which had died before they left for North Carolina; she loved animals and had been asking for a dog for what seemed to her like forever. The boys quickly named the pup Brownie, even though she was mostly white with only a few brown and black markings. Hannah had wanted to name her

Misty, but she was overruled by her siblings. Their father warned them that when the pup grew, she would be a working dog for the farm, not a plaything, but he smiled as he said it. Brownie would just have to fill both roles as she grew.

As much as Hannah wanted Brownie to be her very own pet, the puppy had other ideas. Brownie followed Edward and William everywhere they went. They threw sticks for her to fetch. They chased her around the barnyard; when they caught her, they all tumbled together, rolling on the ground, giggling and laughing.

One quiet afternoon, Mary heard her sons calling from the woods and knew they were playing a game with the dog. Brownie needed to be a working animal on the Jackson farm, helping to herd the livestock and chasing away rats and other pests, but the children often treated her like a pet. She heard Edward run away as far as he could, yelling, "Brownie, here Brownie." His younger brother headed in the opposite direction, also calling, "Brownie, here Brownie."

The dog bounded back and forth between the boys, chasing them as they ran and called. It was a fun game for both the children and the animal. They played until all of them, hot and thirsty, were united in a tangled mess in the middle of the woods. They raced back to the house for water and to collapse at their mother's feet. They talked over each other trying to tell her about their game.

William said, "She came to me, so she likes me the best."

Edward poked his brother and said, "But she came when I called, even when she was on her way to thee, so she likes *me* the best."

Brownie lifted her head and looked at each of the boys. With a sigh, she settled down and fell asleep.

"Boys, I think Brownie likes thee equally well," Mary said. "Chasing thee was a good game for her and for thee. Now, lie down and take a wee nap as thy pup is doing. Then thee can help me gather food for thy supper. Thy father should be returning from the field shortly, and he's sure to be very hungry."

Mary shook her head with a smile because they were unknowingly training Brownie to find them if ever they were really lost or in trouble. Not that Brownie would willingly leave them out of her sight even without learning this game.

Chapter Four

Before leaving Pennsylvania, Isaac had written a letter to Perquimans Monthly Meeting, the oldest Quaker meeting in North Carolina. In Tenth Month 1751, he received a letter informing him that a new meeting had been established at Cane Creek. A large group of Quaker families had settled in the area several years earlier. Already they were a vibrant and growing community; they had been worshiping together informally and asked the Quaker leaders on the coast to recognize them as an official meeting.

The letter suggested that Isaac and the other Friends along the Eno River transfer their membership to this new meeting, the closest to their new home. Isaac and Mary had requested a certificate from New Garden meeting to show proof that they were members in good standing and clear of debts or entanglements. Mary had carefully wrapped the precious document in paper coated in beeswax to keep it safe and dry and packed it in the little trunk that carried the family Bible and her mother's treasured candlesticks.

· · ·

ON A COOL, crisp morning at the end of Eleventh Month, Isaac and Mary set off to present their certificates of removal to this new meeting. Others from their community also went along to deliver their own certificates or just to have an opportunity to worship with the Cane Creek Friends.

The children climbed into the wagon, excited about this great adventure. Mary had promised them picnics and new friends to play with. The meeting was almost thirty miles from their home on the Eno. The group traveled slowly and stopped along the way over two nights. They wanted to arrive at the meeting early on First Day.

Autumn leaves were no longer on the trees, and the scent of winter was in the air, but the temperature was still comfortable. In the evening they found it quite pleasant to sit around the fire with their relatives, the children playing with their cousins, no chores to distract them from enjoying each other's company. They had all been so busy, clearing their lands, building their houses, and planting their gardens. This was the first time to just sit and visit.

At Cane Creek, the Friends from the Eno area were warmly welcomed. Mary took the children to the women's side of the newly built, simple meetinghouse. Isaac joined the men on the other side. The elders, both men and women, sat facing the rest of the congregation on benches at the front. The children sat quietly with the women in the meeting for worship, but the younger ones soon grew restless. William clambered into his mother's lap and started to mumble. Mary held her finger to her lips to quiet him. She motioned to her daughter, and Hannah took her two brothers outside to run and burn off some of their energy, leaving May dozing on a blanket at her mother's feet.

A large group of youngsters in the yard were playing together quietly under the watchful eyes of their older siblings. Hannah looked wistfully at the men and women sitting quietly in worship. Now that she was eleven years old and no longer a little girl, she had been looking forward to being a part of the adult meeting. She did listen carefully when she heard one of the elders speak at length about God's abiding grace. Someday, she dreamed that she, too, would be a respected minister. But for now, her task was to stay with the children.

After the meeting ended, everyone gathered in the yard for a simple yet hearty meal and to share stories with the other Friends. As the women cleared the picnic area and spent time with their children, Isaac went to the elders to present their certificate. Simon Dixon, the founder of the meeting, read it aloud to the men gathered:

"From our Monthly Meeting of men and women Friends held at New Garden in the Yearly Meeting for Pennsylvania and New Jersey to friends and brethren of North Carolina, Greetings: Whereas our Friend Isaac Jackson did some time ago acquaint us with his intention of removing himself and family to North Carolina and Desirous of a Certificate, we therefore do Certify that the said Isaac and Mary, his wife, hath behaved themselves orderly amongst us their Brethren & Sisters where they dwelt and now leaveth us in Unity. They have left this place free from Debts or Defraud to any man & we have Cause to hope and believe that they will so behave themselves for the future, they may Deserve the Religious notice & care of Friends for their good. Signed on order & on behalf of our Said Meeting."

The men settled into worship to consider this request. Finally, they agreed to accept the Jackson family into membership and recorded their approval in the written minutes of the meeting. Mary and Isaac's little community near the Eno River did not yet have a Quaker meeting. The

Jacksons had held worship in their cabin from the beginning, mostly with relatives. Isaac and Mary prayed together every evening before sending the children to bed, but the community gathered only sporadically on First Days. Mary and Isaac were elated to again be members of a Quaker meeting.

IN EARLY 1754, the Jacksons received a request to return to Cane Creek. Mary and Isaac walked their horses slowly down the worn path to the meetinghouse. They looked forward to worshipping with the Friends they had met when they surrendered their certificates. But they were also mindful that their attendance was requested, not just invited; the elders had sent word that they wished to speak with them on a matter of some urgency. This felt serious and a little frightening. They spoke little as they got closer to Cane Creek. After dismounting, they tied up the horses and held hands as they crossed the yard to the meetinghouse.

After a long and deep worship, Mary met with some of the women of the meeting. Abigail Pike spoke up first. "Mary Jackson, we have prayed about the Friends on the Eno River. Thee and thy husband hold meetings in thy home and welcome other Friends in the area. Other Friends worship with just their families or not at all. We believe it's time to begin setting up meeting for worship in thy area. Eno Friends need the structure of a meeting to make sure they stay strong in the discipline of our ways. Recognize that thine will be under the care and guidance of Cane Creek Meeting; Eno Friends are only authorized to hold First Day and midweek meetings for worship. Once thy meeting is well established, thee may apply to us for full

recognition as a Friends meeting able to accept memberships and conduct thy own business."

Mary smiled and nodded her agreement.

Abigail continued, "We have visited in thy area and met
with thee and some of the other women. Many spoke of
their esteem for thee and that they find thee cheerful and
also God-fearing and faithful. After prayerful discernment,
we are clear to appoint thee as the clerk or leader of the
women's meeting. Thee will oversee the women's business.
Aye, but thee will also be an example and a spiritual guide
for them. The men are asking the same of thy husband to
join thee in doing God's work on the Eno."

Mary blanched at the enormity of the work being asked
of her. She stifled a flicker of pleasure at being asked. *Who
wouldn't want to have her gifts recognized in such a visible
way?*

Mary gathered her thoughts before speaking. "I'm grateful
that thee has placed such trust in me. But, dear Friends, I'm not
sure I am ready to take on the leadership of this community.
We're poorly organized in our area. Isaac and I have little
enough influence over our extended family members and even
less over the Friends who are not close relatives. Does thee truly
think the Eno Friends are ready to organize? And I ask humbly,
why must my husband and I be the ones called to this work?"

Sarah Chamness jumped in. "Mary, as Abigail has said,
we are clear that thee and Isaac are the right ones to unite
the Friends in thy area. Thy neighbors already go to thee for
advice and counsel. The worship meetings in thy home are
well-attended. Many Friends say that they look forward to
thy ministry in worship. In Pennsylvania, thee was just
starting to use the power of thy ministry in the work of
Friends. Thee's more ready than thee might believe."

Mary hesitated and sat thoughtfully for a while. "Has

thee considered Rachel Maddock? She's quite strong in her faith, and her husband Joseph is a strong and capable leader."

"Dear Mary, we visited many of the Eno women and held them in our prayers as we sought a way forward with this concern. Thee is the one God is calling. Thee is the one who must work to bring Friends on the Eno into the discipline of the Society of Friends. Ask Rachel Maddock to work with thee, if thee feels she is right to be a boon companion in this undertaking."

Mary asked that the women worship with her while she contemplated their request. For almost an hour, she and the other women silently prayed and listened earnestly for God's will before Mary felt clear to take on the responsibility being laid on her.

"I accept the duty," Mary said, "which thee is laying on me. With thy support and love, I promise to do my best to be faithful to the principles of our Society and to the calling of our Lord."

Abigail told Mary that she and Sarah had been appointed to visit the Eno Friends frequently and to be available to Mary for advice and guidance. That gave Mary more confidence. They were both gifted elders with leadership experience in Pennsylvania before they emigrated and now in their own Cane Creek community.

"This has been a lot for thee to consider," Abigail said. "Let's leave each other for now. Go, talk to thy husband, pray together. Thee will find a way forward."

After the other women walked away, Mary sat alone in quiet contemplation. She was startled when Isaac placed his hand on her shoulder.

"Is thee all right?" he asked gently. "I have just come from a meeting with the elders. They told me of the burden they have laid on the two of us. Did thee accept the call?

Will thee work to establish a meeting among the Eno Friends?"

Mary clutched at his hand and held it against her breast. "Dear Isaac, of course we'll work together in this undertaking. I did accept. I'll do my best to lead the women in forming a strong community."

Isaac sat down beside her. "Mary, thee knows the men of Cane Creek asked me to serve as the elder of Eno Meeting. They had told me that the women were requesting the same of thee. I asked to be released from this request. I fear that our family and our farm would suffer if we were both so engaged in the work of the meeting. I told them of our young children who aren't yet old enough to be a help on the farm. We talked a long time, and the men agreed that I not be called to this work. They will ask Joseph Maddock to serve as a leader with thee."

Mary hugged her husband and was loath to let go. "Are thee sure that I should be the one so named and not thee? Thee's by far the better leader. I fear I'm too frivolous at times, and not at all the spiritual leader our meeting needs."

"And I, dear wife, am too contentious and ill-tempered at times. Mary, my love, we're a team. We will be strong together, but I'll carry on the work of our farm whilst thee needs to attend to the affairs of the meeting. I'll be thy support and helpmeet. Don't fret; it is right. God isn't asking more than thee can handle."

Mary and Isaac rose and joined the others to say their goodbyes and headed up the path. They had a ride of several days ahead of them, but they stopped early to settle for the night. There was much to talk about and much to do to organize the Eno community. Instead, they sat in silent wonder for a long while before lying down on their cloaks for the night.

Mary put her head on Isaac's chest and wrapped her

arms tightly around him. "Don't talk. Just hold me right now. Let's just lie here and warm each other. We'll talk tomorrow and often after that."

Isaac kissed her cheek and squeezed her tightly. "Good night, my love. Sweet dreams."

A FEW WEEKS LATER, Mary and Joseph Maddock called together the Quakers along the Eno River and from the town that was growing up several miles to the south. The Friends gathered in the large room at Maddock's mill. When the clerk visiting from Cane Creek stood and asked that they settle into worship together, he told them of their request and their desire to see the Eno Friends eventually raise their own meeting. A murmur of pleasure coursed through the group. He said that the meeting had prayed about them and were clear to ask Joseph Maddock and Mary Jackson to serve as elders of the new preparative meeting. When eventually they would be authorized to hold their own meetings for business, it was these two Friends who would serve as the first clerks. The local Friends looked at each other and smiled. Most nodded their heads in agreement. The Cane Creek Friends had, they knew, chosen their leaders wisely.

After the worship was concluded, Mary asked that the women gather in the Maddock's house. Sarah Chamness had come from Cane Creek and joined them to explain their responsibilities as a women's meeting. "As Quaker women you have an important role in the conduct of the life of meeting and are responsible for ensuring the well-being of members." They would meet separately from the men to discuss the business of meeting, she explained, including recommending memberships, supervising marriages, disciplining delinquent members, and reporting to Cane Creek Meeting.

Mary added, "The men have their responsibilities, but we don't have to consult with the men when we make decisions in our areas of concern."

One of the Friends spoke up. "In my meeting in Pennsylvania, the men sometimes overruled the decisions of the women's meetings. Is that their right?"

"Aye, they can, if we disagree and the concern warrants them doing so," Mary said. "And, for the near future, we're subject to the oversight of our Friends in Cane Creek. But let's not worry about that now. We shall conduct our own business in prayerful discernment, asking God's will for our community. The men will see this, and we shall not be bothered by any attempt to control us."

Sarah Chamness said she was well satisfied that the Eno women's meeting would be strong and serve Friends well. "Let's all now settle into grateful worship," she said. After a long period of silent prayer, Mary and Sarah shook hands to signal that the meeting had ended. Each woman in the room shook hands with her neighbor. They rose and started chattering with each other. Soon the room was filled with joyful exclamations and lots of hugs. This was an exciting new beginning.

Mary and Joseph Maddock appointed a time for First Day worship and for midweek worship. As they dispersed, everyone was admonished to take care to attend these services and to stay faithful in the discipline of Friends.

Over the next few years, Sarah Chamness and Abigail Pike visited regularly from Cane Creek Meeting to assist and provide guidance. Mary was often chastised for not keeping good records and for not reporting regularly back to

Cane Creek. She chafed silently at this. Mary found it difficult to get the women to record the concerns and decisions of their meeting; it seemed to them an unnecessary burden. The men were also disciplined for their own lax reporting, but that was small consolation to Mary.

Eno Friends were not always diligent in attending their own First Day meetings, and often only a few arrived for midweek meeting. Mary struggled to get many of the women to regularly attend meetings for business. All the women were tired from the work of cooking, cleaning, mending, gardening, and assisting their husbands in planting and harvesting. Many of them were young and just starting their own families, so the added burdens of pregnancy and care of their children kept them from being active in the meeting. Most did try to attend as often as they could and encouraged their menfolk to participate.

It was not an easy task for Mary, but she felt that the Cane Creek elders expected her to persevere in building a strong Quaker meeting in the Eno wilderness. Isaac always encouraged her when she felt the responsibility too daunting, and prayed with her when she feared that she was failing in the work. Mostly, though, Mary found the challenge of leading the women to be energizing and heartening. With God and Isaac on her side, she knew, she could not fail.

Chapter Five

1754

Isaac and Mary had worked hard to build up their Quaker community from the time they moved to the Eno valley and the meeting was finally getting established. In Twelfth Month, they received word that two women ministers from overseas were on their way from Cane Creek Meeting and would arrive late in the afternoon. That these two ministers were coming to stay with the Friends at Eno was cause for great joy. They had so few visitors, other than overseers from Cane Creek Meeting who visited to see if Eno Friends were faithfully following the discipline.

"Edward. William. Stop thy dawdling. We have much work to do," Mary ordered, flustered, as she placed their newest son, John, in his cradle. "The bedding needs to be shaken out and fresh water carried from the well."

The two boys took one more swipe at each other and hurried to their chores. They were excited by the prospect of meeting Friends from England and Ireland. They weren't sure what that meant exactly, but they knew their parents considered it an honor.

Thirteen-year-old Hannah, quietly sewing by the fire, tried to ignore the commotion. She looked up when she heard her name.

"Hannah, run to thy uncle Benjamin's house and tell them the good news about our visitors," Mary said as she bustled about the house. "Say that we will worship together tomorrow morning after taking care of the animals. Tell them to please come. We should all sit in worship with our guests and, if God favors them in our worship meeting, we'll hear the words given to them for us. I know I should not presume God's will, but I do so hope they are called to speak. One of the visitors is from Ireland!" She grinned. "From the land of your grandparents!"

"Mother, shall I go to Uncle Samuel's and Aunt Ruth's houses, also?"

"Nay, Hannah. Ask one of thy cousins to carry the news to them. I don't want thee away from home after dark, and dusk falls so early in Twelfth Month. Besides, I'll need thee to attend to John, so he won't disrupt the news our guests carry. Just go now and come back quickly."

Mary set about making a rich stew. She quickly mixed batter for soda bread, using the recipe handed down from her Irish grandmother, and set it to bake in the oven built into her hearth. Next, she made a sweet cake from her supply of hickory nuts that the boys had gathered in the fall. It was important to her that the travelers would feel welcome, and serving good, nourishing food was the best way to warm them from the cold. She hoped they planned to remain in the area for a long while; she had so much she wanted to ask them, and she was hungry for any news from abroad and from the Friends they had visited along the way to the Eno valley.

This was a wonderful opportunity, and Mary wanted to do everything she could to take advantage of their wisdom and experience.

The two women arrived before dark.

"Boys," Isaac instructed his sons as the two visitors alighted, "take their horses into the barn. Brush them down well and give them some of the corn from the bin."

"Come, come in," called Mary in greeting. "You must be tired. We have stew and warm bread, freshly baked. Welcome to our home. Please, come in." Mary couldn't stop talking in her joy at meeting her company.

Inside the warm house, she took their cloaks. As she brushed off the dust of their journey, she ran her fingers longingly over the fabric. The cut and the weave were much finer than she had become accustomed to in the colonies. She was tired of the coarse homespun she usually wore and, for a moment, allowed herself to wish for a similar garment. She shook her head to rid it of that notion. *She must not let envy take hold.*

After supper the women joined Mary and Isaac before the large stone fireplace. "Please, Friend Catherine, tell us of thy journey to the Carolinas," Isaac urged.

Catherine Phillips settled back in the comfortable chair, a shawl wrapped around her shoulders and her feet up on a warmed brick. "Mary Peisley and I sailed to the colonies in Tenth Month. We spent nine weeks on the ship before we reached Charleston."

Mary Jackson gasped. She vividly remembered the uncomfortable, smelly journey in the hold of the *Sizargh* to Philadelphia from Ireland. She was a young child then, and the misery of the six-week journey threatened to overtake the thrill of moving to a new country. She couldn't imagine spending nine whole weeks on the voyage.

Mary Peisley jumped in. "It's worth the hardship. We truly are doing God's work here in the colonies."

Catharine smiled at her companion and continued, "We made our way to Cane Creek traveling on roads that were little more than trading paths. Fortunately, we often found Friends who offered hospitality, but occasionally we had to sleep on the hard ground. It's milder in Carolina than in England at this time of year, but still, many nights were cold. One night we rested in an itinerant camp and slept under a little shed on a rising sandy ground, which abounded with lofty pines. In some ways, it was quite lovely, and we strongly felt the spirit of our Lord over us in our journey."

Mary Peisley had been silent but added in her soft brogue, "We appreciate thy hospitality. It's gratifying to be able to stay in the homes of Quakers. And," she added with a smile, "to receive a warm Irish welcome at that."

The Jacksons were most eager to hear all the news the two women carried from overseas. *Catherine Phillips was English, but, oh joy! Mary Peisley was from Ireland.* Mary Jackson vaguely remembered her Irish home. Her parents had moved the family to Pennsylvania when she was a small child, but they had kept alive the memory of the old country. Her home was now in North Carolina; she was mostly satisfied with her life in the new country, but she and Isaac had both been born in Ireland, and Irish blood ran in their veins.

Mary Peisley spoke of the famine of the 1740s, in which hundreds of thousands of Irish died. The country was recovering from the loss, but there was rising anger against the British government that controlled the country and was demanding more and more in taxation and usurping more and more power.

Isaac nodded. "I see the beginnings of the same struggles in the eastern Carolina counties under the British-appointed officials who control the industry and trade. The Piedmont is not yet affected. But give it time; their greed for money and power will reach us. As British citizens, we need to accept it, but Friends in the east complain mightily about the government's overreach. We don't look forward to the time when the government decides we also need controlling."

"But we also bring good news," the Irish visitor added. "There are now more than 150 Quaker meetings in Ireland alone."

Catherine joined in, "And there are more and more Quaker meetings in England, although Friends are still persecuted and imprisoned for not tithing to the established church." She sighed. "It's difficult at times."

They continued through the evening, telling the Jacksons about people they may have known from their ancestral meetings. The close of the day was relaxing and cheerful. It was cold outside, but the fireside was warm and inviting, and Mary and Isaac reveled in the ministers' company. After a while, though, the two women yawned. They had traveled by horseback for nearly thirty miles from Cane Creek meeting and were exhausted.

Mary told her sons to take blankets to the barn and instructed the children to sleep there with the animals. The boys were delighted; they would be away from their mother's sharp eyes. She smiled fondly at them, knowing they would take full advantage of their unexpected freedom. "But before you get distracted by play, bed down the animals. Set the lantern up high on the hook so the straw won't catch fire and where you won't knock it over with your lively play." She turned to her daughter. "Hannah, thee will be there, too, to make sure the boys settle down and get some sleep."

She directed the visitors to use the bed in the recess off the kitchen, where she and Isaac usually slept. This space, near the big fireplace, was the warmest part of the house. After banking the fire and trimming the lantern wicks, Mary and Isaac climbed to the children's loft, taking the baby with them.

In the morning, while Isaac and the children fed the livestock, Mary prepared a hearty breakfast of sausage, soda bread, and blueberry jam that she had put up during the summer. The boys were especially greedy about the jam, for their mother only brought it out on special occasions. They wheedled for more, but Mary silently shook her head and they quieted.

Isaac's brothers Benjamin and Samuel Jackson and their broods arrived and joined them as the adults were finishing their breakfast. The children begged leave from the table, and the cousins ran off to play. "Come back when I call. We'll meet in worship shortly," Isaac said as they scampered outdoors.

The cabin was small, but it was deemed too chilly to gather outside for meeting. Chairs, cushions, benches, and chunks of wood were arranged in every corner of the room so that all could squeeze in. The Carolinians hoped that their visitors would be moved to share ministry out of the silence.

After a time, Benjamin rose. He spoke at length about God's grace as the new year approached, citing Exodus 23:16, "And the feast of harvest, the first fruits of thy labors, which thou hast sown in the field: and the feast of ingathering, which is in the end of the year, when thou hast gathered in thy labors out of the field."

He settled back down. After a long silence, Catherine Phillips arose. She took a deep breath, for the message she was about to give was difficult. She began by reminding them that it was the will of the Almighty, measurably to baptize everyone into the state of grace.

She continued, "We could not but suffer in spirit with His pure seed, and it seems as though a drawn sword was delivered to us in this the beginning of our journey, which we're to use against spiritual wickedness."

Catherine then urged them to be more diligent in attending weekday meeting, for it would strengthen them in observing God's laws. She closed with a deep entreaty to lead them out of their indifference and transgressions into a holy state of oneness with the Lord.

That evening, after all but the two guests had departed, Isaac and Mary took a quiet walk together. Mary finally spoke up. She was troubled. "Isaac, we've been trying since we came to Carolina to bring the Friends in the Eno under the discipline of our faith. We've held meetings in our home and visited others in theirs. That this stranger from overseas exhorts us to do more, that she tells us our friends and families are disorderly, hurts me to my very soul. It's an arrow to my heart."

Isaac wrapped his arm around her shoulders and hugged her closely. "I agree with thee, Mary. But the elders and overseers of Cane Creek Meeting have been saying the same things. I'm sure they urged Catherine to try to correct our shortcomings. We must do more."

"But did her message come from God or from the elders? Unless they told her of our difficulties, she couldn't have known."

"Mary, thee must go to them with thy concern. Talk to them. Listen to them."

"Dear Isaac, will thee go with me?"

"Nay, my love. Thee will be able to speak thy truth more freely if thee's just with the women. Be brave. This is important to thee and to our Eno Friends."

Days later, after their visitors had left to visit New Garden Meeting about fifty miles west, Isaac walked into the house and hesitated. Mary was standing at the table kneading bread, or more precisely, Mary was beating the daylights out of a lump of dough. She was muttering, none too quietly, working out her frustrations.

"It's not fair," she muttered, unaware of Isaac's presence. "These so-called Friends come here just to criticize our meeting—to criticize me! Cane Creek Meeting sent elders from their own meeting to tell me what I should be doing. To tell me what I'm doing wrong! *Damnú!* They appointed me as elder. Did they think I was a miracle worker? We know already that Friends in this area don't always live within the discipline. *Ejits!* Don't they know how hard we're working to bring Eno Quakers to lead good lives!"

She paused to take a breath. Isaac started to say something; Mary looked up at him crossly and exclaimed, "*Damnú!* Even the Friends who visited from across the sea criticized us, and we were so looking forward to their visit. I could expect it from Friend Catherine. She's English, and the English are *always* critical of us Irish. But from Mary Peisley—Mary Peisley, an *Irish* woman. She should have been on our side."

Every sentence was punctuated with louder and louder thumps of the dough.

They had been married long enough that Isaac knew it was best to turn and leave quietly. His Mary was usually very even-tempered, but when she started cursing in Irish—

the same language her mother used when her temper got the best of her—there was no stopping his wife until her frustration was spent. He knew that, even when it was not his fault that she was so angry, anything he did or said would only make it worse.

Isaac smiled to himself as he walked away. She looked so charming and righteous in her anger. Rosy cheeks, fire in her flashing green eyes. Her strong, lightly freckled arms working the dough fiercely. It was sure to be one tough loaf of bread. *At least she rarely stays angry for long,* he thought with a grin, *we'll have some good loving tonight when we take to our bed.*

If he had not been a Quaker, Isaac would have whistled as he walked away. And, in fact, he did let out a few cheerful notes, after making sure he was well out of hearing of the elders, if any were nearby.

The next morning, the family awoke to snowfall. The flakes were large, and Mary knew they wouldn't amount to much. Before their move, Hannah and Edward had spent hours with their cousins and friends playing in the deep Pennsylvania snow. This much snow was uncommon here in this part of the Carolinas; usually it only amounted to a dusting. The younger children had little experience with it.

Mary shooed them outside when the snow started to let up. Hannah tried to teach William and May about building a snowman, but it was not the right kind of snow and wouldn't stick together. So, she, Edward, and the two littler ones trundled over to a hillock and climbed to the top. Like little otters, they slid down the slope and raced up to do it again. Finally, even the most intrepid of the youngsters was exhausted.

Hannah bustled the children into the house. She and

her mother helped them take off their cold, wet clothes and bundled them into warm blankets by the fire. Mary gave each a mug of broth from the pot hanging from the crane in the fireplace to warm from the inside.

Mary smiled at her children. She shook her head. *I must stop obsessing about Catherine's criticism,* she thought. *This is a wonderful place to live, and we'll do the best we can with Eno Meeting. That is all God can ask of us.*

Chapter Six

1757

Mary felt the first pains early in the morning, shortly after stoking the fire. Isaac had gotten up before dawn to clear the far field. The children were still asleep. She walked around carefully. She did so want this child. She had lost several babies since they moved to North Carolina, but that was much earlier in her pregnancies. She hoped again that this babe about to arrive would be healthy and strong. She said to the empty room. "Well, at this point, only God knows about my baby. She or he is in His hands now."

She stirred the porridge simmering over the fire, drank a large mug of water, and went outside to the bench on the porch to shell peas. The sun was warm on her face, and she relaxed as she worked.

Before she was finished, the pains were coming more frequently. Hannah was inside setting the table for breakfast and heard her mother moaning. She rushed out and grabbed the bowl of peas before it fell. Worried by the look of pain on her mother's face, she asked, "Are thee well? Is it your time?"

Mary nodded weakly. "It seems so."

Hannah ran over to the sty and threw the pea shells into the pen for the pig. William had been given a piglet as payment for clearing brush for one of the neighbors, and the children delighted in watching the animal grow and fatten. She turned back to her mother. "Let me help thee stand up. Come, we'll go inside."

Mary winced and rubbed her hand on her lower back. She took Hannah's arm and went to sit by the fire. She had already birthed six babies, three of them since coming to the Eno valley, but this one felt different. In Pennsylvania she had lost two babies soon after they were born. She still felt a few feeble kicks now and again and prayed that her new babe would live.

"Edward and William," she called out. "Wake up. I need thee right now!"

The boys quickly tumbled down from the sleeping loft. They rarely heard such urgency in their mother's voice. May, who was almost six, rushed into the kitchen at the same time. "Ma, is it time? How can we help?" she asked.

Four-year-old John started to ask what she meant by "Is it time?" but was silenced with a stony look from Hannah.

Mary started to give them orders. "William, thy father is out clearing land back by the northern bend of the river. Saddle one of the horses and fetch him. Edward, run to thy aunt Elizabeth's house and ask her to come quickly. May, go to the pump and bring in water and set it to boil. Hannah, I want thee to take John and little Isaac out to play in the barn."

Hannah interrupted, "But, Ma, I'm sixteen years old. I want to stay. I helped thee when Isaac was born."

"Hannah, please." Mary's words came through tight lips

as she grimaced through another pain. "Take them outside. When William returns, he can take the children to thy aunt Ruth's to spend the day. She'll be glad of their company. Don't fret. Thee will have plenty of time to help with the birth later. I need thee to do this now."

Little Isaac, barely two years old, sensed his mother's distress. He clung to her skirt wailing. "Me stay, Mama, me stay," he cried.

Hannah gently pulled his hands away and picked him up. John, seeing how upset Isaac was, began to cry loudly in solidarity, although he was not sure why. Hannah bustled the two small boys out the door. May's chin started quivering; she was afraid that something bad was happening. Mary could hear the two boys screaming for her all the way to the barn; she knew they would settle down once they started playing in the hay loft. She hugged her young daughter. "Thee's doing good work, May, thank thee. Now fetch water and set it to boil."

The girl beamed. Her mother rarely praised them for just doing what she asked, and this felt special. She wanted to be a help; she wanted to make her mother smile again.

More than an hour later, a horse and buggy rattled into the yard. Edward clambered down, then held out his hand to help his aunt Elizabeth and an older cousin, Mary. Through the window, Mary watched his solicitous care of these women, and smiled. *Maybe he was growing into a gentle, mindful young man—although that outcome seemed doubtful at times.*

Hannah helped him carry in the bags and boxes that his aunt had loaded into the wagon. One of those contained various herbs and potions that Elizabeth used as a healer. Edward didn't think his mother was sick, but he knew from watching some of their animals that giving birth did not always go smoothly, and hoped that maybe the herbs would help.

Elizabeth had already bustled into the house. She was an experienced midwife, and her daughter Mary was learning to follow in her footsteps. She saw with approval that young May had water on the hearth beginning to simmer and had gathered up clean cloths and blankets to warm on the hearthstones. Elizabeth sent May to the barn and told her to send Hannah back to the house. May smiled gratefully and hurried away. It distressed her to see her mother in agony.

"Oh, and May," Elizabeth called out. "Don't wait for William to get back with thy Da. The wagon is still hitched. Have Edward take thyself and the boys to your aunt Ruth's house. Stay there until we send for everyone to come back home."

May ran off to do as bidden, and Elizabeth turned back to the laboring woman. Mary was in the bed near the fireplace and moaning softly. Her face was damp with perspiration. She smiled wanly at her sister-in-law.

"This time it feels different. I think the baby is in distress," she whispered. "He hasn't dropped as he should, even though my water has broken. And I have been feeling birth pains since early morning."

Elizabeth felt Mary's swollen abdomen, pushing and prodding while Mary winced and tried not to cry out. "Mary, I fear thy baby is facing the wrong way. Why didn't thee tell me thee was worried when we talked on First Day? We must get him turned around and soon. Thee must get out of bed and get moving. Now!"

With the help of Hannah and Elizabeth's daughter, Mary struggled out of bed. She started chuckling. "Was thee telling me, Mary, that the baby was coming in rump first, or was thee telling thy daughter Mary? Or maybe my Mary, that thee sent to the barn? Too many Marys!"

It was not really funny, but Mary was tired and light-headed from the labor, and the humor seemed to help at the moment. Elizabeth nodded her head and smiled back at her. "Both my Mary and thee," she replied. "One to get up and move around, and one to help me turn the baby."

Mary walked around the kitchen, her hands on her lower back and stomach. She wanted to just be able to go to sleep but knew that was not an option.

Isaac burst through the door and rushed to his wife. Birthing could be dangerous, and he did not want to lose his beloved wife. He put his arms around her, mostly to calm down and reassure himself she was okay.

William took one look at his laboring mother and asked where the rest of the children were. He was definitely ready to be away from this room. Elizabeth directed him to take care of the livestock. "Then thee will leave with the other children. Now scoot." He ran out, grateful to have something to do away from the house.

Mary stepped back from Isaac and told him to leave too. "Birthing children is women's work," she said. "Elizabeth, Hannah, and Mary will take good care of me. Be gone with thee now." She kissed his cheek and shooed him out the door.

Mary labored for hours, walking around, squatting, occasionally lying down. Elizabeth periodically massaged Mary's belly, trying to maneuver the baby around. Finally, shortly after dark, the baby turned. Both Mary and Elizabeth sighed in relief. Labor resumed in earnest. Mary squatted, supported by Hannah and her cousin Mary, when suddenly the baby's head emerged. Another son slid out into Elizabeth's waiting hands.

Mary fell back onto the bed and Hannah went to wrap her new brother in a warm blanket. He was weak but alive. The women were happily relieved when he gave a feeble cry. Hannah laid the baby on her mother's breast, while Elizabeth delivered the placenta. Her daughter Mary soon took away the soiled cloths and bedding, dragging it out to be burned, and put fresh, clean straw on the bedstead. Hannah raced to the barn to tell her father about his new son.

On a fine fall day, Mary put the weeks' old infant, whom they'd named Thomas, in his basket and asked Hannah to watch the other children. Thomas had just finished nursing, and he would sleep a long while. She was going down to the river and appreciated when she was able to do that alone. Isaac had carved a bench out of a hickory tree that had fallen, in the perfect place for her to see the river and the hillside beyond. A short while later, he joined her. She smiled, patted the bench beside her, and leaned into her husband once he settled in.

"How I love this time of year," she said. "The changing colors of the leaves, and the sunlight dappling through the branches. Does thee see that one bright red tree?" She pointed. "The light is shining directly upon it so that it glows. This must be the light of God specially come to brighten my day."

Isaac smiled as he looked out over the land. "Thee always did love the golds and reds of an autumn day. And the bright orange skies of a winter sunset. Those colors suit thee."

He turned to face Mary and picked up her hand. "I remember well thy green dress that thee wore in our youth. I saw thee in the meetinghouse yard, watching over the younger children. Thy green dress and thy glorious red hair peeking out from thy bonnet were enticing. I was fair captured by the sight. I believe I was smitten with thee from that very moment."

Mary laughed. "Oh, yes, that dress was my favorite. We found the cloth in Philadelphia at my cousin's mercantile. My mother helped me make it; I think she secretly wished she could wear something other than gray. But the elders of the meeting were not so pleased with me. They said I was too worldly. The dress was plain and simple; it was just the wrong color."

"According to those old busybodies."

"Aye, according to them. I was prideful when I wore it, but it made me so merry. I wish Quaker women weren't expected to dress in clothes of gray. Margaret Fell once asked George Fox to buy her cloth for a red dress. I read in her journal that it's a "silly poor Gospel" if we all dress in one color."

Isaac grinned at her. "If a red dress is good enough for the wife of the founder of our Society, so must a green dress be good enough for the likes of thee. And there is none here who will find thee scandalous. All will admire thee for thy boldness and beauty. I myself shall find thee too hard to resist in thy gay finery."

Mary looked up at him. "Isaac, does thee truly think I could wear a green dress again? I do so admire the Anglican women in their colorful clothes, with ribbons and bows. I know that we strive for simplicity, but must we be so drab?"

"On the next market day, I shall buy thee the cloth that thee desires. I fear, though, that I shall be overly taken with longing for thee again when thee wears such a garment. Will my poor heart bear the temptation to take thee in my arms in front of our children and embarrass thee in the presence of our neighbors?"

Mary laughed loudly as Isaac finished his flirtation with a flourish and a broad wink.

"Aye, I'm quite the reprobate," he admitted, wrapping his arm around Mary's shoulder as she giggled. "And 'tis all thy fault, temptress that thee is."

The sun was starting to set, and they lingered for a few more moments, basking in the last of its warmth. When they heard baby Thomas cry, they headed up to the house, hand in hand.

On a warm afternoon in Eighth Month, Mary sent the younger children to their bed for a nap and set the older children at their chores. She picked up Thomas from his cradle and went outside to sit on the bench in front of the house. For a brief while, she stood with her baby on her hip, admiring her garden. She and her daughters had cleared away the leftovers from the summer and planted some of the winter vegetables. Hannah was now preparing the ground for more planting. Mary smiled at the small shoots of the collards poking up. She had recently discovered this winter vegetable, which grew so well here in the Piedmont. After the first frost, this green would become a mainstay of their winter suppers. Her potatoes, onions, and beets were doing well and would supplement the beans, tomatoes, and summer squash she had preserved. And the bright orange pumpkins and golden gourds were a delight to her eye.

Mary had expanded her herb garden over the past year. She loved the fragrance of the herbs drying in her rafters. A native woman who had come to market with her man to trade their skins had taught Mary about the healing benefits of some of the indigenous plants. The woman gave Mary a piece of wild ginger to soothe indigestion and cramps and told her how to root it. Mary also planted lavender for headaches, mint for digestion, osha root for breathing, and thyme to use as an antiseptic. Her plots were producing so well she knew she should be able to take some of her produce and herbs to market.

"Hannah, thee does fine work," she said. "We surely need the shillings that these small crops will bring. But even if we can only use them for barter, this will help us survive if a drought should come upon us."

Thomas began to fuss with hunger as Mary used her free hand to take off her cap, shake out her hair, and loosen her bodice. She sat, gratefully, on the bench Isaac had built beside the house. While her babe was nursing, she leaned back against the warm boards and closed her eyes. The sun felt so good on her bare head and arms.

Isaac came up to the house and stood gazing at his wife for a long moment. Her hair glinted coppery in the sunlight, and she looked so peaceful. Finally, he spoke, his voice reverential. "If there is a more lovely sight in all of God's creation, I would faint from the seeing of it."

Mary opened her eyes and smiled. "Ah, Isaac, such fine words of thine could turn a lass's head. Thee's such a strong, handsome man to be spouting such nonsense. And I, a married woman with a babe at my breast."

He winked at her slowly in that way that promised more to come. "And I thank the Lord every day that I have been blessed with such a wife."

Hannah, overhearing her parents, sat back on her heels and smiled at them. *I'm sixteen years old*, she thought. *Soon I'll be ready to wed. I hope I find a lad who will look at me the same as me da looks at me ma. Even after all these many years.*

As if reading her thoughts, Isaac glanced at his eldest daughter and grinned. "Get on with thee. Back to work!

Avert thy eyes for I aim to kiss thy mother in this bright sunlight, and I wouldn't want thee to be scandalized."

He sat down beside Mary and kissed her, and then kissed the downy head of his baby son at her breast. Leaning back against the house, he said, "Thomas Fincher stopped by as I worked in the field. He had news from town. There's a new sheriff, a man named Edmund Fanning. He built himself an impressive house in town. He's also planning for building new government buildings, to make Corbin Town the seat of Orange County.

"What does that mean for us?" Mary asked.

"No doubt he's a trusted compatriot of our governor, installed here to make sure we pay our due to the crown. We can only hope that he takes the best interests of the colony and our county to heart. But, I delayed the good news. Thomas Fincher gave me a letter for thee from thy sister."

Isaac pulled it from a pocket and waved it in front of her, enticing her to snatch it from his hand. Mary reached for it, again and again, laughing at his antics.

"Here, husband, take thy babe so I might read my letter in peace."

Isaac stood with his son and watched Mary expertly gather her hair and tuck it back in her cap. Slowly, watching him with a sly smile, she fastened her bodice. Isaac took a deep breath and handed her the letter. He went inside to lay the baby in his cradle.

Mary watched him leave. "Aye, a fine man and a good husband and father," she said to Hannah. "Thee could do worse, so choose thy mate carefully. Men think they are the ones doing the choosing, but we women lead the chase and let them believe they caught us."

Hannah grinned at the picture of her father gleefully chasing her mother until she let him catch her. *I want that same joy and love for meself,* she thought as she turned back to her garden work.

Mary held the precious letter and turned it over and over in anticipation. It had been so long since she had heard from Katherine. She opened the folds carefully. In it, her twin sister shared stories of her growing children, and the friends and neighbors Mary had left behind. She closed by remarking, somewhat sadly, that she and her husband wouldn't be joining Mary and Isaac in North Carolina. Their farm in Pennsylvania was prosperous, and her husband was in a trusted position in the legislature. It was too much for them to leave behind.

Mary allowed a few moments for quiet tears, then stood and brushed down her skirts. In the house, she laid the letter on the mantel. She fixed cups of peppermint tea for herself and Isaac and told him the news.

"As much as I miss my sister and wish to have her near, I'm glad we moved here to the Eno Valley. I love our home and our meeting. We're doing God's work here in the wilderness."

On a cold, wet autumn day, the family stayed crowded in the house. The air was close, and smoke from the cooking fire tinged the air. The door and windows were closed against the wind.

The two youngest children, John and little Isaac, raced back and forth across the small room, trying to keep the table between them as they laughed and teased each other. Hannah and May were mending and squabbling about whose stitches were finer. Mary sat on a bench out of the chaos and leaned gratefully against the back wall, nursing the baby and humming quietly to him. Isaac, who'd been trying to read in the dim light of the lantern, gave up and stared off into the rafters, attempting to ignore the commotion.

Suddenly one of the chairs was knocked over with a loud bang. Startled, Thomas broke from Mary's breast and started bawling. May pricked her finger and began crying too. John and young Isaac immediately stopped running, looking horrified.

Isaac glanced at the chair and motioned for John to pick it up, then sighed, put both hands on the table, and pushed himself up. "Mary, I do think it's time we built ourselves a bigger house."

Hannah looked at him with excitement. "Oh, Da. I remember the most beautiful house in New Garden. With pillars in the front and real glass windows. And it was painted the most lovely shade of yellow. I can see myself living in such a fine house."

Mary smiled at her daughter. "Hannah, dear, the price of paint is too precious. I have a length of fine cloth. Perhaps we could boil some marigolds and dye the cloth yellow to make a curtain for the window in our new house?"

May joined in, "And there is a house, I saw it when we went to market, down near the center of Corbin Town, with broad white steps and a place for a chair...I can't remember what it's called."

Her mother said, "A porch, dear."

"Yes, Ma, a porch across the whole front, with a rocking chair for thee when thee feeds the babe. And the house has two real levels, not just a loft for sleeping."

"And four chimneys," Hannah added.

William looked up, panicked. "That means four fire-places that I'll have to bring wood in for and clean out the ashes. No! We should not have that many chimneys, promise me that, Da!"

Hannah continued, "And it can be white or the color of

the wood. It does not have to be yellow, even though that is such a happy color for a house."

Isaac laughed. "Sorry, my daughters, I don't see us building such a fine mansion for us. We're only farmers in the wilderness. But perhaps we can add a small porch for thy Ma. And maybe only two chimneys, William, one at each end."

Mary patted the baby and said quietly, "I would truly like a separate sleeping room for our sons and another for the girls. And one for us. As far away from them as we can get." She winked saucily at her husband, who grinned and nodded his head.

"Definitely," Isaac agreed. "A room for us on the other side will be a necessity in our grand new home." He then asked if she wanted a room for a loom. His sister-in-law was an expert weaver, and his brother had built her a loom over the winter.

Mary shook her head. "My dear husband, thee knows I'm not a weaver. I've too much to do taking care of thy children, planting thy garden, sewing clothes for thee and thy children, cleaning thy house. Not to mention serving as elder to the women of the meeting. I've little time to spend hours sitting at a loom, relaxing while I weave. Surely, we can continue to purchase cloth from a trader or at market, or even from thy dear sister-in-law."

Isaac and Mary spent several quiet afternoons walking their land, trying to find the best place for the new home. Finally Mary said, "We have to stop this wandering about, Isaac. Thee knows we picked the best spot when we built the house we now live in. Could we just add on to what we have? Keep the main room for our kitchen and add a wing with new sleeping rooms?"

Surprised, Isaac asked, "Is thee sure that's what thee wants, my love? Wouldn't thee want a bright new kitchen with a fireplace?"

"'Tis already a fine cook hearth, and my kitchen has a beautiful view of the Eno. I'm quite content there." She looked at him slyly. "I think I would really like clapboards on our new house, not the old logs with mud chinking like we have now. May I have clapboards, real clapboards?"

Smiling, Isaac nodded. "'Tis a simple request and thee deserves so much more. I set aside some good trees that I felled when I cleared the far field long ago. They will make strong, straight clapboards now that they are dried. There's a sawmill south of us that can process them for me." He clasped his hand to his heart dramatically and smiled at Mary. "Aye, but does thee think a plain clapboard house with the same old kitchen will satisfy our two daughters, who have such visions of grandeur?"

Mary shrugged. "Maybe not, but thee promised them a wee little porch that I might sit upon to feed thy youngest offspring. And maybe someday we can paint the clapboards a happy color to please Hannah."

Laughing, they hugged each other, heedless of who might be watching. Sometimes they were happily willing to shock their children—just a little—with their brazenness.

LATER THAT FALL, Isaac and Mary traveled to Perquimans to attend North Carolina Yearly Meeting, the annual gathering of representatives from all the Quaker meetings in the Carolinas. Mary brought baby Thomas with them, as he had not been weaned. The rest of the children stayed with Benjamin and Susanna. They were thrilled to spend time with their cousins and favorite aunt and uncle.

The Jacksons enjoyed visiting with old Friends and

meeting new ones. The meetings for business were worshipful and productive. On the second afternoon, Mary saw that Isaac had gone for a long walk with a man about their age, dressed oddly in white clothes. His jacket and trousers were plain and cut simply, but were not the traditional Quaker gray or black. Isaac explained to her after his return that the man was visiting from the colony of New Jersey.

"Why is he wearing white? His clothes must be impossible to keep clean."

"Friend John Woolman is traveling under a concern for the abolition of slavery," Isaac said. "Dyes for coloring cloth, particularly indigo, are produced by slaves, and he refuses to take advantage of enslaved people. He came to North Carolina to observe slavery firsthand. He visited with some of the Quaker slaveholders in the Albemarle counties. Thee would like him. He's sincere and of a strong faith."

Mary sighed. "I wish him well. He's taken on a big burden, trying to convince these planters that they should give up their slaves. Their plantations and their profits depend on their free labor."

"John lives his example. If he dines with a slave owner, he gives a small sum to the men and women who serve him as payment for their services. I hear that he won't stay in the homes of any man who relies on slave labor. He would rather sleep on the hard ground outside."

Mary and Isaac walked on in companionable silence until it was time for the next business session. John Woolman was to speak to the women's meeting about his concerns. Mary was grateful that Isaac had prepared her for what to expect.

Later that afternoon John Woolman spoke at length about what he had observed in his travels—African families living in squalor; tiny children put to work in fields in the hot sun; husbands sold away from their wives; women raped by their owners and overseers; men and even women beaten. The women of the meeting wept to hear of such horrors. Most had not realized that these human beings were sometimes treated worse than animals and not free to make their own lives. They wanted to believe that the Quakers they knew who owned slaves treated them well, but maybe they were refusing to see the reality. They had heard reports about the Negro meetings for worship being held in Perquimans, but was that enough? Woolman reminded the women that they had influence over their husbands and sons. He urged them to pray that the enslavers' hearts would be turned to godliness.

After he left the room, the women settled into a deep and worshipful silence. Finally, a woman from New Garden Meeting stood and spoke passionately, urging the meeting to condemn slavery. There were nods of support, mainly among the women from the western meetings.

The representative from one of the eastern meetings stood. She looked around the room angrily. "Thee condemns us without knowing the truth. Friend Woolman did not describe our farm. We rely on the labor of slaves, 'tis true, but we treat them well. We feed them and give them a small plot of land to grow their own food. We give them a new set of clothes every year. My husband has *never* sold a husband away from his wife. Children do *not* work in the fields until they are eight years of age. Africans are simple creatures and so do well with firm guidance and the benevolent care we provide."

Another woman rose to argue with her. Others spoke to their neighbors or shouted over the speakers. The clerk stood, drawing every eye to the elders at the front of the room. "Friends, let's sit in worship and listen for guidance from the Holy Spirit. We're speaking too much from our heads and not our inner Light."

Someone started to say something else, but the clerk raised her hand and firmly said, "Not now, Miriam. Now we pray and listen."

The silence went on until the sun started to go down. It had been a long afternoon. The clerk stood again and said, "Friends, we heard of the horrors of slavery when they are owned by cruel men. We have heard others speak of the care they take of these simple humans. Jane spoke eloquently of being cared for by a Black woman who lived in their home, taught her the ways of the world, and stayed years to later care for Jane's children. Let's close this session in grateful worship." She sat down, put her head in her hands.

After a few moments, a woman shouted, "I want us to disown any Friend who continues to own slaves."

Someone else jumped up, stressing, "Even in the Bible, Jesus did not condemn the holding of slaves. He only urged that they be treated with fairness and compassion. We rely on our African laborers. We would have to disown many of the families in the Eastern Quarter."

The argument continued for several more minutes. The clerk again stood, facing the women with a glare that stopped all the chatter.

"Friends, please, not one more word. We are *not* in unity to abolish the institution of slavery. We're not going to solve this tonight. We'll take this concern up at our meeting on the morrow." She urged the women to pray on it and firmly closed the meeting.

The next morning, the tone of the meeting was much settled. A statement was read by the clerk, stating that Friends should treat their slaves with care. "In verse 2, chapter 18, Saint Peter writes 'Slaves, be subject to thy masters with all reverence, not only to those who are good and equitable but also to those who are perverse. Thy servants are thy brethren whom God has placed under thee. Whoever has a brother of his under him should feed him of the food he eats and clothe him of the same clothes he wears. Never ask them to do what is too hard for them.'"

The women settled into worship, holding these words in their hearts.

Finally, the clerk said that God had led them to this understanding. We could go no further now in our seeking. "We'll write this and send it to the men as a statement of the unity among us."

On the way home, Isaac told Mary that the men's meeting struggled similarly but were not so clear in their unity. "My love, the yearly meeting has much work to do. The wealthy men of the eastern meetings wield too much power and influence."

"Aye, Isaac. I'm glad this isn't our grave concern. We have so few Africans in the Piedmont, and I haven't heard tales of cruelty toward them. I doubt John Woolman will bring this concern to us in the wilderness. We'll report this to Eno Meeting, but I think we have more pressing matters to concern us."

"Ah, but Friend John had written to the western meetings before he came to our colony. I have with me a copy prepared by the meeting scribe. Let's stop for a moment so I can read a few excerpts; I think his words give us much to contemplate."

Isaac took the folded paper from his bag. "To Friends at their Monthly-meeting at New-Garden and Cane-Creek, in North-Carolina. Dear Friends—It having pleased the Lord to draw me forth on a Visit to some Parts of Virginia and Carolina, you have often been in my Mind; and though my Way is not clear to come in Person to visit you, yet I feel it in my Heart to communicate a few Things, as they arise in the Love of Truth."

Isaac paused. "There's a lot of wonderful testimony that will take much time to absorb. I'll skip right to the part on slavery, to my mind the real reason he's writing."

He cleared his throat before continuing with Woolman's words. "I have been informed that there is a large Number of Friends in your Parts, who have Slaves; and in tender and most affectionate Love, I beseech you to keep clear from purchasing any. Look, my dear Friends, to divine Providence; and follow in Simplicity that Exercise of Body, that Plainness and Frugality, which true Wisdom leads to; so will you be preserved from those Dangers which attend such as are aiming at outward Ease and Greatness.

"Treasures, though small, attained on a true Principle of Virtue, are sweet in the Possession, and, while we walk in the Light of the Lord, there is true Comfort and Satisfaction. Here, neither the Murmurs of an oppressed People, nor an uneasy Conscience, nor anxious Thoughts about the Events of Things, hinder the Enjoyment of it.

"When we look toward the End of Life, and think on the Division of our Substance among our Successors; if we know that it was collected in the Fear of the Lord, in Honesty, in Equity, and in Uprightness of Heart before him, we may consider it as his Gift to us; and with a single Eye to his Blessing, bestow it on those we leave behind us. Such is the Happiness of the plain Ways of true Virtue. The Work of Righteousness shall be Peace; and the Effect of Righteousness, Quietness and Assurance forever. Isa. xxxii. 17."

"Isaac, John Woolman's letter gives us much to ponder. I'll share it with the women, but for today, I think our minds are full enough with all we heard at yearly meeting. Let's just enjoy being together on our ride home. I look forward to hugging our children again."

ON A COLD, crisp winter day, Isaac gathered his family together around the hearth. They had been enjoying their new house for several months and had started the habit of listening as their father read from the Bible in the evening.

"Today is the twenty-fifth day of Twelfth Month. Our Anglican neighbors call this day Christmas and, on this day, they celebrate the birth of our Savior. We Quakers don't celebrate this occasion."

John piped up, "I know, I know, Da. We believe every day is holy."

"That's right, John. We want to worship God at all times. There is a story in Scripture that I'll read to thee about the birth of a little baby."

Little Isaac piped up, "Jesus, Da. Baby Jesus."

Isaac smiled at his young son and started telling the story of Joseph and Mary traveling to Bethlehem, of how Mary was with child and rode into town on a donkey.

William started laughing. "Remember our Ma before the baby was born. She was big and fat. Can thee picture her riding around on our old mule?"

The children laughed with glee. Isaac grinned back at them. Mary, sitting in the back with her infant, shook her head and smothered a smile. It would have been a funny sight, she knew. And very uncomfortable.

Isaac gestured for the boys to settle down. He continued telling them of the search for a room in an inn. May furrowed her brow at the thought that there was no place for them; she was the most empathetic of the children and seemed to worry about everything.

"It was all right," Isaac assured her. "They found a barn to bed down in."

"Like ours, Da?"

"Well, maybe like ours. But they lived in a far-away place, so it might be a little different."

"Did they have animals like we do? Cows and horses and chickens?"

"I imagine they did."

Mary said, "Come, children, let thy father finish the story."

Isaac told them of the birth of the baby and of the shepherds who heard the angels and went to worship the baby Jesus. They finished with a restless moment of silence.

Isaac finally spoke. "Children, off to the table and mind thy manners. Thy mother has made thee sweet oat cakes. And she opened a pot of the lovely raspberry jam that she made last summer. Although I don't know how she had enough berries, since William and Isaac put more in their mouths than in their pails." At that, the boys blushed, and their sisters and older brother laughed.

On the way to bed that evening, May looked out a window and said to her mother, "I wish we had a shiny star in the sky to light us and angels to come to us."

"Dear ones, we have something better. The Light of God is all around us all of the time, and the Light is also within us. We don't need angels to tell us the good news. We hear it in our hearts, if we only listen."

Little Isaac said, rather sleepily, "And that's why every day is holy, isn't that right, Ma?"

Mary nodded and patted her son's shoulder. "Yes, so it's. Off to bed with thee now. Sleep well."

Chapter Seven

1758

Isaac walked into the house, reading aloud from a long, handwritten paper. "Are Friends careful to attend their meetings for worship, both on First Days and other days of the week appointed for that service? And are they careful to meet at the hour appointed? Do they refrain from sleeping in meetings?"

He held the paper out to his wife. "Mary, Joseph Maddock bade me give this to thee. He has received word that Eno Meeting hasn't forwarded answers to the queries. He said—and we already knew this, didn't we?—that neither the men's meeting nor thy women's meeting wrote the answers to the questions they posed to us."

The yearly meeting, the regional body of elders that oversaw Quaker life in all of the Carolinas, expected them to reflect on the questions that were posed, as individual Quakers and to consider them also for their community. The answers were used to assess the meeting's faithfulness in observing the rules in the Discipline. The elders at Cane Creek Meeting frequently urged the Eno Meeting members to respond in writing, and now the yearly meeting was weighing in. Mary and the other Eno elders felt that if they answered the queries honestly, the process would only emphasize their problems—and be one more justification for meddlers from other meetings to criticize the Eno Friends.

The women's meeting had discussed the questions last quarter, and Mary said that she saw little need to spend time on the matter again. She had reported to the men's meeting that most of the women attended First Day meetings with their husbands and children, except when confined by pregnancy or illnesses among their children. Not many consistently tried to attend weekday meetings, most considering it too far from their homeplaces, when they had too much to do. Some of the older women were faithful in attending meetings for business; younger women found this difficult with babies and children tugging at their skirts.

The women of the meeting had dealt with several transgressors and most were resolved satisfactorily, either with discipline or disownment. They certainly didn't see the need to advertise their delinquent members outside the borders of the Eno Meeting.

Mary knew the women said that they strove to train up the children in plainness of speech and righteous behavior, but they all knew that too many of the youth strayed from the primitive testimonies of Truth. And a disconcerting number of young people had married out of meeting.

Hearing her husband's words, Mary paused and frowned at her eldest son.

Edward sputtered, "Why is thee glowering at me? What did I do?"

He truly hoped one day to be an important elder in the meeting, like his father. But he confessed—only to himself— that on more than one occasion, he had enjoyed games and sporting with his companions. Even George Fox, the founder of his religion, had written in his journal about his misspent youth; this was probably not what his mother wished him to glean from reading such important spiritual works.

Mary shook her head as she thought about the careless behavior of young men. She looked at him with a sad smile. "Take that as a caution, Edward. Thee's only thirteen and thee's quite a responsible boy. Perhaps it's time we set thee out as an apprentice. Anyway, thee has let me get diverted."

She turned to her husband. "Thee knows that, for the most part, the women of this meeting have struggled with their men and youth to maintain the discipline, and some Eno members have left to go with the Baptists or Anglicans. Is this what we want to report again? And open ourselves to more judgments from outsiders? It's hard enough to do what we can without others complaining constantly that it isn't enough. And now this from them on the coast who don't understand how we struggle to make our way in this wilderness?"

She took a deep breath. "Isaac, we came here to start a new spiritual community." Isaac nodded and patted her hand. He started to speak, but she cut him off. "Yes, I know, we came for the land and the chance to start anew. But we sincerely wanted to create a peaceable kingdom out of the wilderness. At least I did."

"Me also, my love," Isaac murmured.

Mary pushed on with her rant. "I did *not* come here to give succor to a bunch of hooligans! Some of the young men have become fiercely independent. They are out from under their parents' control and out of sight of the elders in our yearly meeting. And further, they think they don't have to be under the discipline of the local meeting. These people grew up as Quakers! They learned from an early age how they should behave and their responsibility to live faithfully in the spirit of Truth. Instead, they act like children squabbling in the schoolyard!"

Isaac chuckled at her imagery. He tended to agree with her and did so enjoy watching her get all het up. *Was it wrong to appreciate thy wife getting her dander up in self-righteous indignation?* he wondered. *Well, as long as it wasn't because of something he did that triggered her tirade.* Again, he leaned back and sighed, appreciating anew his good fortune in marrying a fiery Irish lass.

Mary finished with, "But nor do I want to report their misdeeds far and wide. They are *our* concern, not the yearly meeting's."

Isaac needed to bring her back to the new request from the yearly meeting. He gave her a quick hug and patted her back. This was all the affection he tried to allow himself in front of the children, but his love of his wife sometimes overflowed his good intentions.

He told her, "This year, we have a new query to consider." He took up the paper Mary had tossed onto the table and read, "'Are all that have Negroes careful to use them well and encourage them to come to meetings as much as they reasonably can?' I think emancipation is becoming a topic among Friends."

Ten-year-old William had been listening carefully. He piped up, "But, Da, no one we know owns slaves. The slaves we hear about are on the big plantations in the east. We only have small farms here on the wilderness."

Isaac reminded him, "A small number of Eno Quakers do own slaves to help with their mills and workshops."

Edward jumped in. "But the Africans that work in Maddock's Mill aren't slaves, are they? They are free men. They must be."

His father shook his head sadly. "A Legislative Act

many years ago forbade owners from attempting to set their slaves free. While Maddock's workers might appear to be free, under the law of the colony, they are still slaves. And the widow Martha Stubbs has a Black girl to tend to the house and garden. She's a slave under our colony's laws. I think, though, that most Friends in Eno Meeting who do use the labor of enslaved men and women try to provide them fairly with the outward necessaries."

William said, "I don't see any African boys when we go to our aunt's house for learning. Didn't the yearly meeting say we're to educate them?"

His father answered, "William, the laws of this colony forbid us from teaching slaves to read and write."

"Not even their names?" William was incredulous.

"Nay, William, not even their names. Friend Maddock does teach his workers to read and do their numbers. He says it's necessary for their jobs at the sawmill. But he does not tell the authorities—"

"But that isn't honest!" William interrupted. "And the commandment requires us to be truthful."

"Aye, William, so it does," Isaac agreed. "But what is the lesser of the evils?" He held up a hand. "No, don't answer now, just think on it. I know Joseph Maddock cares for their souls and requires them to attend meeting on First Day. He even allows them to hear the Baptist preaching on Third Day. The sin of his dishonesty, however necessary, is his alone. His African workers are not at fault."

Isaac went on to explain to his son that several hundred African men and women had been brought to the area since they moved here, before William was born. A few of them were freed men, but their position was precarious under North Carolina law, and they needed to carry their papers when they went about their business. It was difficult to free slaves, so not many had been given their freedom, even if the owners wanted to do that.

William started to continue his argument, but his father cut him off. "Let this go for now, young William. Someday, they may be freedmen, but not at this time. This needs to be changed, but it won't be easy. Not at all. And it will be even harder to change the hearts of the slaveowners on the big plantations. The economy of the east is so dependent on their labor. Sadly, there's not much we can do from here."

William sat back in a pout. "This is not right, Da. This isn't right at all."

"I know, Son. I know."

William got up and left the room, hurt and angry. He told himself that when he grew up, he would work to make sure that his colony would no longer have slaves. In meeting he heard that God loves all people. That must include Africans; they were God's people too.

Isaac shook his head sadly as he watched his son stomp outside, slamming the door. Mary started to go after him, to soothe her young son, but Isaac stayed her with a wave of his hand. "Ah, Mary, 'tis the burden of youth, to see things as right and wrong so clearly and so painfully. I fear his concern for the African people in our colony may trouble him for a long while. That isn't a bad thing. Not a bad thing at all."

Chapter Eight

In the spring of 1759, Isaac sauntered into the house one afternoon and dropped a bundle on the long table where Mary was working. She looked up from shelling beans and smiled. "What has thee brought for us, Isaac?"

"I shot a fine, fat wild turkey on my way back from a meeting at Maddock's mill. And I also bring great news. William Comb is leasing a five-acre plot northeast of Corbin Town—oh, I mean Childsburgh." Isaac shook his head as if trying to shake a thought into it. "I can never remember that our town's name now honors yet another of Lord Granville's land agents. Silly! Anyway," he continued, "the property is on the Great Road and will be for the use of our meeting. Mary, we can finally build a meetinghouse of our own. After meeting in each other's homes for nigh on eight years, it's time. There's even enough land to have our own burying ground and, soon, a school for the children."

Mary looked up thoughtfully. "I'm truly glad, but I had hoped it would be closer to our land. I do so want to be able to attend First Day and midweek worship more regularly. But I admit, this is progress."

"Mary, 'tis only about five miles. The road is good because of all the customers Joseph Maddock is bringing to his mill. A group of men is already working on plans for the building of it, and several carpenters have offered their skills."

"I know Friends don't believe we need a special building to worship God," Mary said, "but maybe this is what we need to bring the community back into the rules and practices set out by our yearly meeting in our Book of Discipline. I'll have to call on the women of the meeting about the good news. Many in the Eno Meeting have strayed from good order, according to the elders from Cane Creek. I know, I've seen it also, but I hate being reminded of our weaknesses by outsiders." She paused. "Hmm, perhaps having our own meetinghouse will show those elders that we're faithful and will convince them to leave us alone."

She went back to her task, but not before sending her husband a mischievous glance. "One more thing—who will pay for this fine structure? When the Anglicans built the little brick St. Mary's Chapel a few miles north of here, our taxes were increased to pay for it. And several Quaker carpenters and bricklayers helped construct it." With twinkling eyes, she asked, "Does thee think they would mind raising a few shillings to pay for our worship house?"

Isaac laughed at her impertinence. "Certainly, dearest, they will be falling all over themselves in their haste to see the Quakers properly housed—throwing around shillings and lining up to assist in the building of it."

Mary set aside the pan of beans and gathered up the trimmings to throw to the hog they were fattening before winter. Then she picked up the turkey and took it outside to begin plucking it for supper. Isaac followed.

"In all seriousness, Mary, we have to accept that we are British subjects and the Anglican church is the official church. We Quakers have always been outsiders and have had to fend for ourselves. At least here in the Carolinas, we're allowed to worship in the open, without persecution and prosecution. We just have to do it all for ourselves with no help from the colony. But no matter. It's still great news, and we'll find a way to pay for it."

For several months, the men of Eno Meeting worked on the new building as much as they were able. The farmers donated what they could to purchase nails and other building materials. Each family contributed sturdy trees from their acreage to be used in the new building. The first structure was a small framed meetinghouse enclosed with stripped logs, just one large room with a removable dividing wall down the center aisle, to allow the men and women to conduct their business meetings separately. Two doors, one opening into each side of the room, were accessed from the wide porch across the front. The members hoped that eventually, given enough time and money, they would be able to establish a larger brick meetinghouse with actual windows to let in the sunlight, and maybe a balcony for additional seating. That was the dream, anyway.

The men carved crude benches made from split logs. There were four rows of benches facing the front of the building and a row of facing benches on which the elders would sit.

The meetinghouse was completed by the end of summer. Fortunately, Quakers did not require fancy edifices in which to worship, and this simple, plain structure was more than adequate for their needs.

. . .

IN EARLY NINTH MONTH, Eno Friends invited Quakers from nearby meetings to gather in their new meetinghouse for fellowship and celebration. Not everyone could fit inside, but with the doors open wide, all could be a part of the worship. Several Friends preached at length, and their messages were well received. Afterward, the women set out meats, vegetables from their burgeoning gardens, and plentiful cakes and pies. Everyone ate their fill, and the conversations over the plank tables and on quilts spread on the ground were lively and excited.

Daniel Maddock, Joseph's brother, silenced everyone so he could tell them about the other project the men envisioned. Some of them had paced off an area for a graveyard and selected a site for the school. The schoolhouse would have to wait for a year or two until more funds could be raised. In the meantime, they needed to hire a teacher to set up classes in the meetinghouse. This would provide a more proper, rigorous education for the children. They'd been gathering in Benjamin Jackson's parlor for informal classes, where Susanna Jackson taught them to read, write their names, copy passages from the Bible, and do basic arithmetic, but Susanna didn't feel qualified to teach much more than that.

Mary thought she had a solution. Her sister Katherine had sent a letter introducing a young woman in her meeting who might be willing to move to the Eno community. Katherine wrote, "Rebecca is plain of countenance. She is a sober, hard-working spinster of twenty-three years, who is good with the children here in New Garden Meeting. I wonder if her spinsterhood is due to the rather unfortunate, large burn scar on her face from a childhood accident. Rebecca can be stern but has a ready smile for her charges. She has completed her schooling and is competent in ciphering, writing, and reading. Her parents have both died, and now that she no longer has to care for them, she would like to move on. We believe she would be able to train your children up in the fear of the Lord and the discipline of our Society."

Mary read the letter to the women's meeting for their consideration. After a brief discussion, they agreed to recommend to the men that Rebecca be hired. As Rachel Fincher said, "Katherine is Mary's twin sister. We can accept that her reference of this Rebecca is as well-advised as if our own dear Mary had recommended her."

The men agreed. Joseph Maddock then sent word to Pennsylvania that Rebecca would be hired if she came to Eno Meeting. She would board with his family until a small cabin could be built for her next to the school.

When Rebecca was informed of the meeting's offer, she accepted readily and packed for her new home in the south. The young woman joined a large family group from nearby Buckingham Meeting who were also readying for their move to North Carolina. The future of the Eno meeting community looked so hopeful.

The next summer, Rebecca arrived to take up her position as teacher. The younger children joined her for lessons shortly after her arrival. And following the harvest, the older youth started learning their letters and arithmetic.

ONE AFTERNOON MARY'S son Isaac came home from school, crying. When he settled down enough, Mary coaxed the story out of him. Another boy, Nathaniel, had been teasing him cruelly. And the harder Isaac cried, the redder his nose became. So, Nathaniel had teased him even more about his nose matching his hair, until Isaac pushed him down and ran away. Their teacher had seen the scuffle and grabbed both boys by the arms. She led them under a tree and sat without speaking for a long while, looking at them sadly.

"Using thy fists and calling names," Rebecca had said, "isn't the way to solve problems. We Quakers don't treat each other unkindly, nor do we resort to violence in any instance, even when provoked. And thee, Nathaniel, I heard that thee provoked Isaac. And thee, Isaac, thee let thy anger get the best of thee. Now go home, both of you, and tell thy mother and father what thee did today. Tomorrow, come back ready to apologize to each other."

Isaac had started to say something in his defense, but Rebecca held up her hand. "I don't want to hear a word from either of you. Go home. Confess to thy parents. Ask God for thy forgiveness, and tomorrow forgive each other. Go now. Go," their teacher had said. Isaac dragged his feet, but eventually made it home.

Mary looked at her son and hugged him. "Now, Isaac, stop thy sniveling and tell me exactly what caused such great tears."

Isaac told her how unfairly Nathaniel had treated him. How Nathaniel had called him names and chased him to taunt him more.

Mary stopped him mid-story. "And what did thee do to provoke such treatment?" she asked quietly.

"Nothing, Ma. I did nothing. He said he didn't like me. That's all, and when I tried to walk away, like Da told us to do, he followed and said mean things. I tried to get away from him, I really did."

Mary gave him one more hug. "Now," she told him, "Go wash thy face. Thee will have to tell thy father about what happened. And thee knows thy Da won't put up with any whining about it."

Later that night after the children were in bed, Mary and Isaac were talking about what had happened with their son. Isaac said, "Mary, sometimes boys have too much energy, and it gets the best of them. I think Isaac has learned his lesson from this incident."

Mary looked at him. "I've heard rumors—nay, more than rumors, complaints—that Nathaniel's father has been seen beating his wife and children out of anger. Their neighbor says that it seems to be increasing. Nathaniel's mother, Hester, often sends the children to her friend, to protect them when her husband is on a rampage. Perhaps Nathaniel is acting out what he learned from his father. If this is the case, the problem is bigger than a schoolyard scuffle."

Isaac sat deep in thought for a long time. "Mary, has thee had a chance to meet with Nathaniel's mother?"

Mary nodded. "I met with Hester several times. I gently probed, but she denies that there is a problem. She would never speak ill of her husband. I think she tries to hide the bruises. Susanna went with me the last time to try to help her see reason, but Hester does not see any way out. She has children and no other family in the area. The meeting needs to step in to protect her. No man should be allowed to get away with what she has had to endure."

Isaac sighed. "I had no idea. Thee's right, my love. I can't imagine a man deliberately causing harm to his wife and the mother of his children, but I know that some men do. I'll take thy concern to heart, and a couple of us will go to labor with Micah. I'm not sure it will do much good if he has so much anger in him. But perhaps it will give her a respite if he knows people are watching him."

Mary hugged her husband, then said, "And now to the problem of thy own son."

Isaac grinned. "Aye, when he misbehaves, he's my son. When he's at his angelic best, he's thine."

"Well, he is *thy* namesake," Mary said with a laugh.

"But seriously, how do we teach him to react to hurt with love, rather than retaliation?"

"My own love, no young boy thinks of loving his opponent. He only wants to stop the attack any way he can, and that's usually to react in kind. I'll speak to him again about turning the other cheek. Now, let's join our children in slumber. We have a lot to do before this concern is behind us."

Mary rose to check on the children while Isaac banked the fire. So many problems seemed more manageable after a night together in their marriage bed.

Isaac and Daniel Stubbs met with Micah as promised. Like most of the farmers in the area, he found the drought and the corruption increasingly stressful, and Hester was bearing the brunt. The man declared that he was no more violent toward his wife than was his right as a husband. They counseled him to be gentle in dealings with his family members and warned him that the meeting would be watching him.

When Isaac returned home, he told Mary that the visit was not satisfactory. "Daniel and I considered disowning him, but chose not to ask the meeting to do so. We'll keep an eye on him, but for now, that is all we can see to do."

The oversight of the meeting was not enough to curb Micah's behavior. One afternoon, Hester and her two children arrived at the Jackson home in great distress. Hester was bleeding from a deep cut on her forehead and had a broken arm. Nathaniel was injured too, having tried to stop his father from beating his mother. Mary hustled the family into the warmth of her kitchen. She tended to their injuries with healing herbs and clean bandages and braced Hester's arm with sturdy sticks and soft cloth ties.

"Hester, please, I know thee loves thy husband, but thee can't return to his house. His anger is escalating. We'll send thee back to thy home in the north as soon as we can find a family traveling that way. In the meantime, thee may stay here with us. My Isaac will protect thee from Micah as best he can."

Hester started to assure Mary that Micah meant no harm, but she stopped, recognizing that the other woman was right. She would have to leave her husband. Perhaps Micah would realize he needed to change his ways and would come to get her.

Mary sat with young Isaac and Nathaniel to help them work through their differences. "You two need to find a way to get along. We don't allow anyone in this house to harm another person." After much hemming and hawing and a few scuffles, the boys came to an uneasy truce.

Mary sent word to Hester's brother in New Jersey, her only relative, and he urged his sister to move in with him. The family stayed with the Jacksons for several months, until a small group from Cane Creek invited them to travel north with them, at least as far as Philadelphia where her brother could meet her.

Micah blamed Isaac for sending his family away and refused to have any more dealings with Eno Meeting. He refused to meet with the elders and was eventually disowned.

Isaac admitted, "Mary, I wish we could have done more to heal that family, but Micah's anger runs too deep. He's no longer a member of our meeting, not that he cares anymore. I'll look in on him occasionally, but only as a neighbor. A sad, sad thing, to be sure."

.   .   .

WEEKS AFTER HELPING Hester return to her brother's family, Mary was in her drying shed hanging up basil and thyme. She was pleased with her dried rosemary bunches and looked forward to the lavender being ready to pick. She also looked forward to selling some of the herbs next market day, so they would have coin to pay their taxes.

Thomas came running into the shed, breathless. He bent over with his hands on his knees until his breathing slowed a bit. "Ma, come quick. Martha Embree is in the kitchen, and she's crying awfully hard. I told her to sit by the fire, and I ran as fast as I could to get thee."

Startled, Mary put down the basket of herbs, brushed her hands down her apron, and headed out of the shed. Again large with child, she moved slowly. "Thank thee, dear Thomas. Now run ahead and tell May to take down the teapot and make us some tea. I think there is a little left in the tin. I'll be in shortly." As he raced away once more, Mary muttered, "I wonder what has Martha so upset. This isn't like her at all. She's usually so peaceful and undaunted."

She walked into the house and saw her guest at the table, crying and hiccoughing softly. Mary took a seat across from Martha and reached for her hand. Concern filled her voice. "Oh, dear Friend Martha, whatever has thee in such a state?"

Martha shook her head and spoke through tears. "My oldest, Jamie. Mary, my son... he drowned...in the Eno." Mary drew a sharp breath and Martha paused. "His brothers were playing around with a birch bark canoe they were trying to build. They had seen some native boys on the river in one and wanted to make one of their own."

She paused again, sobbing. "They didn't know what they were doing. They're just little boys."

May quietly set down the teapot and mugs, and Mary

silently waved the girl outdoors. Martha tried to take a sip of the warm, soothing tea, but her hand shook so much she had to set it down. She buried her face in her hands and started crying harder. Mary moved to sit next to Martha and handed her a clean, soft cloth to wipe her eyes. She wrapped her arms around the weeping woman and held her until she was able to stop sobbing. She let go, and they waited several minutes in companionable silence.

Eventually, Martha was able to continue, "Jamie...he fell in. I think they dragged the canoe to the river and let Jamie climb in. How could they know they should have made it watertight. The canoe got caught in the current and started sinking. Jamie went under. His brothers tried to save him." After hiccupping once more, she took a deep breath. "They yelled for Jamie from the bank, but they're too little to go in the water. They know that. My neighbor heard the shouting. He jumped in the river to try to save him, but Jamie was caught in the rapids. Other men joined in. They ran up and down the banks trying to find him." Her voice dropped to a whisper. "By the time they found him and pulled him out, he was gone. They brought my poor battered baby to our home."

She put her arms on the table and dropped her head, spent from the telling and the crying. Mary gave her a few minutes before asking softly, "Martha, where are thy young boys now? And thy husband?"

"The woman who lives down the road from us kindly offered to sit with my children. She brought them fresh-made cookies, and gave them some warm milk. I truly hope they fall asleep. They were so upset." She started shaking. "Oh, oh, my poor husband does not yet know! He went to Childsburgh early today to talk with the sheriff about the fees they have been charging us. Oh, how will I ever tell him what has befallen us? He was already unhappy when he left this morn."

Mary stood up. "Martha, let me get my cloak. I'll go with thee and help thee prepare Jamie's earthly body. He has no need of it now. His soul is already winging its way to God. We'll tell thy husband together, and thee can be of comfort to thy little ones."

Before leaving with Martha, Mary instructed Hannah as to what needed doing while she was away, and to tell Isaac and the other children she didn't know when she would return.

As Martha and Mary washed the boy's broken body and dressed him in clean clothes, they talked about when to bury the boy and have a memorial worship meeting. Martha and her family needed to publicly mourn their son and to thank God for a life well lived, no matter how brief it was. When Martha's husband, Jonathan Embree, returned, Mary stood silently as he learned the devastating news, wishing Isaac were there to help comfort the distraught man.

The next Fourth Day, Friends gathered in worship and remembrance as Jamie was buried in the graveyard beside the meetinghouse. Martha and her husband's extended families had come from New Garden and Cane Creek meetings, and filled many of the small meetinghouse benches. Most Friends from Eno Meeting joined them, many standing at the back or along the sides. The Embrees were well loved by all who knew them.

As was the custom, after the burial, the Friends gathered in worshipful silence, waiting upon the Lord for guidance and solace. Jonathan Embree sat stoically beside his wife, Martha, unwilling to show any weakness in front of his family and neighbors. He clasped her hand tightly, their other sons crowded beside them. The little boys were still in shock from the loss of their older brother. By then Martha had cried herself out, but many of their relatives were sobbing quietly.

After a while Jane Dowell stood, holding tight to the back of the bench in front of her. "Young Jamie was a sober and affectionate child, obedient to his parents, and active and cheerful in his disposition. I spent time with him on First Days, and I saw that he quickly gained the esteem and affection of the other children. Although he evinced a serious turn of mind, he was ever ready to join in light-hearted play. I have no doubt he was taken into the kingdom of heaven. God rest his soul." She sat back on the bench, and the meeting settled back into worship. Her husband gently patted her hand, and her young daughter snuggled against her arm. Jamie had been a friend to the girl for as long as she could remember.

Some moments later a little boy stood. He looked at his father, who nodded to him for encouragement. The child spoke softly, his voice catching. "Jamie was my friend for my whole life. He was a good person. We had fun. God must want him terrible bad to take him away from me." He turned and buried his head in his mother's arms, sobbing uncontrollably. His father reached over, pulled the lad onto his lap and patted his back until he calmed. Many Friends had to wipe their eyes after this testimony.

Presently an older man, one of Martha's relatives, rose, hat in hand. "Life is a gift from God. Our children are all gifts to be savored. Although today may be full of sadness, each moment that young Jamie shared with us illustrates the beautiful gift of life." He quoted from Joshua: "Be strong and of good courage; do not be afraid, nor be dismayed, for the Lord thy God is with thee wherever thou goest." Then he preached at length about how he found this passage to give him solace in the face of young Jamie's death. Mary thought his words were rather ponderous for the memory of a dear little boy and that he went on a bit too long, but Jamie's father seemed to find his words edifying.

Friends shifted restlessly on the benches before settling back down into a comforting silence. After a few more thankfully briefer messages, Isaac rose to close the meeting, reciting several passages from the Psalms: "The Lord is a refuge for the oppressed, a stronghold in times of trouble. Those who know Thy name trust in Thee, for Thou, Lord, have never forsaken those who seek Thee. And, truly my soul finds rest in God; my salvation comes from Him."

Chapter Nine

Eleventh Month, 1759

Mary and Isaac sat on the hickory log overlooking the Eno, enjoying the sunset over the water. The sky was especially vibrant this time of year when the sun was low on the horizon. Isaac wrapped his arm around Mary, and she leaned into him.

"Isaac," she said, "although our youngest, Elizabeth, isn't yet a year old, our children are growing up. Has thee wondered why Hannah is so eager to go to Cane Creek? I have, and I believe I know the reason. She seems fond of Thomas Wright. Thee knows he has been to our meeting several times. I fear he comes not just to worship, but to court our daughter. I think he will soon ask thee permission to wed her. Perhaps, thee should sound him out when he next comes."

Isaac smiled at his wife. He, too, had noticed a growing affection between the young couple and agreed to speak with Thomas if the young man approached him. Isaac leaned back and contemplated how dull his own life would be without his beloved Mary by his side. Of course, he wanted the same happiness for his children. Hannah was his eldest, and part of him was unexpectedly sad that she would probably not be with them at this home on the Eno River much longer.

By the end of the month, Mary's prediction came true. Thomas approached Isaac after First Day meeting and sought his blessing. Isaac questioned the young man about his family, about his plans for the future, how he intended to support Hannah. Thomas told about land his father had given to him on the banks of the Haw River, more than twenty miles away from the Jackson home. He planned to build Hannah a fine, snug house come the spring. If they are found clear to marry, he'd like the wedding to be held as soon as their new home was ready.

Watching from a distance, Mary saw the men smile and shake hands. She called to Hannah to come with her. When Hannah also saw her father and Thomas, a huge grin broke across her face. "Mother, does thee think Da has agreed that Thomas and I may be wed? Oh, please, say yes!" she whispered, daring to hope.

Mary smiled and nodded. "Yes, I do believe thee's becoming betrothed. Let's invite Thomas and his family to dine at our house. Very soon, thee needs to meet with our women's meeting so they can assure themselves that thee's clear to marry. And Thomas needs to do likewise at his own meeting. Only then, may thee set a date for thy wedding."

IN TWELFTH MONTH, Hannah approached the women's meeting and asked that she meet with them to tell them of her desire to marry. Mary usually served as clerk of these meetings, but Deborah Stubbs convened the clearness process. They talked with eighteen-year-old Hannah for a long time, reminding themselves of her work with the young children of the meeting, and her regular attendance at First Day and midweek meetings for worship and at quarterly meetings. Afterward, Deborah announced she would check at the courthouse to make sure Hannah was free from other encumbrances.

The wait seemed interminable to Hannah, but soon the committee was able to show her the written statement that they found her clear to marry. This document would be forwarded to Cane Creek Meeting the next time someone traveled in that direction.

Thomas went through the same process with his meeting, and the elders likewise sent a statement to Eno Meeting that he, too, was clear to marry.

The young couple was ecstatic. They immediately began planning for their new life together. The elders gave permission that the marriage be accomplished at a meeting for worship on the second First Day of Fifth Month. Thomas and Hannah would become the first couple to wed in the new Eno Friends meetinghouse.

All winter Mary and Hannah worked extra hard, making new quilts and to put aside other household goods the young couple would require. Mary had saved some of the money from selling her herbs and the quilted blankets she made to earn coin for taxes, and gave this to Hannah to buy an iron cooking pot and a sturdy kettle.

Isaac occasionally went to help Thomas and his brothers clear the land and build the house to which he would bring his bride after the wedding. As the weather warmed, Hannah took two of her brothers with her to help her prepare the land for her kitchen garden. It would be time to plant vegetables and herbs soon after she moved in, and Mary promised to provide cuttings and seeds as soon as the ground was warm enough.

Finally, the wedding day arrived. Hannah and her sister

May were both giddy with excitement. Soon, Hannah would no longer be Hannah Jackson, she would be Hannah Wright. She was unable to contain her happiness as she swung her youngest brothers around and around until they were dizzy and squealing with delight.

Dressing for the ceremony, Hannah pinned a bright sprig from a redbud tree onto her best white shawl. Mary started to object to such frippery on this solemn occasion but stopped herself. The bright pink flowers looked lovely beside the dark green of the new dress she had made for her daughter. *After all*, she thought, *a wedding in the family is a happy occasion, a day for outward and inward celebration.*

May gathered all the boys together, Mary carried little Elizabeth, and the family piled into the wagon for the trip to the meetinghouse. Hannah, who would be leaving for the Haw River house with Thomas afterward, had sent her housewares and belongings ahead. She carried only a small valise with new nightclothes and undergarments. At the meetinghouse, she helped the younger children down from the wagon and smoothed her dress. She wanted to run into the meeting and hug Thomas, but she held back. She was now an adult and would behave as a wife should.

Hannah and Thomas sat side by side on the facing bench. This was almost too exciting for her to bear—usually men and women sat on opposite sides of the room, but today they were able to touch each other in reassurance. Hannah couldn't stop grinning; Thomas, though, tried to tamp down his look of panic. They both realized this was a momentous undertaking. They struggled to settle into solemn worship and to refrain from glancing too frequently at each other.

The meeting quieted. The only sounds were the cacophony of cicadas that had emerged that week and an occasional muffled cough from someone in the congregation. After what felt like a nerve-racking period of silent worship, in the manner set out by early Quakers, Hannah and Thomas rose to stand alone in the front of the Friends. The Quakers did not have a minister or elder to conduct the wedding ceremony, and the couple had to recite their vows to each other when they were ready to be joined. Hannah's palms were sweaty, and she feared she would faint from nerves, but her voice was clear and assured.

"In the presence of God and these our friends," she intoned, "I, Hannah Jackson, take thee, Thomas Wright, to be my wedded husband, promising with divine assistance to be unto thee a loving and faithful wife as long as we both shall live."

Thomas, likewise, made his promise to her, his words echoing hers. They sat down and settled back into the silence, in awe of what they had just done, and done so quickly. One of the elders brought them a small table with their marriage certificate prepared by a woman in Cane Creek Meeting. Below the beautifully handwritten text Thomas affixed his name. Hannah signed her name, using for the first time, her new surname. Of course, she had been secretly practicing writing Hannah Jackson Wright for months, even before her father had approved of Thomas's proposal, and she reverently touched her new signature after the ink was dry.

Thomas had asked his father to be the one to read aloud the words on the certificate. Daniel Wright rose and walked to the front. He smiled warmly at his new daughter-in-law, picked up the signed document, cleared his throat, and read: "Whereas Hannah Jackson, daughter of Isaac Jackson and Mary Miller Jackson of Childsburgh, in the colony of North Carolina, and Thomas Wright, son of Daniel Wright and Margaret Terrell Wright of Haw River in the colony of North Carolina, having declared their intentions of marriage with each other to Eno Friends Meeting of the

Religious Society of Friends held at Childsburgh, their proposed marriage was allowed by that meeting."

He continued, "Now this is to certify to whom it may concern, that for the accomplishment of their intention, this thirteenth day of the Fifth Month, in the year of our Lord 1760, they, Hannah Jackson and Thomas Wright, appeared in a meeting for worship of the Religious Society of Friends held at Childsburgh. And Hannah, taking Thomas by the hand, did, on this solemn occasion declare that she took him, Thomas, to be her husband, promising with divine assistance to be unto him a loving and faithful wife so long as they both shall live. And then in the same assembly, Thomas, taking Hannah by the hand, declared that he took her, Hannah, to be his wife, promising with divine assistance to be unto her a loving and faithful husband so long as they both shall live. And moreover, they, Thomas and Hannah, did as further confirmation thereof, then and there, to this certificate set their hands. And we, having been present at the marriage, have as witnesses hereunto set our hands."

As he set the paper down and prepared to remove the little table, he reminded all those present that they were to sign the marriage certificate at the rise of meeting. This was the good order that had been ordained by George Fox and the early elders in the Society of Friends. In so doing, they were assuring the young couple that they were more than witnesses—everyone in attendance was a participant, with the charge that they keep the marriage under their care and guidance.

Mary's eyes were misty as she looked across the room at her own husband. She was remembering when they had stood in front of their own family and friends at New Garden Meeting and recited the same vows. Isaac turned to her and smiled. He winked at her, a gesture which, after all these years, still managed to cause her heart to leap. Others in the meeting smiled at the newlywed couple and nodded their support. This was a joyous occasion for everyone.

Thomas and Hannah both were pale, considering the enormity of what they had just done. Thomas held his bride's hand tightly as if he was afraid to let her go. But there was relief on their faces. They had gotten through it. They had said their vows to each other without stumbling over the words. They had signed their names to the wedding certificate with only a little nervous wobble in their signatures. Hannah wanted to touch Thomas, to calm him, and to steady his hand as he struggled to hold the quill in the midst of his emotions, but she was just as shaky.

The meeting quieted again and settled back into worship. An elderly woman, a long-time friend of Thomas's parents, stood to share a message. She spoke of the responsibilities and the joys of married life, and concluded by a reading from the Song of Songs. Upon hearing her begin "My lover is like a gazelle or a young stag," both Hannah and Thomas blushed deeply. Their families smiled at the couple's discomfort, and a few chuckled softly, as the Irish Friends were not at all hesitant to celebrate the earthly delights with their spouses.

Several other Friends rose with messages of encouragement and hope. One man gave a long-winded prayer, asking the Lord to look favorably on this union. Usually Mary was a little frustrated at the man's pomposity, but today, she reminded herself, was a day for happiness, not annoyance.

After what seemed like an interminable time of both silence and witness, two of the elders shook hands, indicating that the period of worship had ended. Those in attendance lined up to sign their names to the certificate. Their families clustered around the new couple, hugging and laughing.

Finally, everyone was able to escape to the meeting-house yard. The women set to laying out a feast on broad board tables: hams and stewed chickens, crocks of brightly colored pickled vegetables, bowls of baked root vegetables, cakes, and pies. The children ate quickly and scampered off to play. The adults ate and talked well into the late afternoon. Eventually, everyone gathered up their things, loaded their horses and buggies, and headed home. Hannah and Thomas were eager to head to their new house. They were followed by his brothers, teasing them mercilessly. Even the rude calls of the young men could not quench the happiness they were feeling.

Mary rode on the wagon bench beside Isaac with the children piled in the back. The younger ones promptly fell asleep. May mentioned dreamily that she hoped she would find such a fine spouse, at which her older brothers hooted and poked at her.

Mary leaned onto Isaac's shoulder and touched the hand that held the reins. She sighed contentedly. "What a lovely day this has been. I'm so happy that Hannah has found a young man to love, who loves her so deeply. I pray that they will be as happy as we have been."

"Aye, my love. And this is but the first of many meetings for marriage. The day will come when all our children will be settled with their own spouses and families. And it will be just thee and me, as when we started."

Chapter Ten

1761

Ann Jackson, the fourteen-year-old daughter of one of Isaac's relatives, soon moved in to help May with the younger children. With Hannah married and in her own home, Mary appreciated the extra hands. Ann was a hard worker but also quite lively. Mary hoped that the girl's joy in life would rub off on her often too-sober daughter, and that May's steadfastness, at age ten, would tamp down the more frivolous side of her cousin. She looked forward to seeing both of the girls grow into adults.

Mary's sister-in-law Susanna occasionally called on her to assist in delivering babies, though Mary had no desire to become a midwife herself. When Ann said that she was interested in midwifery, Mary took her along on a few births and, soon enough, Ann was assisting Susanna, freeing Mary from having to rush off in the middle of the night, something the adolescent didn't mind at all.

Over the ten years since they had arrived in the Piedmont, Mary had become well known among Friends for her gift of ministry. She was a beloved elder for many of the women, who came to her for advice and guidance. Her youngest child, Elizabeth, was now three, and Mary felt a bit more freedom to extend her work beyond Eno Meeting, to visit the women and families in other meetings in the Piedmont.

On a lovely fall day, Mary arrived home after several days at Cane Creek Meeting. She and Deborah Stubbs had traveled there at the request of the women's meeting. Late in the evening she finally had an opportunity to share what she'd learned with her husband. It was not news she wanted any of the children to overhear.

"Isaac, the meeting is in turmoil—not just the women's meeting, the entire meeting community! The women's meeting has disowned Charity Wright for having carnal knowledge of a man before she was wed. She's only fifteen years old. She's younger than our son Edward, and thee knows he does not always make the wisest decisions at his age. The girl strongly denies what they are saying about her. But if 'tis true, did she really have a choice or had the man forced himself upon her? There truly is a difference, but not to those elders, it seems to me."

Isaac smiled. "Thee's right about Edward, but, Mary, the women's meeting has the duty to discipline children who don't act in accordance with the dictates of our faith, and—"

Mary interrupted. "Jehu Stuart was also disowned for bragging about all the girls he bedded, including Charity. He deserved the censure, and I'm glad he didn't try to excuse his own behavior. Charity, on the other hand, vigorously denied that she fornicated with the young man, but the women of the meeting decided that she was not sincere enough. Not sincere enough! How sincere does a young girl have to be when confronted with such accusations?"

"She must have appealed to the quarterly meeting," Isaac started to explain.

"She did, or at least her mother did for her. The men—not the women—the men of the quarter, upheld the disownment, saying that she didn't fight back hard enough. As if it was her fault that he pushed himself on her, if he even did! She denies that it happened at all."

Mary sighed. "It gets worse. Rachel Wright has also been disciplined for objecting to her daughter's treatment at the hands of the meeting and the quarter. Those Friends have gone too far. Rachel is a well-respected elder of the meeting and a recognized minister of the gospel. They have treated her so badly. Their whole family intends to pick up and move to South Carolina. She was one of the founders of Cane Creek Meeting, and now they are driving her away. It's shameful!"

Mary spun around to face Isaac with a scowl. "Isaac, I've traveled with Rachel, and I find her to be serious and resolute in her ministry. She's more than an acquaintance. I count her among my dearest friends. She's hurting because of this mistreatment."

"Dearest, has thee finished thy rant?" Isaac asked quietly, starting to reach his arms out to her.

Mary looked at him in disgust that he would call her righteous anger a simple rant. Isaac wisely stepped back and dropped his hands.

"Nay, there is *still* more. Rachel asked her meeting for a certificate of removal, stating that she was a member in good standing. She intended to leave and wanted to take her membership with her. She was denied, again because the meeting didn't think she was sincere enough in her apology for rising up in anger when the meeting disowned her daughter. A lot of members have taken Rachel's side, and they are also being disowned. The elders at Cane Creek refuse to listen. This is why Deborah and I were asked to come down to see if we can smooth the ruffled feathers."

"My love, was thee effective?" Isaac asked softly.

"Nay! I think the meeting will be in disarray for a long while. 'Tis a shame to see such a fine meeting descend into conflict. Deborah and I'll give them some time before we go back to labor with the women's meeting, to see if we can help them find a resolution. We can't do much about the men who have chosen sides, but at least we can try to help the women find peace."

She finally allowed her husband to put his arms around her. They held each other, silently asking God to be with the meeting and with Rachel and Charity in these struggles.

Joseph Maddock observed the controversy at Cane Creek and was concerned about the lax behavior of some members of Eno Meeting. He became even more demanding that there be a strict adherence to Quaker discipline, lest their own became embroiled in a similar discord. Many of the most egregious offenses, in his estimation, occurred when members married a non-Quaker, engaged in sexual relations before marriage, or committed adultery, behaviors which fell squarely under the purview of the women's meeting. He demanded that Mary take a firmer hand in her discipline of the women and families under her care.

Mary was called on many times to labor with members of the meeting who were felt by some to be disorderly in their behaviors. At the request of the men's meeting, she spent too many hours, in her estimation, admonishing women or families for missing worship meeting too often, although she was very forgiving of young mothers who fell asleep during the worship they did attend. She remembered the overall exhaustion of tending to infants and young children and her home.

Although Joseph Maddock began to stridently insist that members be disowned for what Mary thought were seemingly minor strays from the discipline, she did not like having to take someone to task for singing or dancing or even an occasional nip of alcoholic spirits. She herself believed that God wanted his children to enjoy life, not to see it as a drudgery, but some in the wider Quaker community felt that Friends should be held to a higher standard and not waste time in idle pursuits. So, she met with Friends who had misbehaved, urged them to make apologies to the meeting, and reported her satisfaction—or lack of it—to the women's meeting.

Loving her own dear Isaac as she did, she most enjoyed meeting with young people who were considering marriage. Seeing courting couples brought back such sweet memories. She was grateful that Hannah had found a sober and faithful partner, and looked forward to seeing her other children choose spouses.

She even appreciated the chance to labor with young couples who were putting themselves in the way of temptation. Young people had a way of pushing boundaries when it came to expressing their love. She was reminded of the way that Cane Creek had cruelly disciplined Charity Wright and promised to be more caring, less judgmental. After all, these young people were just following their natural healthy instincts and needed guidance, not punishment.

She was also mindful of the harsh way that Cane Creek Meeting had dealt with one of their members, Phoebe Cox, and her relatives when she married Herman Husband; he had been disowned for speaking his mind during the Charity Wright case, but he still attended meeting for worship. Since the meeting decreed that the marriage would not be in good order, the elders decided to disown anyone, even the bride's mother, who attended the wedding.

The discipline of the Society was clear that members should not marry out of meeting, but attraction and proximity sometimes caused a couple to leave their meeting rather than give up the person they loved. It was a hard choice that the couple had to make, one that affected them for the rest of their lives. It was Mary's job to instruct them in the ways of the Society of Friends, when often she would prefer to console them for the difficulty of their positions.

She particularly remembered, quite fondly, one young couple who was discovered in a compromising position on a blanket in the woods near the girl's home. This was not a forced coupling, such as that which led to Jehu Stuart being disowned. The young couple had every intention of forming a family and establishing themselves in the meeting community. They had declared their intention to marry, and their meetings had found them clear to do so. Knowing so, Mary reprimanded them gently. "You only have a few more months to wait until the proper time to have relations with each other. You don't want to risk having a child out of wedlock."

The young woman answered, "But thee can't possibly understand how hard it is to wait when we love each other so much!"

Mary smiled to herself at this fervent declaration. She was not so old that she forgot when she and Isaac were courting and the sweet agony of suppressing their desires. Occasionally, they even came close to pushing the boundaries of their own budding relationship. She understood very well how the temptation of their passions could override obedience to the discipline. She truly recognized how hard it was for this young couple. However, her job as an elder of the meeting was to help them understand the purpose of the discipline, not to condone their disorderly behavior, no matter how much she sympathized with them. More than once, she thought, *Sometimes, I feel like a mother to the whole meeting and an overly strict one at that.*

She and Deborah Stubbs continued their work with the women's meeting at Cane Creek. This was not as enjoyable a labor as spending time with young people in her meeting, but the two women knew their advice and prayers were of great help. The women of Cane Creek had been supportive when Mary was starting Eno Meeting, and she was glad that she and Deborah could return the favor.

In the spring, Mary and three women from Eno Meeting traveled to New Garden Meeting, fifty miles west of Eno. They gathered with other women Friends in Western Quarter to further consider the queries from the yearly meeting on slavery and the treatment of the enslaved.

The meeting was lively and the discussions fruitful. The gathering was a time of both friendship and fellowship. Mary reveled in the depth of the worship among these devout and respected women. She was able to relax from the pressures of leading Eno Meeting and trying to support the women of Cane Creek.

On the fourth day of the meeting, she received a letter from her husband. Thomas, her ten-year-old son, had fallen and hit his head. The bruise had swollen. He was delirious, and a fever was rising. Isaac urged Mary to come home. The note was three days old by the time a traveler had gotten it from Childsburgh to New Garden. Mary didn't know whether Thomas had already recovered or if he was even alive.

She was torn. She believed that God had called her to New Garden. She needed the time of respite and support to enable her to continue the work of ministry within her own meeting and among the nearby meetings. But she also loved her children dearly and felt she needed to be with Thomas.

She didn't want to force the other women from Eno to leave the conference early. They had all arrived together in the Maddock's carriage; if she took it, they would have no way to return home at the end of the week. Then Richard Mendenhall from Jamestown Meeting offered to take her to her home. With his sons' help, he could drive her in a wagon, and they would get her there in little more than a day.

After sitting in prayer, seeking the Lord's wishes for her, she decided to accept Richard Mendenhall's kind offer. If Thomas was still ill or even if he were better, her son would want her to be with him. If he had died, and Mary prayed that God had not taken him, then she needed to be with her family and community.

The journey home was uneventful. The Mendenhalls maintained a brisk pace, stopping at the home of Friends in Haw River to let the horses rest overnight. Mary found conversation with these new acquaintances engaging and fruitful, and she made plans to arrange a longer visit when she was less anxious.

Isaac heard the carriage pull up in front of the house. He and Edward rushed out to greet them. Before Mary could alight, she called out to hear the news of Thomas.

Isaac reassured her. "Young Thomas is still abed, but is recovering nicely. I would have sent another message, but thee would have been on thy way home by the time thee received it. We're thankful to God that our little boys have such hard heads."

He helped her down from the carriage and gave her a warm, quick hug. He stayed to thank Richard Mendenhall while she rushed into the house. May and Elizabeth jumped up and ran to their mother.

May said, "Ma, Thomas is in our room. We wanted to hear him if he got worse in the night. Cousin Ann is sitting by his bedside now in case he needs us."

When Mary walked into the bedroom and Thomas saw her, he started to cry.

She hugged him gratefully for a long time, then asked, "Why is thee crying now? Thy Da says thee's almost mended."

Sniffling and coughing, Thomas said, "Thee was not here. I hurted myself and cried for thee."

"Oh, Thomas. Thy father and thy sisters took good care of thee. Thee will be up and running around soon. Thee will forget the hurt."

Mary stayed in the room, consoling her son for a few minutes more. With another hug, she left and found Isaac had welcomed Richard Mendenhall and his sons into their home.

"Friend Richard," he said, "I'm most grateful that thee brought my Mary home. Her children missed her terribly. Please, tarry a while. May has made some stew, and there is fresh baked bread. Sup with us and tell me the news from thy meeting."

"Aye, Isaac, we have pushed the horses hard these two days, and they could use a long rest."

"Then stay with us for as long as thee desires. Thee's welcome to bed here. William, help our visitors unhitch the carriage and tend to the horses."

William and the two Mendenhall boys did as he bade

and led the animals into the barn. Isaac and Richard sat down by the fire to chat. May was stirring a pot of delicious-smelling soup, and she smiled shyly at Richard Mendenhall. Her younger brother John was sitting in the corner, whittling on a piece of soft wood.

"John," she called to him, "run and fill the pitchers with fresh water. Young Isaac, thee and Elizabeth help me serve our guests."

Four-year-old Elizabeth carefully carried spoons to the table and laid one in front of each seat. She next placed a mug and a plate beside each spoon and stood back proudly to see what a fine job she had done. Isaac, now six years old, moved the chairs and benches into place around the long, wide table. There was enough room for all of them if they sat close together.

May handed Elizabeth the loaf of freshly baked bread. She held out the knife to her brother.

"Put these on the table, in the middle if thee can reach it. Isaac, be very careful of the sharp knife. Walk slowly and hold the knife by the handle."

Soon, William and the boys came in, making loud noises and joking with each other.

May looked over to the doorway. "Shh! Thomas is abed and is sick. You must not disturb him with your foolishness. Sit, sit. I'll serve you some stew. Have you washed your hands and face? Or are you bringing in the stink of the barn?"

The boys looked at each other and laughed. They hurried back outside to wash at the trough in the yard. By the time they returned to the house, they were clean—of sorts—and settled down.

Mary came into the room and looked with approval at the effort her children had made to welcome the guests. She said, "John, take a small bowl of stew to Thomas and help him eat. He says he isn't very hungry, but I'm sure he'll want a few bites. He loves May's stew. Let Ann get away from the sick room and join us." She looked at Isaac. "Tell me, husband, how did this happen, that Thomas was so badly injured?"

"He and his brothers were playing on the woodpile. Thee knows they have been told repeatedly not to do so, but thee also knows how our boys are. Their play got a little rough. A few of the logs shifted and brought down young Thomas. He screamed and screamed. His brothers stood there crying. They weren't much help, 'tis true. I don't know if it was from fear or from shame at having disobeyed our rules. I rushed out of the barn and carried him into the house."

She smiled, "Well, it looks like he'll live, this time."

The Jacksons and Mendenhalls settled around the long wooden table. At the hearth May carefully spooned stew into the wooden bowls her father had carved. She handed one to Elizabeth, and the child slowly and carefully carried it to her mother.

"Nay, Elizabeth, please serve our guests first. I'll pass this bowl to Richard Mendenhall."

Elizabeth's chin started to tremble. Her mother gave her a quick hug and said, "Thee did a good job! Come sit beside me and let May carry the rest of the stew."

When May reached over to hand the bowl of stew to Daniel, Richard's younger son, the boy, who looked to be near in age to May, blushed and stammered his thanks. Mary noticed that he couldn't look May in the eye when she smiled at him. She knew May did look appealing. Her cheeks were rosy from the heat of the kitchen fire. Her rich auburn hair was tied back in a long braid and a few curls had escaped from her cap. Her dark green dress brought out the green in her lively eyes. Her lightly freckled arm accidentally brushed against Daniel's, and he snatched his own arm away as if it were burned.

Isaac looked at Richard, his eyes twinkling. "I do believe thy boy is smitten. May is only thirteen years old and already as beguiling as her mother."

Richard smiled as he replied, "Daniel isn't much older than thy daughter. They still have a few years yet to beguile each other. She may be the first young woman to give him such a sweet look, but I fear she won't be the last."

Laughing, Richard's other son, Jacob, punched Daniel's shoulder. "Brother, thee's drooling at our friend May. Close thy mouth. Thee prattled non-stop in the wagon, but now thee can't even manage to say thank thee without stuttering."

Daniel looked down at his bowl, mortified at the teasing. He couldn't look at his father and brother and especially tried to ignore May.

Mary gulped in realization that May was coming into her womanhood. May was not much younger than Charity Wright had been when the meeting accused her of not fighting off her attacker. Mary would have to be diligent in reminding May to avoid disorderly conduct. But then, she fervently hoped, Daniel Mendenhall was no Jehu Stuart.

The families settled into prayer, grateful for the meal placed before them. Before the children became too restless in a long silence, Mary picked up her spoon and said, "Everyone, please eat." While they enjoyed their meal, she told them about the women's gathering that she had hurriedly left. She entertained them with some lighthearted stories until the younger children were excused. Then she became serious.

"The Moravian community about twenty miles beyond New Garden has received refugees from the Cherokee wars in the west. This is only a few years after a typhus epidemic ravaged their community, and they're still recovering. Some of the Friends from the quarterly meeting are going to help. The Moravians are in need of supplies—blankets, bandages, food. They are doing God's work, and I think we should help. Richard, if we gather up some things, may we put them in thy carriage? I'm quite sure that the Friends in thy meeting and New Garden Meeting will carry them to the Moravian community so that they can distribute them."

He quickly agreed.

Mary looked at her older children. "May, go to thy Aunt Susanna's house and ask her if she and thy other aunts have anything to contribute."

Jacob grinned. "Perhaps Daniel would go with her to help carry her parcels."

Mary nodded. "That's a good idea. May, take thy brother Isaac with Daniel and thee."

"Ma, does Isaac have to tag along?" she wheedled. "He always wants to stop and pick up some disgusting thing he found."

Mary simply said, "May..." and gave her that look she had perfected over her years of raising lively, independent children. May grimaced. She seemed to be the focus of that look more often nowadays and accepted that there was no use arguing.

Isaac laughed. "I think I know why some parents put their children out to apprentice when they turn thirteen. Perhaps it's time that we consider doing so."

May glared at her father and started to say something to him.

Mary jumped in. "And thee, William, can help Jacob hitch up their wagon and go to the Maddock's house. Use our mules so their animals can rest. Ask the Friends near them to contribute, if they're willing. Elizabeth and Ann will clean the dishes, and I'll see what I can find to send in the carriage. I've plenty of healing herbs put up that I can share."

Jacob and William hurried toward the barn. May headed out briskly, her younger brother skipping along behind her. Isaac was always thrilled to go on an adventure with his older sister and was excited to be sent on an errand with their special visitor. Daniel hung back but then walked quickly to catch up with them, wondering what would he say to her as they walked.

But he needn't have worried. May was more than glad to chatter all the way to her aunt's house, and Isaac chimed in whenever she stopped talking to take a breath. On the way home, Daniel was even able to get out some complete sentences without stammering, but he wasn't sure he could remember what he said.

The next morning, when the Mendenhalls were ready to depart. They had a carriage full of blankets, foodstuffs, medical supplies, and, a good supply of Mary's healing herbs.

"Thank thee again for thy hospitality," Richard said, shaking Isaac's hand. "I'll deliver these goods to our committee for the care of refugees. We have a fine day for our travel back to Jamestown, so we should be able to make good time."

"If thee thinks it useful, Eno Meeting could send a small work party to assist thy committee and the Moravians. We have several young, unmarried adults who would love to be of service in the Lord's work. And, incidentally, who would enjoy the chance to meet other young people that they didn't grow up with. As we saw yesterday, our children are maturing, despite our wish to keep them protected and chaste."

Waving to their departing guests, Isaac put his arm around his wife and sighed. "I truly enjoyed Richard's company. What a pleasure to talk with someone so knowledgeable about the goings-on in the western meetings and with the Indians. And such a fine sense of humor." He squeezed Mary's shoulder as they turned back to the house. "It's good to have thee home again, my love."

MARY OFTEN WISHED she had been called to travel in the ministry, more than just to quarterly and yearly meetings. She prayed that God would send her to preach in Ireland—or at least Philadelphia—but so far, it hadn't happened.

On the whole, she knew she was doing good work in her community and meeting. Her niece Ann and young May were old enough to make it possible for her to spend long hours away from home tending to other Friends when they needed her. Most days, though, she spent time with her own sweet children and, most nights, she was home to lie with her Isaac. "My life is complete, even without the call to preach far and wide, and I am content," she told Isaac, and she almost believed herself.

Chapter Eleven

1764

Isaac stood at the edge of the far field. He took off his hat and rubbed his eyes at the dismal scene. The corn stalks were too short for this time of year; many did not even have ears set on them, and the ears that did manage to start were dried and lifeless. The beans he planted to wrap around the cornstalks as they grew were only small brown shoots. The ground cover of pumpkins was crunchy as he stepped on the dried-up vines to check the corn. He had planted them to hold in the water, but there was no water.

He was especially dismayed at the state of his tobacco fields. The crown had ordered that a large part of a settler's fields should be devoted to this one crop. The leaves could usually be sold to raise money for taxes. Plus, tobacco was the main cash crop Isaac could use to buy things that couldn't be grown on the farm. Not only that, the Indians were willing to trade baskets and seeds for tobacco, one of their sacred herbs. Isaac feared he would only get one tobacco harvest this year and that of an inferior grade.

Dispirited, he slumped to the ground and leaned back against a tree near the cornfield. Even the forests were feeling the effects of the drought, and leaves were dropping early. Mary wandered out to the edge of the woods and sat down beside her husband. She leaned her head on his shoulder and reached for his hand.

He smiled wanly and said, "Mary, my love, this drought has gone on too long. I fear we'll have no crops to take to market this year. I rejoiced when we were spared from the damaging winds of the hurricane that struck our friends in the east several years ago. Perhaps my hubris is catching up with me." He sighed. "I don't know what to do."

She replied softly, "Isaac, this drought didn't happen because of thy pride. Thee isn't so powerful that thy thoughts have an effect on the weather. Thee is not alone. The children and I've kept the kitchen garden watered and weeded. The Eno hasn't dried up."

"Yet," said her husband.

"Yet," said Mary, nodding, "The spring is down to a trickle, but we have been able to get water from the Eno every day. Thee knows we even filled the rain barrel and have several filled bladders stored in the old spring house in case the well runs dry. We'll have enough to eat this summer, and I should be able to put up enough vegetables for the winter. Far less than last year, though. We'll get through this, my love."

Isaac shook his head. "We need to be careful when we send the children to the river. Coyotes and bears have been seen in great numbers. They are coming down from the hills, and they need water. The wild animals may be hungry enough to find our young ones quite tasty. At least we'll have an easy source of meat when I go out to hunt."

Mary laughed. "Their flesh may be tough and stringy, but even small bits of meat will flavor the broth."

They sat quietly for a long while. Then Isaac reminded her that the tobacco crop was also failing. She knew he counted on the income to make a payment toward the debt they took on when they had expanded their fields. They needed sterling coins to pay the taxes to the crown, and the tax collectors weren't known for their leniency. Mary squeezed his shoulder.

"My herb garden has taken a lot of hard work to keep it thriving, and it's producing well. We should be able to sell a goodly portion of herbs, if anyone has any shillings to buy them. And May and I can take on more sewing, if anyone can pay us. Maybe the people in town can still afford our herbs and labor. The tax collectors and government officials, and of course, the sheriff, all have plenty of money—our money and that of our neighbors."

Isaac patted her hand and sighed deeply before going on, "Thy coins will help somewhat, but they won't be enough to pay the taxes on our land and goods. The British government doesn't seem to care that we're struggling because of this terrible drought. They want more money and they want it in shillings. The tax collectors are getting ruthless and demanding more and more in coins. We'll survive this disaster, I pray, but only God knows how."

Mary sat quietly, remembering the news of the famine that Mary Peisley brought from Ireland when she and Catherine Phillips visited ten years ago. Mary had told them of the dire conditions that caused the death of hundreds of thousands of Irish men, women, and children. *God won't let that happen to us,* Mary thought. She frowned. *But I'm sure our Irish cousins felt the same way.*

She sighed deeply. She reckoned that most of their community could survive several years under drought conditions, especially if they helped each other from their food stores. However, the increased taxation was most worrisome. The authorities were demanding that taxes be paid in British coin, but few farmers had enough extra crops to take to market—*We certainly do not*, she thought—and most received goods in exchange, rather than money.

"It would serve them right!"

Startled, Isaac looked at her with a frown.

"Oh, did I say that aloud?" Mary asked, startled herself. "I was thinking that soon even the merchants would suffer if no one had any coin to buy their goods. Some of our neighbors have borrowed heavily already to get through this drought. And the lenders are taking them to court and winning." She frowned. "They don't care about us. They deserve to struggle too." Her voice dropped. "And I know that isn't very Christian of me to wish them ill, but I do."

THE DROUGHT WAS NOT their only concern. The colonial government in Childsburgh was becoming conspicuously corrupt, and most of the farmers blamed Edmund Fanning. He had settled in Childsburgh three years before and was a close friend of Governor William Tryon. Fanning quickly got himself elected as a commissioner of the town and one of two representatives of their county to the colonial legislature in New Bern. He had wealth, which he used to purchase several other important positions in town, including public register and judge of the Superior Court in the Salisbury District. As soon as he had moved into the area, he began acquiring lots in town as well as land in the countryside to the south and east of town. This gave him considerable power, which could only grow in the coming years. And that power made him even greedier.

Fanning surrounded himself with men who shared his greed and saw an easy path to increased riches. He imposed high fees for deed registrations and other legal services, higher than the rates published by the legislature. At the same time, Governor Tryon demanded that the western counties step up their tax collections to satisfy the British crown. The governor also demanded that residents give more money so he could build a showy mansion in New Bern, a town many days of hard riding away, one that few of Mary and Isaac's friends and neighbors had even visited. Tryon called it his palace, as if he were royalty rather than an appointed bureaucrat.

Adding to the discontent, some of the sheriffs charged with the actual collections were increasingly rapacious and imposed additional fees on top of the taxes, extra money that went into their own pockets. Fanning and his cronies were getting wealthier at the expense of the farming families, including the Quakers who had settled in the area a decade earlier.

Farmers and craftsmen in the Piedmont countryside were unhappy with their tax monies being swindled or used for such a frivolous purpose as a far-distant palace. They were only a few years beyond hacking their way through the forest to clear their land, and most still lived in simple log houses. The Jacksons and their neighbors had very few luxuries. They still considered themselves loyal British subjects and were willing—albeit begrudgingly—to send some of their hard-earned money back to England, but they bristled at increasing the wealth of bureaucrats not only in their own town, but also in the wealthier coastal towns.

All of this went through Isaac's and Mary's minds as they sat near the parched cornfield. Isaac looked at Mary sadly and said, "If we can't earn enough coin to meet Fanning's demands, the tax collectors could take our supplies, our livestock, and even our land. Worse yet, they alone appraise everything before they take custody. Then, they value it lower than it's worth, so that they can take even more of our property. Mary, my love, 'tis a vicious cycle they've put us into."

He paused. "Oh, and did thee hear that the name of our town has been changed again? We no longer live near Childsburgh. Now, the closest town is to be called Hillsborough!"

Mary smiled and replied, "Well that's good news, anyway. 'Tis a lovely way to remind us of the hills and rolling meadows in this area. They truly are beautiful, especially at sunset."

"Nay, it isn't for the rolling meadows the town name is changed. It's to honor the Earl of Hillsborough, William Hill! And a relative of William Tryon. Tryon is giving away our town, piece by piece. Now even our name belongs to him. Sometimes it feels as if it's all just too much to handle. We hoped when we left our friends and family in Pennsylvania that we would be away from this nonsense."

He shook his head ruefully and continued. "My love, I heard in the market that some of our neighbors are threatening to march on the town, burning the government buildings and running off the tax collectors. This worries me as things could get ugly, and fast. As if we don't have enough problems as it is."

Mary slowly stood, brushed off her skirt, straightened her shoulders, and held out her hand to her husband. "Enough of this morose talk. Thee's starting to sink thyself into a despair. Come, love, let's go back to the house. Being with our children will remind us of why we came to this beautiful place, and why we'll muddle through. I love our home on the Eno. I love our land. I love our family, and we have each other. I promise, there is a bright side. We just can't see it yet."

They stood a few moments longer, looking at their sad crops, the dusty, cracked soil, and the relentless sun. Isaac put his arm around his wife. "Thee's right, my Mary. We have our children and each other. And I do so love thee."

He shook his head to clear it of his maudlin thoughts. "Enough of this. Homeward let's go. We'll put on smiles for our children and thank God for our blessings."

THE DROUGHT CONTINUED through the summer. One humid, gray afternoon, two men rushed into the Jacksons' house carrying a young man who was covered in blood and missing his leg below his knee. Thankfully, he had passed out.

"Goodwife Jackson, I heard that you are a healer," one cried out. "We're not of your religion, but we desperately need help. Tom here was attacked by a black bear when he was fishing in the Eno. He's grievously harmed."

Mary shook her head in sorrow as she dried her hands on her apron. "Black bears are usually afraid of people. She must have been very hungry or protecting her young. Put him here on my table and help me remove his clothing so I can see his injuries. Thy friend may not survive, but I'll do my best."

The man's body was covered in scrapes and bruises but most were minor. Mary knew they would eventually heal, after being thoroughly cleaned and packed with an herbal poultice. Of course, the significant problem was the missing leg. One of the other two men had bound the stump with the woolen shirt off his back and used a strong cord as a tourniquet, but the wrapping was already soaked through. She'd need warm water to remove the cloth without tearing the skin further.

Mary called to her children. "Thomas, get fresh water so I can clean the wounds. May, go to the shed for clean cloth strips. Bring me yarrow to stop the bleeding and boil some willow bark into tea for the pain should Tom awaken. William, dig up clean clay for me to seal the stump, and find large oak leaves to wrap the limb. Hurry now!"

Mary worked on his battered body for more than an hour. Tom did not wake up through her ministrations but moaned softly in his fitful unconsciousness. Eventually, she stepped away, put her hands at the back of her waist and stretched, bending backward as far as she could. She groaned at the relief in her aching back from having leaned awkwardly over her work for too long.

She then turned to the injured man's companions, who had watched nervously. "Friends, I'm afraid that's all I can do for him. His life is in God's hands now. If fever or infection doesn't claim him, he may come through. He'll be a cripple, but alive."

By then Isaac had entered the house and set up a pallet in the warm corner near the hearth. "Do you think you can help me move him to the pallet?" he said. The three men settled Tom gently on it and tried to make him comfortable. He moaned and thrashed before settling back into a restless coma.

"Sleep is the best thing for him now," Mary said. "Does thy friend have a wife to come sit with him? Or a mother or sisters? They'll want to be here with him if he passes, and to help him in his healing if he comes through."

The older of the two men replied, "No, he came alone to North Carolina from Virginia to hunt and trap. He told us he has no family left after a band of roving Indians burned his village."

Isaac frowned. "My wife and daughters will watch over him and use cooling cloths to try to keep the fever down. If he survives, we'll find a family to take him in while he heals and gets stronger."

"Yes, until then, he can stay here," Mary agreed. "Go

out to the pump and wash thy hands and faces. My husband will find a clean shirt for thee," she said to the man who had first bandaged Tom's leg. "I'm afraid that the one I cut off thy friend's stump is beyond salvaging. There is soup in the kettle and fresh bread on the shelf. You are both welcome to stay and sit by thy friend or to rest up on a blanket in the barn before you go on your way."

Mary then set May and her brothers to scrubbing the table with lye soap and rinse it until the water ran clear. She covered it with a layer of straw and a clean cloth; it would be a while until it could dry. The men did as they were told and gratefully sat down at the covered table. May silently set steaming bowls of soup in front of each and put a loaf of bread and a sharp knife on a board. The men ate heartily, then checked on their wounded companion and announced that they'd be on their way.

"We're trappers," one said. "I'm sorry that there's no way that a message will be able to reach us quickly. However, we'll come by again and check back with you in a few days. Might we leave you some cleaned and scraped beaver skins as payment for your kindness?"

Isaac said, "That isn't necessary."

The older man spoke again. "We're grateful to you for your care and food. Come. Choose some of the skins for your use or to sell in the market. We know this drought has been difficult for you farmers."

Isaac took a few skins and nodded his thanks. "Thy friend is in good hands."

Tom was feverish for almost a week, but with Mary's care and prayers, he survived. When the trappers eventually returned, he was stable enough to leave with them nestled in the cart among the beaver skins. They promised to take him to Virginia to a family who may know of his kinfolk.

Isaac wrapped his arm around Mary's shoulder as they stood in the doorway, watching the men go down the lane. "Aye, my love. Thee did all that thee could. Tom is in God's hands now."

In early Eighth Month, Mary was delighted to welcome Katherine White, who had come from Piney Woods Meeting, one of the earliest meetings on the North Carolina coast. Katherine had sent word in advance that she was traveling, at the request of the yearly meeting, to visit Piedmont meetings. Eastern Carolina Friends had heard about the difficulties that the rural western meetings were experiencing and had asked her to bring back news.

Mary and Katherine had met several times at gatherings of women Friends, as well as the occasional yearly meeting. This was the first time they were able to sit and visit. Katherine settled gratefully in a comfortable chair by the fire. Mary handed her visitor a tightly woven lap rug to help her warm from her journey. She bustled around the kitchen, preparing a pot of herb tea and thick slices of freshly baked bread with jam. Setting the tray on a low table between the two chairs, Mary finally sat down.

She reached over and patted the hand of her guest. "Katherine, I'm so glad that thee has graced us with thy visit. Pray tell, how is thy family, and what is the news from the east?"

The two women spent a fine hour talking about their children and grandchildren—Hannah and Thomas had blessed Mary and Isaac with a wee grandson the year before. The women laughed over some of the exploits of the more adventurous of the youth they talked about. They shared stories of weddings and others' new babies. Then they took a few minutes to hold in prayer their members who had taken ill, and to tell of Friends who had recently died. Mary rose to add another log to the fire.

Sitting down again, she turned the conversation to the difficult subject of how the year's drought had affected the farmers. She described some of the dealings of the crooked tax collectors and other government officials, and how this was leading to the growing unrest in the Piedmont region. Then Katherine changed the subject once more, sharing news of the recent devastations along the coast. Another brutal gale had struck a month earlier, but only light rains had made it to the Piedmont. Many coastal areas were severely damaged by the high tides and extreme winds. In New Bern, whole neighborhoods were underwater and many residents were killed. All over the region, trees had been knocked down. Farmers saw their fall harvests destroyed; vegetable and tobacco fields were inundated with salt water. Rice plantations in the low-lying marshlands were especially hard hit, with the salt water flowing into the fields and the crushing waters destroying both crops and the rice stored in warehouses. Even worse, too many slaves living on these plantations had lost their lives.

"Mary, I fear that some of these farms will take years to recover. I hear that the salt from the flood waters has soaked into the soil and will prevent crops from thriving and not just this year. Oh, it's too sad to contemplate."

"Katherine, we got some of the high winds from thy gale, but they were not so devastating here. We're finally getting some rain and are beginning to recover from the severe drought." She sighed. "But now, the cruel and dishonest tax collectors and sheriffs are taking our crops and livestock for taxes to pay for the governor's palace."

She paused again and asked, trying unsuccessfully to hide a small but detectable smirk. "Oh," she asked, "did the governor lose his palace in the gale? Did God look down and smite William Tryon for his arrogance?"

"No," Katherine replied. "It's well constructed and not yet furnished. Little damage, I'm told, but I'm quite sure they will demand more money from the rest of us to make the repairs. Not like the ordinary people whose homes and livelihoods were destroyed. No money is forthcoming for them."

Mary paused to hold the New Bern folk in her heart while silently wishing she could curse the governor and his people who were not suffering as greatly. She shook her head to dispel the wish to cause harm. Her temper, she knew, was from her Irish heritage and not worthy of the Quaker she tried to be. She sent out a tiny curse anyway.

"But we can help somehow," she offered. "We can gather some foodstuffs, good seeds, maybe some household supplies."

"That isn't necessary. Our meetings are taking care of Friends and our neighbors. Many of us are trying to help the Africans who survived, but some of the plantation owners are obstructing us. They fear that we're trying to convince their slaves to escape from their servitude. We aren't. We just want to take care of their needs. But their owners' great wealth depends on the labor of the Africans. They simply can't conceive that Friends would try to help people in need out of the goodness of our hearts. They, themselves, would expect some kind of payment in return if they were ever led to provide succor."

Katherine sighed and looked away. She hesitated to disturb the companionship that was developing between her and Mary. After a pause she said, "Mary, we understand thy struggle, and we truly want to hear more about the drought and the difficulties thee and thy neighbors are experiencing with the officials in Hillsborough. That is but one reason that the yearly meeting sent me to thy meeting."

Mary looked at her warily. "One reason? Are there others?"

Katherine nodded slowly. "Thee knows why the yearly meeting is concerned about Eno Friends. Thy meeting isn't sending in annual reports. Thee hasn't sent the answers to the queries. Reports are reaching us about Friends being read out of meeting because they joined a group that is considering an uprising against thy government officials. The news from thy meeting is sparse, but what we hear isn't good."

Mary sat back. She should've known that this visitor was not here just to share news. Maybe some Friends cared about their struggles in the Piedmont, but the yearly meeting was more concerned about their own rules. *I understand why the yearly meeting wanted to discipline Eno Meeting,* she thought, *because Friends here didn't always obey the dictates of the yearly meeting or the quarterly.* The Eno Friends hoped to be left alone to survive as best they could, worshiping God in their own way, and attending the meeting when they were able. Keeping records and sending in reports had very little priority.

Mary tried to deflect the criticism she knew was forthcoming. This was one more in a long history of complaints against her meeting. "Katherine, thee has heard all of the reasons from us through the years. We aren't going to change, no matter how many times we're disciplined. The clerk of our meeting and I have tried. We have few members who are experienced in record keeping. I can't force those who write well to do our reporting. They would rather stop attending our business meetings than to give up more time in unnecessary paperwork."

"Mary, the records and reports aren't unnecessary,"

Katherine challenged her. "They're a part of a discipline instituted by George Fox himself, when the early Friends were imprisoned for not tithing to the Anglican church and bowing down to the king and their so-called betters. Reports are just as important now for overseeing the life of Quakers in North Carolina."

"Katherine, thee says that we can't be good Quakers without filling out papers. I disagree," Mary argued. "I can't continue to lead the women's meeting and serve as an elder to our members if I also have to write reports. I have a large family, a household to maintain, and gardens of herbs that I must tend, to sell to raise money to pay the exorbitant taxes."

She sat back and closed her eyes. Katherine started to say more, but Mary stayed her with her hand. After several minutes of silent reflection, Mary again spoke. "I'll listen to thy concern no more. Thee can report back to our yearly meeting that we'll continue as before. If there are consequences, then so be it."

She rose and began to clear the tea things. "Katherine, thee's welcome to join us for supper and, if thee desires, to remain for a night or two before thee continues on thy way. We're happy to have thy company. If thee wants to hear about our struggles, I will continue to converse with thee."

Katherine nodded. "I thank thee for thy hospitality. I won't say more about thy meeting's lack of discipline. I would enjoy supping with thy family, but I must continue on my way. Rachel Maddock is expecting me. We have long been friends from back when we both lived in Pennsylvania. I'm bringing Joseph a report from the yearly meeting. Maybe he'll be more receptive to the concerns I carry. The request for answers to the queries and annual reports isn't just a burden laid on the women of thy meeting."

Mary helped her visitor gather her belongings and

called to her son to saddle Katherine's horse. As he did so, she thought, *How very sad that the conversation turned to criticism. I did so look forward to building a friendship with this Friend. Why must everyone be so difficult? Aren't we all doing God's work?*

As she waved good-bye, Mary frowned. Maybe the problem was not just with Katherine and the yearly meeting. Perhaps she herself was too quick to take offense, too quick to find excuses for her own behavior. She had much to share with Isaac.

Chapter Twelve

1770

On the way back home from a visit to Cane Creek Meeting, Isaac stopped the wagon in a small clearing at the bend of the river. He and Mary climbed down, helping the younger children jump to the ground. Isaac unhitched the horses and led them to the river to drink. At the meeting, the older boys and girls had enjoyed visiting their counterparts, shyly seeking boyfriends and girlfriends who were not their own cousins; now they moved to a shady tree to compare notes. The younger children had worn themselves out, playing while the adults worshiped and conducted business, but still had enough energy to wade and splash in the shallow pools.

The stop by the river gave them a chance to wind down and clean off the dust from the day. Isaac set up camp, building a fire for Mary to cook a quick supper. She pulled out food that was left over from the fellowship lunch, and the children added some wild strawberries that they had found. After eating, the youngsters settled down for the night in quilts and blankets around the fire. The ground was hard, but they were soon sound asleep.

Mary and Isaac sat leaning against a wagon wheel. The night was clear, and they enjoyed sitting quietly together. A shooting star crossed the sky. Isaac noticed it and smiled at his wife. As a Quaker, Mary knew not to believe in old wives' tales, but her Irish side was still a bit superstitious. She made a silent wish on the star. To be safe, she turned the wish into a small prayer. It was not only for herself, but for all the struggling people in their county. Maybe God would grant her this one thing.

"Isaac, my love, I truly wish that the ugliness that has taken hold of our town would just go away. Is that so terrible a thing to want?"

Isaac looked down at her earnest face and smiled. "Ah, if only it would be true. But I fear it won't be so easy to achieve."

He leaned over and pulled out a small printed sheet of paper. Simon Dixon had handed them out to anyone who would take one. The author was Simon's brother-in-law, Herman Husband, who had made a name for himself with his writings and now turned his pen to the current political situation. Simon was torn between his Quaker tendency to stay neutral in such doings and his pride at the clear statement his wife's brother had published.

The men at the meeting had read and discussed this paper but couldn't agree to join in solidarity with Herman's views. Several Friends said that such a statement could only inflame the violent tendencies on one side and antagonize the town officials on the other. Isaac and a few others, including the author of the statement, hoped that such a direct and simple presentation of grievances would provide a basis for reasoned discourse between the two sides. Still, he had no idea which view would prevail and feared that any attempt to negotiate with the officials could escalate, rather than appease, the tensions.

Isaac smoothed out the wrinkles on the paper. "I have this statement from Herman Husband for us to consider." He brought the lantern closer so that he could read the words to his wife and a couple of the older children who had come closer when they overheard their parents.

Nineteen-year-old May interrupted, "Wasn't he read out of meeting because of Charity and Rachel Wright?"

Mary replied, "Yes, he was disowned, but he still goes to meeting for worship, and he considers himself a Quaker. But he hasn't made sufficient apology to the meeting, according to the women I have talked with. In fact, when he married Phoebe Cox, she was disowned, for marrying out of meeting. And then they disowned any member, including Phoebe's mother, who attended the wedding. What a mess! Now, thee has gotten me sidetracked. I still get angry when I remember the bad treatment Charity and Rachel received at the hands of their meeting."

She raised her hand and shook it softly. "Hush now, let Da read the paper."

"Herman Husband wrote a list of grievances against the abuses by corrupt British officials and tax collectors," Isaac first explained. "Some people see his words as a justification to use violence to achieve their ends, but Friend Simon insists that Herman published this document in hopes of finding a settlement without violent means. Maybe they are both being naive, but there is always hope that this document will speak to the better good of the government officials."

He began reading, "We, the underwritten subscribers, do voluntarily agree to form ourselves into an Association to assemble ourselves for conferences for regulating Public

Grievances and Abuses of Power in the following particulars, with others of like nature that may occur—"

May interrupted again. "It does sound as though he's urging peaceful settlement. Why won't Edmund Fanning and his men just sit down and listen!"

"May, dear, thee's right," Isaac said, "but people aren't always open to listening to each other. Let me continue. By the way, they call themselves the Sandy Creek Association, although there's already a Sandy Creek Association among the Baptists. Who knows why they're using the same name. Friend Simon did say the Baptists who are struggling just as much as we are have joined with the Quakers. Might I continue?"

May sat back and nodded to her father. She had no intention of being silenced about the injustices she saw but was willing to listen.

"'First. That we will pay no taxes until we are satisfied they are agreeable to Law and Applied to the purpose therein mentioned, unless we can't help it and are forced. Second. That we will pay no Officer any more fees than the Law allows, unless we are obliged to it, and then to show a dislike to it and bear open testimony against it.'"

Again, May spoke up. "The tax collectors have been truly unfair. My friend Jacob's parents lost almost half of their land and two of their best milk cows because they didn't have enough currency on hand. And Mama had to give up the candlesticks that our grandmother brought with her from Ireland to Pennsylvania. And she treasured those candlesticks as a reminder of our dear grandmother and Mama's homeland! No wonder people are upset."

Mary hugged her daughter. "May, settle down. Those candlesticks were precious, true, but they're only worldly things. We can survive without pewter candlesticks. Let thy father read on."

"Aye, that is true enough." Isaac patted his wife's knee fondly and continued. "Third. That we will attend our meetings of Conference as often as we conveniently can or is necessary in order to consult our representatives on the amendments of such Laws as may be found Grievous or unnecessary, and to choose more suitable men than we have heretofore done for Burgesses and Vestrymen, and to petition His Excellency our Governor, the Honorable Council and the Worshipful House of Representatives, His Majesty in Parliament, et cetera, for redress of such grievances as in the course of this undertaking may occur, and inform one another and to learn, know and enjoy all the Privileges and Liberties that are allowed us and were settled on us by our worthy ancestors, the founders of the present Constitution, in order to preserve it in its Ancient Foundation, that it may stand firm and unshaken."

Isaac looked at Mary and May. "I think what Friend Herman is trying to say is that the farmers and small merchants in our area want to be represented in the government of our colony and, even if we're not, for the authorities to listen to our grievances. A bit wordy, but he had to use such language and flowery titles to even get the British officials to listen."

Again, this time rising on her knees, his daughter spoke. "He should've stayed true to our testimony of simplicity in our dealings and used plainer language. This sounds like he's trying too hard to appease the other side."

Mary shook her head slightly and sighed. She leaned in closer to her husband and wrapped her hand around his arm. At everyone's nod, Isaac continued, "Fourth. That we will contribute to collections for defraying necessary expenses attending to the work according to our abilities. And, fifth, that in cases of difference in judgment we will submit to the Majority of our Body." Isaac refolded the paper. "Herman Husband ends with his fervent expectation that he and others will continue in this work until all of their grievances are satisfied."

This time, it was his wife who rose in indignation. "Since when do we ever submit to the majority in any of our meetings? We prayerfully wait on the Lord for clarity before going forward. We never just vote. That's the way to ensure hurt feelings and animosity toward others who don't have the same opinions. Why ever would Friend Husband include such a statement?"

Isaac reminded her gently, "Herman Husband isn't speaking only to Quakers, but to all the aggrieved farmers and merchants, including Baptists and Anglicans and, especially, to the representatives of the King and Parliament."

They sat silently for a long while, considering the words. Mary decided that she needed to bring this document to the attention of the women of Eno Meeting for their discernment. Too many families were affected by the cruelty and dishonesty of the government officials, and many of the women had husbands, brothers, and grown children who were itching to cause trouble.

May started to say something more, but she was silenced with a wave of her mother's hand. She and her older brothers got up and went back to their bedding. May was certain that the authorities would dismiss the grievances, if only they could be convinced of the grave unfairness. She assumed her parents agreed with her; at the same time, she recognized that they couldn't condone rebellion even if that was the only way to accomplish their goals. Some of the boys in her community, her cousins included, had decided that they'd fight if they had to. But maybe that was just silly posturing; at least she hoped so. She lay awake for a long time before falling into a fitful sleep.

. . .

SEVERAL DAYS after returning from Cane Creek, Mary sent word to the women of Eno meeting that they should gather. Mary, having been appointed clerk of the women's meeting more than fifteen years earlier, was still looked up to by the women as their leader. They, too, feared what was happening in their town and wanted to hear what she had to say.

The women were unusually restless on that gloomy afternoon, only a faint light coming in through the small window of the meetinghouse. An infant was suckling lustily while the women nearby smiled in remembrance. Another baby cooed as he played with a lock of his mother's hair. One young mother paced around the back of the room, trying to quiet her fussy child. The older children, in the schoolhouse across the yard, were bent over their lessons under the watchful eye of their teacher, Rebecca. Even while doing the important business of the community, women still had to take care of their young families and duties.

From the clerk's table, Mary looked at each of the women sitting in the dim meetinghouse. She implored them to settle into expectant worship, asking the Lord to be with them in their considerations. Her voice trembled with urgency, but she knew to wait until the moment was right. Eventually the creaking of the floorboards and nervous shifting on the benches settled. Most of the infants were finally soothed, and several slept peacefully with gentle snores. When Mary was quiet in her own mind, she read to them the proclamation that Isaac had carried from Simon Dixon. Several of the women started to talk to one another and raise their voices in alarm.

Mary raised her hands from the table to still them. "Let's hold this in our hearts and listen to God in worship. There will be time to speak when we have prayed on it."

After a long, uneasy silence, she felt that Sarah Chambers was ready to speak and called on her.

"Friends, this is a long time coming," Sarah began. "Our farms have been decimated, our household goods and tools confiscated in payment, our livestock carted away without any consideration given to feeding our children or supporting ourselves. And oftentimes, the amount they demand is far more than what is owed. This is unsupportable greed. We must do something."

The other women murmured among themselves and nodded in agreement.

"Yea, it's time we rose up together and demand our rights," a young mother almost shouted. "My husband says it's time to fight, that fighting is the only way the authorities will listen."

A few of the older women were visibly shocked. One of the elders rose and looked around the room. Everyone quieted when she started speaking. "Since the beginning of our religion, Friends have taken a stand against violence and making war. George Fox told Oliver Cromwell that he couldn't in all good conscience join him in battle. It's our lot to show, with patience and forbearance, that we stand firm in our demands without resorting to fighting. Jesus told us to give unto God that which is God's and unto Caesar that which is Caesar's. Perhaps our property isn't ours to withhold."

Another woman jumped up in anger. "Maybe if our Caesar only demanded a fair share, but Edmund Fanning and his men are taking our livelihood, our homes, our land! Some of our husbands and brothers have been thrown in prison, not for our faith like the early Friends, but for not paying exorbitant tax demands. This is *not* giving to Caesar, as Christ commanded us, but lining the pockets of greedy men. My husband won't stand for it. He's ready to go to battle and some of my cousins also. We *must* take back our lives!"

Mary let the women continue to rail against the injustices. A few others agreed that their menfolk were also ready to fight, but most were torn between their faith, which demanded a peaceful resolution, and their livelihoods, which demanded restitution. Then Mary quietly asked that they all sit together in prayer. She had hoped that the women would take a firm stand against the rising tendency to violence, but realized they were not ready.

After a long while, an elderly woman stood, quivering. She was faithful in attendance at meeting for worship and meeting for business, but had never spoken in either, as far as Mary knew. She mostly kept to herself. The women quieted in surprise that she felt led to speak. She continued to stand for a few minutes, clearly nervous.

Finally, in a soft, halting voice, she spoke. "My dear Friends. Paul in his letter to the Colossians said to us, 'Put on therefore, as the elect of God, holy and beloved, bowels of mercies, kindness, humbleness of mind, meekness, long suffering; forbearing one another, and forgiving one another, if any man have a quarrel against any: even as Christ forgave you, so also do ye. And above all these things put on charity, which is the bond of perfectness. And let the peace of God rule in your hearts, to that which also ye are called in one body; and be ye thankful...And whatsoever ye do in word or deed, do all in the name of the Lord Jesus, giving thanks to God and the Father by him.'"

Her trembling words were the reminder that the women needed. They were humbled by her sincerity and the words of Scripture she recited from memory. The gathering settled into a deep and rich worship, trying to quiet their own fears and their anger and listen to the still, small voice of the Lord.

When the children could be heard being released for the day, the women gathered up their things, bundled up the infants, and went outside to collect their children. They had no more to say to each other; they needed time to ponder and pray about the right path forward. Fortunately, the children demanded their attention and relieved some of the tension. There would be more to say at another time.

OVER THE NEXT WEEKS, the desire for a confrontation, violent if necessary, continued growing among the farmers and merchants around Hillsborough, and many of them began calling themselves "the Regulators" because they demanded the right to regulate their own affairs. Isaac was torn about whether to join the Sandy Creek Association, but he definitely kept up with their efforts. They claimed they didn't wish to change the form of their government; after all, they were British citizens. They simply wanted to make the colony's political process fairer. They wanted better economic conditions for everyone, instead of a system that solely benefited the colonial officials. As Isaac had feared, the more headstrong men were turning the group toward violence instead of the peaceful negotiation that Herman Husband advocated.

Under the auspices of the Sandy Creek Association, the leaders issued the following advertisement in Eighth Month, 1766:

"Let each Neighborhood throughout the Country meet together and appoint one or more men to attend a General Meeting on the Monday before the next November Court at a suitable place where there is no Liquor (at Maddock's Mill if no objection) at which meeting let it be judiciously enquired whether the free men of this Country labor under any abuses of power or not and let the same be notified in writing if any is found and the matter freely conversed upon and proper measures used for amendment; this method shall cause the wicked men in power to tremble, and there is no damage can attend such a meeting nor nothing hinder it but a cowardly, dastardly Spirit which if it does in this time while Liberty prevails we must mutter and grumble under any Abuses of Power until such a noble spirit prevails in our posterity for take this as a maxim that while men are men, though you should see all those Sons of Liberty (who has just now redeemed us from tyranny) set in Offices and vested with power they would soon corrupt again and oppress if they were not called upon to give an account of their Stewardship."

Isaac and his brothers decided to attend. They all hoped that the authorities would come to hear their grievances. He told Mary that this meeting was an attempt to rein in the more violent impulses before they appeared at the court in Eleventh Month, when it was next in session.

About a dozen men met at the mill, far fewer than expected. Some were self-proclaimed Regulators, while others, like Isaac, were not ready to join the movement. James Watson was the only colonial official to attend, saying he was a representative of Colonel Fanning. Watson further said that Fanning had written a statement, but he decided not to present it at this meeting. He told the small gathering that the wording of the meeting notice was inflammatory and showed clearly that the men were not interested in reconciliation. He left early. The men argued halfheartedly among themselves but couldn't agree on the way forward.

A couple of weeks later, Joseph Maddock rode up to Isaac and Mary's house. Nine-year-old Thomas ran up to their visitor and asked, "Is thee here to speak with my ma about meeting business?"

"No, I wish to speak with thy father about a matter of some import. Is he about?"

"Aye, he's in the barn. I'll go get him for thee."

Thomas took off for the barn. Joseph followed closely, rather than wait.

"Greetings, Friend Isaac."

Isaac looked up and smiled. "My horse has come up lame. Mary prepared a poultice, and I want to get his leg wrapped before it cools down."

"May I speak with thee in private?"

Isaac nodded. "Thomas, bring Joseph Maddock some water, and then tend to his horse."

Thomas was curious what could be so important, but he did as his father bade.

"Isaac, as thee knows, the Regulators announced a meeting at my mill without my permission. Thee was there as were thy brothers. I didn't stop it from happening. I should have. Edmund Fanning's men have made threats against me and my family. He thinks I'm a leader in the Regulator movement and plans to confiscate my property."

Isaac, his face concerned, finished his task and motioned for Joseph to follow him to the bench outside the barn. The weather was still mild. Thomas handed over a mug of water. He looked at his father for permission to stay, but Isaac shook his head and motioned for the boy to leave.

Joseph continued, "I'm caught between those who urge me to join the Regulators and the officials who are blaming me for inflaming the violence. I fear one side or the other will destroy the business I've built up."

He rubbed his hands over his face and exhaled deeply. "My mill has been struggling for several years. More mills have been built along the Eno. We're too far from the town of Hillsborough, so residents of the town go to those that are closer. I relied on the Quakers in our community to support the mill, but, as thee knows, the farmers still suffer from the drought. They haven't had as much use for my services as in the past."

Again, he sighed. "Friend Isaac, I want thee to know first. I'm selling my property and leaving North Carolina. Last year, my cousin and I traveled to Georgia. The governor there welcomed us and offered us a grant on a large tract of land. We'll be able to start over."

The previous summer, Maddock and several other Eno Quakers had made the three-hundred-mile journey to eastern Georgia. They had heard that the county was offering farmland similar to the Eno region with numerous creeks on which to build mills and other industries. They asked the governor of Georgia, Sir James Wright, for a grant of twelve thousand acres. It was awarded, providing that settlers cleared the parcels and built homes and farms within the year. When the group returned to Eno Meeting, they set about convincing their neighbors to leave North Carolina, rather than continue to be abused by the colonial authorities. They described in glowing terms the welcome they had received from the Georgia authorities and the possibilities of building a new community.

Hearing that Joseph had made the decision, Isaac looked at him in alarm. "Joseph, who among us has enough money to buy thee out? Thy mill and orchards are valuable, and thee owns many acres on both sides of the Eno."

"I need to move quickly before my property is confiscated. Edmund Fanning has been saying he will do so as soon as he has the warrant from the court. I'm thankful to have received a very good offer from Thomas Hart. He's buying up land to establish a plantation here, north of Hillsborough. And I've already sold a large tract to Robert Burnside."

"Oh, Joseph. I'm sorry for thy dilemma, but Thomas Hart—please, not Thomas Hart. He will likely bring enslaved men and women to work this plantation. His crops will overwhelm the markets, and we'll receive lower prices for our tobacco. It will be even harder to raise the shillings we need to pay our taxes."

"Isaac, I, too, am sorry. I see this as the best way for me and my kin. About twenty families will be going with us." Joseph looked at Isaac. "We would like thee and thy family to come also."

Isaac thought for a moment before speaking. "Friend, thee has given me much to think about. I'll need to talk with my wife. Thy land will no longer have Quakers living there. What will become of our meeting? We've worked so hard to establish our Quaker community here. Oh, my Mary will be so sad. She cares so for this land and these Friends."

Isaac stood and moved to shake Joseph's hand, thanking him for telling him of the decision. As his visitor left, Isaac walked slowly to the house. He wasn't looking forward to breaking the news to Mary. They would have to talk about Joseph's invitation and pray to seek a way forward.

Both Isaac and Mary were torn. They had made a home in the countryside near Hillsborough. Mary loved the house they had built, with the view of the hills and river. A few years back, they had purchased more acreage, so there was plenty of land for their children to establish households and farms. Eno Meeting was struggling, yes, but also growing slowly. They had a meetinghouse and school. Their brothers and sisters, cousins, and other relations lived nearby. Mary, especially, did not want to move again and start over. She was almost fifty years old and had borne eight children, five of them still at home. Hannah's daughter was growing up. Mary wanted to enjoy her old age where she was. She wanted to play with her grandchildren, and, she hoped, eventually their great-grandchildren, and continue to work in her garden.

Several of their relatives joined Isaac and Mary in their discernment. Some restless days later, Mary and Isaac made their decision: to remain on their farm. The twenty or so families who were moving to Georgia would be a terrible loss to the community, but the Jacksons had faith that, with God's help, Eno Meeting would continue to prosper in spirit if not in wealth. And that, with God's help, they would get through this terrible time of discord.

ONE AFTERNOON, in Ninth Month, Isaac walked into the house and called for Mary. She was upstairs cleaning the children's sleeping loft and came down the ladder to give him a hug.

"Mary, Herman Husband is coming to Hillsborough to present the Regulator's case in court. He doesn't think it will be safe to stay close to town, so I invited him to stay with us."

Mary said, "Isaac, does thee think that is wise? He's at the center of the controversy, and the sheriff has a warrant for his arrest."

"It's our Christian duty to help him. He's been disowned by his meeting, but he still practices as a Quaker. And he's a life-long pacifist."

When Herman Husband later knocked on the door, Mary invited him into the warm kitchen. Isaac told his namesake son to go out and care for their visitor's horse. Young Isaac jumped up to do his father's bidding, excited to be able to help their guest. He had seen the pamphlet that Herman Husband had written. He couldn't yet read well enough to understand it all, but he had never met someone who actually wrote something that was printed and made into a book.

Herman smiled at the boy and said, "No, that isn't necessary. There is no horse, as I arrived here on foot. But thank thee for thy kindness."

Young Isaac sat back down, feeling proud at being thanked by such an important man. His mother frowned at his self-satisfied smile and looked over at their guest. "Friend, that's a long way to walk. Didn't thee have a horse to carry thee here?"

"My horse drew up lame about nine miles back. I stopped at a farmhouse. The farmer and his wife are sympathetic to our cause and said they would care for her until she's able to be ridden again. They didn't have a horse to spare. They offered to drive me here in their wagon, but I said I would walk. They were doing enough to care for my mount."

"Well, come in and sit by the fire," Isaac invited. "Thee may hang thy coat on the peg near the door. My wife will give thee something warm to drink, and later we'll sup together. Mary has set up bedding for thee in a warm corner."

Herman leaned back in the chair and closed his eyes, weary from his long walk. The Jacksons let him rest. There would be plenty of time for conversation later in the evening. The warm fire and hot tea did much to restore him, and over the meal of venison stew and freshly baked bread, he became lively and talkative. He and Isaac discussed the challenges of clearing the land and farming in the heavy clay soil of the Piedmont. Mary asked about Cane Creek meeting and the Friends she had met there. And Herman brought stories of some of the children in the meeting to draw the younger Jacksons into the conversation.

After supper, Mary sent the children to bed and got them settled in for the night. The three adults sat by the fire to continue their conversation.

Herman said, "Friends, I must talk seriously about what is going on with the settlers' grievances. And I desire thy consult. Thee has perhaps heard of the list of grievances that I published at the direction of many from my community?"

Mary and Isaac nodded. Isaac said, "We appreciate the clarity and wisdom presented in thy document."

Herman continued. "I'm deeply troubled. I'm a Quaker even though my meeting found me lacking and disowned me. I've been a Quaker all my life. I love the words of George Fox, when he wrote that he lived in the virtue of that life and power that took away the occasion of all wars, and that he had come into the covenant of peace which was before wars and strife. And Jesus in the Scriptures said 'Blessed are the peacemakers' and to 'turn the other cheek.'

"I wrote those words in my declaration of grievances in hopes that we can arrive at a peaceful resolution. I had hoped my words would change hearts and bring Edmund Fanning to reflect on his transgressions. But some who read my words have used them to organize a movement and are itching to fight to get their demands met. I cannot countenance the use of force and violence, but I fear it may come to that. Tomorrow, I'll try to prevent the Regulators from erupting, but I've been led to believe that the authorities won't be receptive to our pleas. I only hope I can prevent bloodshed—on either side."

He looked to Mary, then to Isaac. "If my words are used to incite violence, I'm as responsible as if I called them to stand by my side to go forth in battle. How can I live with my participation in this, if it comes to rebellion?"

Isaac and Mary took his concern to heart. The three sat

in silent prayer for a long while before Isaac broke the silence. "Friend Herman, thy concern is real that the rebellion may turn bloody. But thee isn't responsible for the actions of others. If thy words were directed by God in prayer, then stay true to thy leading. 'Tis a gift thee has been given, to be able to phrase the demands so clearly and simply. Thee *is* a leader. Keep urging thy followers to remain peaceful, to not stir up trouble."

Mary added, "We'll pray that thee is steadfast in this work."

In the morning, Isaac hitched up the horse to the wagon and told Mary he would take Herman to the courthouse and would stay to bring him back after he presented the Regulators' demands.

At the courthouse, Isaac watched as Herman told the guards he had an appointment with the judge, but the guards denied his entrance. He refused to leave and standing on the steps, loudly read the list of grievances to all who would listen.

The authorities knew that Herman Husband had only a tenuous control over the Regulators who accompanied him. Before Herman could finish speaking, the guards swooped in without provocation and started swinging their clubs and muskets at those who had gathered. Appalled, Isaac looked on as the Regulators retaliated. Herman tried to halt the destruction, but he was arrested and hauled into the jail. On a rampage, the crowd broke windows and destroyed several buildings in the town. They also rushed into Fanning's house, pulled him outside into the courthouse square, and beat him. The sheriff's men managed to intervene and spirited Fanning to safety. Dissatisfied that their prey had been removed, the angry rioters completely destroyed Fanning's house, including his furniture and clothing.

The mob continued, unabated, while the militia grabbed as many as possible and jailed them. Finally, the unruly gang of Regulators retreated and left the town.

Shaken, Isaac returned home alone. He told Mary of the mob's actions.

"Herman did try to stop them, but he was arrested as the ringleader, even though he was urging the men not to use violence. They were caught up in bloodlust and ignored him. The militia increased their attacks, which only incited the Regulators to even more disruption." His voice trembled. "Mary, it was a cycle of increasing violence, too horrible to countenance."

Mary grimaced as she gently dabbed at a gash on Isaac's forehead. She tried not to hurt him, although privately she felt like kicking him for being so stupid as to get caught up in the melee.

"Oh, Isaac. How could thee get involved?" Mary began sputtering, too angry to express her rage, her relief, and her fear for Isaac. "Thee is a *Friend*, an elder of our meeting. Thee *knows* that violence is never the way to solve problems. Thee *must* set a good example."

"Mary, dear Mary, thee knows I don't condone violence. Thee knows I have done everything possible to urge the men in our community to stay calm and be patient."

Recovering her composure, Mary jumped into her argument, which she knew aligned with the complaints of the Regulators. "Jesus taught that we should give Caesar what is due to Caesar, but Edmund Fanning has gone too far. Thee well knows I think many of the men sent by the British to govern us are greedy and dishonest. And they're getting worse every day. They're doing to the colonies what the British did to our grandparents in Ireland.

"Still, couldn't thee have made a peaceful protest?" she asked. "That was the plan. Thee told me our neighbors were going to present the Bill of Rights that Herman Husband wrote in his pamphlet. He had expressed our concerns so eloquently and simply."

Isaac shook his head sadly. "Nay, Mary. We tried. Herman had an appointment to do just that. We went to the government office in Hillsborough with copies of Friend Herman's declaration. But William Tryon's men tricked us. Instead of being able to calmly present our demands, he set a militia against us. Edmund Fanning watched from the window of the tavern where he'd taken refuge. He wouldn't even come out to meet us. He's not only greedy, but cowardly."

"Isaac, now, no need to call him names. Thee's better than that. Thee should have refused to engage with the guards."

"We tried. At least I tried, and the other elders of our meeting tried. But some of our neighbors—yes, even a few of the Friends—began making loud demands. That's when some in the militia started firing their muskets into the air. I think they were looking for a battle. More than one fired directly at us. No one died, by the grace of God, but some of our men were knocked down and trampled by the horses. Many were harmed far more than I. All we had were our words, which were useless against men on horseback brandishing muskets and bludgeons."

"Then how did thee get this great, gaping wound, if thee was so careful not to engage in the fighting?" Mary demanded.

"I tried to intervene. I yelled to the captain that we had an appointment to present our Bill of Rights. William Tryon's men went after me, thinking I was the leader. I promise, Mary, that I wanted to stay out of the fighting. I didn't fight back, but that only angered them more. Yet I couldn't stand on the side while others were being beaten. I tried to help our fallen neighbors."

Mary finished tending the wound. She put down her sewing needle and the bloody rag, walked to the door, tossed the soiled water outside, and threw down the pan in disgust. She bit back a comment. Isaac was in such a mood she knew nothing she said would ease his pain.

She sat back beside him and placed a hand on his knee. "Isaac, I'll bring this up at the next women's meeting for business, and thee should do the same with the men. We must seek a peaceful solution. We must listen for God's will for us." She paused. "I hear some in Cane Creek Meeting are disowning members for joining the Regulators. Should Eno do the same?"

"I know our meeting has been discussing this for months," Isaac said, "but now we're drawn into the conflict. The colonial government is here in Hillsborough, less than six miles from our home. How can we tell our neighbors not to protest? If we don't have the right to stand up to such greed and dishonesty, who does?"

THE NEXT MORNING, Isaac gathered a small group of elders from Eno Meeting to seek bail for the jailed protestors. Mary and other women assembled bandages and herbs to care for the men who had been injured before being jailed. They also brought bread and water, blankets, and other provisions to the jail, rightly assuming the authorities would have done nothing to tend to the men's wounds or to ensure their comfort. The women demanded that they be allowed to care for the prisoners. They were permitted to enter only after the jailors searched their baskets and confiscated much of the better food for themselves. Many of the women cried when they saw the condition of their menfolk, bloodied and discouraged.

In the meantime, the men from the meeting attempted to negotiate for the freedom of the incarcerated, arguing that the men had intended only a peaceful protest, wanting only to present their demands. The bailiffs were not impressed with their arguments, but the local magistrate intervened. Herman Husband, who had not directly participated in the fighting, was still accused of inciting the attacks but freed under the condition he not return to Hillsborough and, further, he must leave the colony posthaste. Some of the other men were similarly allowed to return to their farms under the threat of further punishment if again caught conspiring with the Regulators. A substantial number of the men were left to languish in the jail until they could be tried for their roles in destroying Fanning's home.

Wagons were brought as close as possible to the released prisoners, and the women helped the more wounded of them get comfortable in the wagon beds. Once all were aboard, they left to go north to their homes. To the authorities, the departing group appeared a dejected and beaten lot. Some were and blamed Herman Husband for encouraging them to think the officials would actually listen to them; a handful of these men were ready to give up, maybe to move to Georgia with Joseph Maddock. Others declared they would have to meet violence with violence, and saw this as incentive to escalate the war against the corruption.

Mary and Isaac rode home silently with Herman Husband and other Jackson relatives in the back of their wagon. No one spoke as they traveled. *I am not going to let discouragement stop me,* Mary thought, *but it's oh so hard to stay strong.*

· · ·

IN THE FOLLOWING WEEKS, the county authorities continued to harass the Quakers. Because Herman Husband was outwardly a Quaker, the members of Eno Meeting were then singled out as troublemakers, especially Joseph Maddock. Because of the pressures being put on him, he decided he needed to leave North Carolina quickly.

Mary's son Edward announced to his parents that he planned to follow Maddock to Georgia.

Mary was frantic. "Isaac, thee has to stop him! Tell him he must stay. We have land for him. He can't leave home. We need him here. I...*I* need him here."

Isaac looked at his wife. His voice was as sad as his face when he said, "My love, our son is nigh on twenty-one years of age. He's old enough to make up his own mind. Thee knows he's courting one of the Maddock girls. She wants to be with her own family and her own mother. That is only natural for a young girl."

"But, Isaac, thee set aside a large tract of our land for him, to build a home and raise his family. How can we bear him being so far away? And he's our eldest son. He's thy heir. Do something, please! For me, please!"

Isaac shook his head. "Nay, my love, I won't stop him. We have four other sons to work the land. Perhaps he will return someday and settle here. Perhaps he has the same wanderlust that we had in our youth."

Mary rested her head on her husband's shoulder for a few minutes, then stood and brushed off her skirt. "Isaac, I'm in need of a cup of strong tea. Does thee want some? May I get us both something warm to drink?"

Isaac nodded. As she turned away, he smiled. He knew she would be in a better mood after she had time to pray on it.

One morning after she had set the children to their chores, Mary decided, on an impulse, to visit Katie Fincher, who lived about three miles north of the Jacksons. She picked up a loaf of fresh baked bread and wrapped it in cloth. She placed it in a woven bag, put on her coat, hooked the straps of the bag over her shoulder, and headed down to the road. It was a fine day for a walk, so Mary didn't bother saddling up her horse.

When she arrived, she brushed down her skirt and called through the open door. Katie looked at her in surprise and welcomed her warmly. Mary handed her the loaf of bread and smiled. "A bit of a gift for you, Katie. I have been experimenting with adding herbs to my breads. This has rosemary and thyme and, I think, it's quite tasty."

Happy to have a visit from Mary, Katie bustled around and fixed a pot of tea. She sliced a few pieces of the loaf and gestured for Mary to sit with her. With Katie's first bite, her face lit up. "Mary, this is delicious! Maybe thee should add baked goods to what thee sells at market."

As they snacked, they chatted about their children, the weather, and the work Katie's husband was doing in the far pasture. Finally, Mary got down to the reason she came.

"Katie, my concern for thee has been weighing heavily on my heart. I heard Isaac and Daniel Stubbs talking about disowning thy husband from the meeting. Katie, thee needs to know the meeting will revoke his membership if he does not stop meeting with the Regulators. The Regulators are no longer satisfied to negotiate with Edmund Fanning. They are bent on wreaking violence. Thee knows our discipline requires we refrain from participating in wars of any kind, even one as local as this."

Katie rose and walked over to the fireplace. With her

back turned to Mary, she pretended to stir the ashes. She sighed deeply. Eventually, she turned back to Mary and sat down again.

"Friend Mary, I won't go against my husband. We've lost so much to the corrupt officials, and now the sheriff is threatening to take our land for back taxes. We have no more to give."

"I'm sorry for thy suffering," Mary said. "We've all been abused by Edmund Fanning's men, but thee seems to be especially hard hit. Thee knows if thy man is disowned, thee's still welcome in our meeting and—"

Katie interrupted. "No, Mary, if the meeting expels my husband, I'll never feel welcome. None of us will darken the meetinghouse door again."

Mary put her hand on Katie's arm, but the woman pulled away.

"Thee does not understand. If the sheriff takes our land and the meeting turns its back on us, then we'll have nothing. Nothing. All that we have worked for will be gone." She paused a moment. "We're talking about following Joseph Maddock to Georgia. Or, I have a distant cousin who is settling in the west, and we might go there. My husband will do as he is led and, right now, he's led to muster with the Regulators. I hope it doesn't come to be a war, but if it must, then so be it."

Mary started to say something more, but Katie stopped her. "Please, just go. Go now. I thank thee for the bread. Thee told the truth when thee said it was tasty. I don't want to talk about the Regulators anymore. This is my husband's business, not mine. And definitely not thine."

Mary put on her cloak and headed to the door. She turned to Katie. "Thee will be in my prayers. I'll ask God that thee shall be guided in the right path."

Katie shooed her out and shut the door. Mary looked

back once more, then trudged homeward. Her heart was even heavier than when she started out that morning.

She thought, *Who am I to judge? I don't know what Isaac and I would do if we were struggling as they are. Lord, please take Katie and her family under thy loving care. Help them see that violence is not the answer if that is thy desire.*

Chapter Thirteen

1771

Mary's body began trembling. Her underarms were wet, although the meetinghouse was not particularly hot. She looked around the dim room. She felt under the weight of the message God was commanding her to deliver, but no one seemed to notice her distress. She tried to ignore the stirring within her. She often preached at Eno Meeting and had even given messages at neighboring meetings. The women at Cane Creek considered her a gifted minister, although she certainly didn't feel up to the burden placed upon her at today's First Day meeting. But this was the most consequential message she had ever been given to deliver.

She waited for what seemed an interminable time, growing more and more anxious. A fly buzzed about her face, and she swatted it away. Someone a few benches over coughed loudly. A child fidgeted with her mother's handkerchief, folding it and unfolding it over and over, humming quietly to herself. An elderly man shifted in his seat, dropping his cane to the floor with a bang. An older woman fanned herself with a small card. The normal experiences of the meeting continued around her and did little to calm her distress.

Finally, with weak knees, Mary rose. Still, she hesitated to speak and stood in silence for several minutes. Closing her eyes, Mary began, her voice soft. "Friend William Penn instructed us in his writings that 'True godliness does not turn men out of the world, but enables them to live better in it, and excites their endeavors to mend it; not to hide their candle under a bushel, but to set it upon a table in a candlestick.'

"Friends in Christ, we're at a crossroads." Mary's voice grew stronger. "We can take the righteous path and accept the suffering imposed on us by corrupt men appointed to govern us. Or we can join in the protests against the evil in this colony, protesting as a part of the mob with shouts and stones. This may be the only way they will listen to our grievances, but we must not succumb to violence. We must work in quiet ways, by example and exhortation to mend the world, not to destroy it and our very souls by bloodshed and brutality.

"As Paul said to Timothy, 'Yea, and all that will live godly in Christ Jesus shall suffer persecution. But evil men and seducers shall wax worse and worse, deceiving, and being deceived. But continue thou in the things which thou hast learned and hast been assured of, knowing of whom thou hast learned them.'"

Mary sat down and bowed her head, crying silently. Was this exhortation too little in light of the enormous challenge ahead of the meeting? "What more can I do, Lord?" she entreated silently. "What more can I do?"

Men and women shifted nervously in their seats when they heard these words, some in guilt, some in renewed conviction. Soon, the meeting settled once more in expectant waiting on the Lord. No one spoke for more than an hour, until John Stubbs rose and urged, "Let love and faithfulness never leave thee; bind them around thy neck, write them on the tablet of thy heart." Using this proverb, he preached long and urgently about the necessity of holding fast to the testimony of peace in their hearts and in their lives. He looked directly at several of the men who, earlier in the week, had been encouraging revenge against the British government.

One of the elders on the facing bench looked around. Several men appeared ready to jump up and speak in favor of joining the rebellion. Listening for the still, small voice of God seemed out of the question and loud debate more likely. Wisely, the elders chose to end the First Day meeting. They shook hands with each other and rose to leave.

Several of the angrier men confronted John Stubbs on his way out. When the crowd grew more and more agitated, Isaac stepped up to try to calm down the situation, and some of the men turned on him also.

The women hurried away to set up the mid-day meal on the wide board tables in the yard, mumbling among themselves. Mary knew the women should do more to rein in the men's wild impulses, but she felt helpless in the face of such anger and passion. For now, a hearty meal and the laughter of the children were all they could provide.

DESPITE THE EFFORTS of the elders of both the women's and the men's Quaker meetings, the anger among the Regulators, including those Friends allied with them, continued to escalate. In First Month, 1771, the government passed the Johnston's Riot Act. Isaac and Mary were especially concerned as this Act gave Governor Tryon the authority to command the colonial militia to maintain order. They realized there would be very little they could do to prevent a bloody confrontation.

The court judges in Hillsborough, increasingly frightened by the violence of the Regulators, called on the governor to invoke the Act. In Fourth Month, Isaac received word from a nephew in Cane Creek Meeting that the governor's militiamen were assembled and marching from New Bern to Hillsborough. On the way, they were joined by other troops, and within a month, the militia had grown to more than one thousand men. General Hugh Waddell, who left Salisbury intending to join Tryon's troops in Hillsborough, was turned back by Regulators at the Yadkin River. The farmers were able to accomplish this with no bloodshed, but many were itching to do more than just hold the line. Isaac and Mary knew it was only a matter of time before the conflict escalated.

A large group of Regulators and sympathizers had already started gathering on the banks of the Haw River near Alamance Creek. Isaac and Mary heard that their son William, now living near Cane Creek near his wife's family, had marched with the local farmers. Mary was particularly worried that he would be harmed. She didn't know if he was going as a pacifist in support of more negotiations for peace, or if he had been caught up in the gang that was out for blood. Herman Husband asked Isaac to join with him and the Regulators, hoping that he and a small group of Quakers fervently opposed to the fighting could try one more time to broker a resolution. At Mary's urging, Isaac chose not to attend. Several of their cousins and nephews would be there when the group attempted to arrange for peace and would keep an eye on young William.

No violence resulted, and uneasy weeks passed.

. . .

ON THE ELEVENTH of Fifth Month, Tryon and his forces left Hillsborough, heading southwest. Most of the Quakers lived north of the town. A large group gathered at the meetinghouse, and Mary and Isaac settled them into worship. They were grateful that nearby Hillsborough had been spared from further violence and prayed for their brethren in Cane Creek Meeting. The militia was heading directly there.

The two sides were in a standoff. Neither the Regulators nor Tryon's more experienced militia wanted to make the first move. Across the fields, the men on each side could hear the other side milling around, preparing for battle. Tryon's general used the time to muster the troops and make their battle plans. The Regulators were impatient for a fight; their anger had built up over a long time. Many of them argued that they shouldn't wait for Herman Husband to attempt one more negotiation. The more rational, older men cautioned against taking action, knowing their clubs and axes and hunting muskets would be heavily outmatched by the army's cannons and artillery.

The impasse continued for several days, with Herman and his colleagues going back and forth between the forces. Finally, the military leaders, as well as the Regulators, could stand the inaction no longer. Preparations for battle heated up on both sides.

Herman was clearly not successful this time, just as his earlier attempts had failed. With his head hung low and his heart turned to prayer, he left for his home.

On the sixteenth of Fifth Month, the battle was on.

WITHIN DAYS, a young man staggered into Mary and Isaac's yard. Covered in blood and muck, he leaned heavily on a sturdy branch, holding it up with one arm. He had a sling holding his other arm close to his chest, and there was a bloody, makeshift bandage on his left leg.

John had been working nearby, trying to mend a broken axle, and raced to catch him before he fell. He urgently called for his mother. Mary ran outside and helped her son carry the man into the house to a chair by the fire. She wrapped him in a heavy quilt; the man was shivering, even though it was warm outside.

"What is thy name?" she asked. "Where is thee from?"

The man groaned, unable to answer. Mary sent Elizabeth to the spring house for honey and set to brewing willow bark tea. He grabbed the warm cup gratefully with his good hand and inhaled the healing steam.

After a few sips, he spoke, his voice ragged. "My name is Samuel. I'm...I'm on my way home. My ma and pa live eight miles to the north of Hillsborough town. I'm so sorry. I don't have the energy to go further. I'm glad for this tea, but may I beg you for something to eat? It's been so long."

Mary nodded at Elizabeth, who quickly brought him drink and food. As he took them, he said, "I'm not a Quaker, but I heard that you are leaders among the Eno Friends. Perhaps you would share with your neighbors what I have to tell you."

"Wait just a moment. Please eat some of the bread that my daughter brought to thee," Mary said. "My husband will also want to hear your message. My son Thomas went to the field to get him."

At that moment, Isaac and Thomas were at the door, stomping dirt from their boots and brushing the dust off their clothes. When they came in, Mary held up her hand to stop them from demanding that the young man answer their questions. She beckoned for her family to sit and bow their heads. As Samuel munched on the bread, he watched the five of them pray in silence for a long time before Mary nodded to her husband.

Isaac leaned toward Samuel and asked gently, "Tell us, Friend Samuel, what has happened to bring thee to this state?"

The young man trembled, looking into his cup. "I was with the Regulators. We camped in a large field for several days. There were militia—I heard the Governor sent them— a short distance away, near Alamance Creek. We heard them drilling and shooting their muskets. They probably were trying to scare us, and it worked."

He stared into the hearth before speaking again. "We didn't know how many they were, but from the echoes across the field, it sure sounded like there were a lot of them. There were hundreds of us, maybe even two thousand. I'm seventeen years of age, and some were boys even younger, maybe even as young as twelve. We weren't drilling while we waited. We didn't have a leader. We got ourselves all riled up and ready to fight. But mostly we got ourselves scared." He looked at Isaac. "As I told your missus, I'm not a Quaker, but there were many from your churches with us."

Mary leaned over and raised the cup to his lips again. He sipped, then went on. "Your Quakers tried negotiating with Governor Tryon and his men. They wanted to avoid bloodshed, but many of the Regulators were too eager to fight. I guess Tryon's men were too. The Quakers couldn't convince both sides to compromise. Tryon gave us only one hour to disperse, but we held our ground. At hour's end, he shouted for his men to attack us. It was a slaughter."

Tears were running down his cheeks, and the tea left in his cup sloshed. John took it from him and set it on the table. Finally, Samuel was able to continue, his voice trembling. "The battle was awful. We didn't stand a chance. Our leaders were disorganized. Tryon's troops were much more disciplined and experienced. We were simple farmers wielding clubs, pitchforks, and muskets. Tryon's militia had guns and cannons. What could we do? They marched on us and kept coming. They kept coming!"

He shook to clear his head and started crying. "The battle was over in an hour, if that much, and we lost badly. Many Regulators were killed. Hundreds of us were wounded. I lost my best friend to a musket ball. The other side didn't look like they suffered the losses we did. We stood no chance against their heavy guns and cannon balls!"

He sighed. He reached for his cup and gulped the now-tepid tea. "Tryon wanted to teach us a lesson, I think. His men took prisoners. They hanged poor William Few from a tree right on the edge of the field where we had been fighting. There was no trial. They just grabbed him and strung him up."

Mary gasped. William Few was from Hillsborough. He lived along the Eno, and his family operated a gristmill. Mary and Isaac knew William and his family well.

Samuel shook and began crying harder. "I've never seen a man die like that. He died, right there. He died in front of us. And the soldiers...they just laughed. They shook their sabers at us and threatened to do the same to the rest of us. I ran.

"Mr. Few was brave during the fight but no more a leader than anyone else. But Tryon wanted to make an example of him and send us a warning as we fled back to our homes. I'll never be able to get away from the sight of his body trying to gain purchase until his neck broke. They mocked and humiliated him. They wanted to set fear in our hearts. Believe me, the fear was already there. He was a good man, a friend of my parents. What will I say to them?"

Shocked, Mary leaned toward the young man. "Our son

William might have been there. Did thee see him, our William Jackson?"

"Ma'am, we were hundreds, maybe thousands of men, so many I didn't know. I stayed with my kinfolk until I lost them in the mess of the battle. You have to understand, ma'am, I was just trying to stay alive. I didn't expect to see so many men wounded or dead. I may have lost some of my kin, I just don't know. I just don't know." He hung his head and wept softly.

"Enough," Mary said, rising and taking Samuel's empty cup. "Let's let the child rest."

That evening, she invited Samuel to join them at supper. They all bowed in silent thanksgiving before digging into the simple meal. Isaac cut off hunks of bread, and Mary dished out thick, rich bowls of venison stew. Samuel slurped gratefully. It had been many days since he had had a warm meal. Afterward, Mary invited him to stay the night before he continued on his way.

"My mother will be so worried. I must get home to her," he said. "I thank you, but I'm rested enough to continue by night."

Mary nodded. Samuel was not even as old as most of her children. She would be worried, too, about one of them. Isaac told John to hitch up the wagon and told Mary that he and John would drive the young man the remaining miles to his home.

When her husband and son returned, they had more to tell. "We passed by the Few farm on our way back," Isaac said. "The house and barn were burning fiercely, and the crops and animals destroyed. Some of their livestock managed to escape to the woods, but the militia hunted them down. The family was helpless. They watched as everything was destroyed. They had lost their eldest son in the hanging, and then Tryon's men destroyed their home and livelihood as more punishment. Young William's father had openly supported some of the leaders of the Regulators. They knew they were being singled out for punishment."

Isaac collapsed into a chair and ran his hands through his hair in frustration. "Mary, I asked what we could do for them, bring them food, clothing, tools? They're leaving. They have nothing left. Tonight, they will go to Friend Few's brother's house. They don't think they can stay there but the night. They don't want to bring danger to their brother. I think they will close their mill and move far away. Mary, dear, there is so much they need and so little they will let us give."

Mary prayed silently in sorrow for the Few family and for the families of all of those men killed in this senseless battle. No matter on which side a man fought, there would be mothers and fathers, brothers and sisters, and young children who would weep for their loss.

Kneeling before him, she asked, "Isaac, my love, how can we go on? The pain is too great."

There was no answer. She and Isaac could only sit and hold each other.

Chapter Fourteen

The next day, a Friend who lived in Hillsborough came by the Jacksons' home with a warning. He had heard that Tryon's militia was hunting down the leaders of the Regulator movement, looting their farms, and burning their houses to the ground. It was not just the Few farm that was targeted, although theirs had been the first.

He told Isaac, "Be careful and don't go near town. Many folks are calling the Regulators lawless desperadoes, and are praising William Tryon for stamping out the rebellion. They are calling him a hero. Even those who supported the Regulators are now hiding behind their condemnations. They just want to protect themselves, but it makes things even more dangerous for the Regulators who can be identified."

"But I was not part of the violence," Isaac protested. "I was simply trying to help Herman Husband negotiate a peaceful end to the violence."

"Herman Husband is especially being vilified by Tryon and Fanning's men. Thee was seen with him. Even though thee wasn't at the battle, thee may be at risk."

Mary listened to the men talk with her hands over her mouth in horror. Her Isaac was at risk! Her Isaac might be lumped in with the most violent of the Regulators. *What if the militia burns our house and farm? What if Isaac is captured and imprisoned? Or worse?*

The attacks on the farms of suspected Regulators continued. Then in Sixth Month, hundreds of men were arrested and charged with treason. Many of the people in Hillsborough were loyal to the British government and cheered the news. Mary was devastated. Several of those who had been rounded up were Quakers, although they had been disowned from their meetings for joining with the Regulators.

"Isaac, I know their wives," Mary said one morning at breakfast. "I know their families. I need to go see them, at least the few who live in our area. I promise I won't go as far as Cane Creek."

May said, "Mother, thee should not go alone. I'll go with thee. At twenty, I'm old enough."

Isaac shook his head. "My love, this is too dangerous. We were warned. The militia is on a rampage. They're armed. They're looting and burning farms."

"I'm going anyway," Mary insisted. "I need to comfort the wives. I need to sit with them, pray with them. They should know that they aren't alone."

Isaac sighed, aware that he couldn't change his wife's mind. "I shall worry about thee and May. But, please, take John and Isaac for protection."

"Nay, Isaac. I fear that having young men with us will put us in even more danger. The militia will be less likely to harass two women alone."

"Then I shall worry all the more. But I fear thee's right."

Elizabeth pleaded to go with her mother and sister, but Mary wouldn't hear of it. She sent the girl to the barn to ask her brothers to saddle the horses. Upset that her mother wouldn't let her go too, out of her parents' earshot Elizabeth grumbled, "I'm almost thirteen years old. I'm not a child."

Mary hastily wrapped fresh baked loaves of bread in clean cloths to pack in her saddle bags. The visits wouldn't be easy, and food was always a welcome way to ease some of the tension. She put in extra loaves, some butter and small crocks of blueberry jam. As much as she hated the idea of bribery, these might be useful if they were indeed stopped by any of the British mar.

As they climbed onto their horses, Isaac said, "Head to the west, but don't stop at the Few farm. Our friend said the family has escaped and is heading to South Carolina, where they have relations. Perhaps the militia will have passed through and is heading further east by now. I hope thee doesn't encounter any stray militia men."

"I'm going to visit with three families," Mary said. "Two are west of us. May and I'll try to visit them today. If needs must, we may tarry overnight. The third family is closer to Hillsborough. I'll come home before I visit them and spend a few days with thee. If I learn it's indeed dangerous to go to Hillsborough, I'll take thee or our sons with us."

"Mary, my love, I do wish thee would reconsider. Please do not put yourself in this danger. Stay home."

"Isaac, it isn't my lot to question why God is asking this of me, only that I accept the burden He has laid upon me. I must go. Don't fret."

"Then I shall put thee in God's hands. However, I'll worry and worry until thee's returned safely to me."

Mary and May left the barnyard without looking back. Despite their brave talk, both women were nervous and afraid that if they turned to wave goodbye to Isaac and the boys, they would stay home.

For the first couple of hours, the ride was uneventful.

They passed a few places where militia, or perhaps the Regulators, had made camp on their way to Alamance, leaving behind the remnants of cooking fires, broken pieces of crockery, and other debris. The fires were cold and didn't look to be recent.

When they were almost to the home of Catherine Wilson, three of Tryon's men stopped them. All were wounded and moving slowly. Two were dragging the third man on an improvised litter. Mary stopped and dismounted.

May looked at her in dismay. "Mother, this isn't safe. We should go on. These men can't harm us."

Mary looked at her daughter. "These men need our help. I have some bandages and herbs in my pack, and I must tend to their wounds. And thee must help."

The wounded men looked at her gratefully and set down the litter.

"Please, ma'am. Look after our brother. He's most grievously wounded."

Mary asked them to open his pants leg so she could tend to the bloody stump. She packed it with herbs and wrapped his leg in clean cloths. The blood still seeped through the cloth, but it was the best she could do. She bandaged the cuts on one of the men who could walk. May poured water onto the wound of the other and packed it well with cotton batting; fortunately, a musket ball had gone through his front and out his back so she didn't have to dig it out. She used a little of the remaining water to rinse her hands and wiped them on her skirt—not ideal, but that would have to do.

May took out a small loaf of bread, tore it into three pieces, and spread it thickly with butter. The men grabbed it gratefully. They had not eaten in several days and fresh bread was in short supply.

"Ma'am, we're more than grateful for your care and your food. You may have saved our friend's life."

"Thy friend is still losing blood and may not live," Mary cautioned. "Have thee far to go to see thy own medic? He needs more care than we can give him on the side of the road. God be with thee."

The women mounted their horses. As they turned to the west, May looked back and then at her mother. "Ma, God was with us that those men were in need of our care, rather than giving us trouble."

"And God was with them, that we were able to offer care and food when they needed it most."

They arrived in a short while at Catherine Wilson's house. One of her young sons stepped through the door, pointing his hunting rifle at them. He was shaking with fear, but faced them bravely.

Mary looked at him sadly. "Daniel, put away thy weapon. Thee knows us. We met thee and thy mother at quarterly meeting. I'm Mary Jackson from Eno Friends Meeting, and this is my daughter May."

Catherine Wilson looked out. "Daniel, we're fine. Go, help Mary Jackson down, and her daughter. Then find thy brothers and take care of the horses. These are Friends. We don't have to fear them."

Inside the cabin Mary handed Catherine a loaf of bread and a crock of jam. Catherine accepted the gift with a smile. "Friend Mary, may I get thee some warm soup to eat with this fine bread? There is no meat in the stew, as soldiers have taken it all and all our animals."

"Catherine, that would be wonderful. We have ridden for many hours. Isaac told us to avoid the roads where we might encounter militia, so it took us longer than usual to get here."

As they supped, May told Catherine and her sons about

meeting the wounded men and how her mother had cared for them and given them food. May was still shaken from the incident. She was not as brave as her mother.

Mary was embarrassed that her daughter seemed to be bragging about her. "Aye, May, I'm not so brave as thee thinks. I only did what needs must." She turned to Catherine. "My dear Catherine, how fared thee and thy husband?"

Catherine began to shiver and weep. "He has been arrested! Yesterday, five soldiers came—five!" she sobbed, "brandishing their guns and shouting foul words. They grabbed Seth and threw him to the ground. Then they clapped cuffs on him and hauled him rudely into their wagon. They said he would be tried for treason. They stole the last bit of meat hanging in our shed and broke some tools and crockery just for spite." Aghast, Mary reached out and placed a hand on the woman's arm. "I think we're fortunate," Catherine whispered, "that they didn't burn our house down, as they did the Few's. Maybe they left me alone because I'm with child, I don't know. I can't leave because I'm too close to when our babe is due. So all we can do is hope they move on and leave us alone."

"Does thee have someone to be with thee when thy time is come?" Mary asked.

"Aye. My cousin from Virginia is on her way to stay with me. Unless she heard that Seth has been arrested and fears for her own safety."

"I'll send my sister-in-law, Susanna Jackson. She's an excellent midwife; she has delivered me of five children since we moved to the Eno. Have one of thy sons send word when thy time is near."

The women sat in companionable silence for a long while before Mary stood and said, "We must be off. May and I are next to visit Jane Terrell. She's but a short ride from thy home."

"Nay, thee needs not go there. Thee didn't hear?" At Mary's puzzled look, Catherine explained. "After they arrested her husband, James, they burned down their house. Jane and the children escaped with little more than burns and scratches. They stopped here to let me know they aren't going to stay; they're going to New Garden. She has cousins who might take her in. She asked me to look in on James, and to pray that he was not put to death. But I can't ride to Hillsborough to see him in jail. Or my own Seth. Will thee go for Jane? Will thee watch out for both of our husbands?"

"Aye, Isaac and I'll go to the prison and bring them food and warm clothes, if the guards let us near. I'll pray for thee and thy children, and definitely for thy men."

Mary and May headed directly home. Isaac was relieved to see them ride into the yard. "Tell me, dear wife, how did thee find thy friends?"

Mary told him about her visit with Catherine, and about the Terrells. She downplayed the encounter with the men on the road to keep Isaac from worrying.

"May," Isaac said, "I know thy mother is hiding something. What happened that she isn't telling me?"

May told her father about the wounded men, this time without embellishing the event. "Don't fret, Da, we were safe. The men were grateful for Ma's ministrations. I suppose grown men still want a mother's hand on their brows when they are hurting, even if it's not their own dear ma."

"There is one more thing we must do," Mary said. "In the morning we must go into town to visit James and Seth."

"Mary, the men are still being held in the prison camp. They have not yet been taken to the Hillsborough jailhouse. We must wait. I'll ask our friends in town to let us know when they arrive."

· · ·

Days later a large group of the prisoners was taken to the jail in Hillsborough. The rest were asked to sign a loyalty oath, and those who did were released. Word came that James Terrell and Seth Wilson refused the oath, as contrary to the dictates of their Quaker faith. They were among the men still being held by the British.

Mary packed a basket with food, some warm clothes and blankets, bandages and healing herbs. In town the guards reluctantly let Isaac into the jail but refused entrance to Mary. She crossed the road to the yard in front of the courthouse and sat on the grass to pray.

She soon was joined by other women, all of whom sat in silence for a long while before an elderly Baptist woman began to sing a mournful hymn. This was strange to Mary, whose only experience with worship was in the silence of a Quaker meeting. But she knew all of the women were suffering and needed God's comfort, even though their prayers were offered in different ways. When several of the women joined their voices in the hymn, Mary closed her eyes and let the sweet sound of their music wash over her.

Later that afternoon, Isaac came and tapped Mary on the shoulder. She rose to greet him. He said, "Mary, I plan to stay in town until these men are brought to trial. I can be a help and a comfort to them. Take the wagon and go home. Thee's needed there to tend to our family and animals."

A bit of fear ran through Mary, but she didn't protest his decision. "God be with thee, dear Isaac. Send word to me when the trial is over so I may come to take thee home." She grasped his hands tightly. "I love thee truly."

Several days later the prisoners were again offered the opportunity to swear an oath of allegiance to the British government. More than six hundred of the rebels had already complied. Still, that left fourteen captives—either they had refused to sign or were being held at Tryon's order. These men were to be tried at a special sitting of the Superior Court.

Isaac had hoped to get inside the makeshift courtroom, to reassure himself that the trial was conducted fairly, but was unable to squeeze through the crowd trying to push its way in. He stood along with a small group of men and women outside the courthouse, waiting for the verdict, praying their neighbors and relatives would be released. After what seemed to be too short a time for such serious deliberations, twelve of the men were convicted of treason and sentenced to death. Many of the women began wailing, and a few fainted when the verdict was read to the crowd. The hanging was scheduled to happen before week's end.

Rather than send word to Mary, Isaac hurried home on foot. He needed to hold his wife and see his children. The past weeks had seemed interminable, and he knew that being present for the condemned men would be more than difficult.

Mary ran to Isaac as soon as he walked in the door. She was filled with gladness at his return until she looked at his pale and drawn face. She stopped. "The news isn't good, is it?"

"Nay, my love." Isaac hung his hat on a peg near the door, then sank into a chair. "Twelve men have been convicted of treason. They are sentenced to death by hanging in two days' time. Two are Quakers from Alamance that I didn't know before meeting them in prison. Thy friends' husbands, James and Seth, have been released. I don't know if they signed the oath the governor was demanding or if they were freed for some other reason. I didn't get a chance to talk with them before they hurried to be with their own families."

Mary stood silently for a moment, overcome by Isaac's terrible news. Finally, she drew herself up and said, "I'll go with thee to the hanging. I need to be a witness and to comfort the women I prayed with at the courthouse, even if they aren't Friends."

THE MORNING of the Nineteenth of Sixth Month, on the day the English court called June 19, the weather was warm but not so hot. The sun shone brightly. Flowers were in full bloom. It was too lovely a day to hold the pain of what was to happen.

Isaac and Mary were taken into town by his brother Benjamin. They could have brought their own wagon, but Isaac was concerned for the safety of his horses in such a great crowd. Benjamin, who didn't want to attend, dropped them off outside of town and immediately turned around toward his home. The couple walked in silence to the field where the hanging was to take place.

Mary stopped suddenly and stood staring at the gallows. The scaffolding had been hastily constructed just a few hundred yards from the county courthouse. She and Isaac soon learned from those who had already gathered that six of the twelve had been pardoned the night before. The other six stood on the sidelines with ropes around their arms and legs, waiting nervously, surrounded by armed men to prevent their escape.

Isaac pointed out to Mary one of the Quakers from Alamance although his meeting had disowned him for associating with the Regulators. "He does not deserve to die," Isaac said, his voice tight. "None of them do. They're all just angry, desperate men, caught up in being part of the mob.

Oh! If only the women had been able to convince their husbands and sons not to join in the violence, Mary thought.

As an elder, guiding the moral and spiritual life of the women and children in her community, she knew that many of the women had urged their men to step back, to pay the taxes no matter how onerous, no matter how unreasonable. *And they did try. Most truly did try. How had it come to this? What more could Isaac and I have done to prevent the rebellion?*

Although, to be honest, she knew that Isaac had been a willing participant in the early days of the protest against the British officials. He had met with the condemned Quakers yesterday and assured her that the accused men were resigned; they were in God's hands now. Mary wished she could've been back in their meetinghouse praying, but like Isaac, she felt called to witness this atrocity. She hadn't been able to do enough to prevent the rebellion, and now she must see it through.

Looking around at the crowd, Mary noticed many of her neighbors, Quakers as well as non-Quakers. Most of the people in Hillsborough, and even others from nearby towns, had come to see the spectacle. Enterprising merchants set up stalls along the main street, selling cakes and fruit and beverages. Some folks brought picnic lunches and settled in to watch the hangings as entertainment. Children too young to understand the gravity of the events were running around, laughing and shouting. And, of course, the militia was in full view. One of their leaders had yellow rosettes made for the men to wear on their caps. This badge emboldened the men as they milled about, their weapons at the ready, laughing and joking amongst themselves, occasionally taunting a weeping woman or mock-threatening a boy too young to have fought. The whole town was too festive for such an occasion. Mary shuddered and turned back toward the gallows.

The first man was dragged to the noose, crying and

pleading. Mary knew that even the bravest of men could break when faced with a painful mortality, and this man was past being brave. One of the authorities intoned the condemned man's name in mock sincerity, "The traitor, Robert Matear." He was given the opportunity to speak his last words, but instead, his sobs tore through the air and pierced Mary's heart. Some in the crowd shouted curses and jeers at his cries; others stared in shock at the cruelty of the hangmen. As his feet lost purchase, his neck snapped loudly; the crowd cheered until his body quieted in death.

Isaac couldn't believe so many in the town believed that the Regulators deserved their punishment. They had not experienced the desperation of the farmers who had lost their lands or the craftsmen whose tools of their trades were confiscated for unpaid taxes. Some were cheering just because of the bloodlust that being part of a mob brought out. Mary prayed harder. She wanted to close her eyes, to walk away, but believed it her duty to bear witness.

Mary was grateful that the broad brim of her Quaker bonnet hid the tears flowing down her cheeks. She could no longer hold them back. Weeping silently, she prayed for his soul. She wrapped her arms tightly around her waist. She needed to set a good example for the other members of her meeting.

The next man walked to the gallows and the noose was put around his neck. Captain Benjamin Merrill held his head high as his name was pronounced. He spoke of his peace with God and recited a psalm. He directed his eyes to the heavens, resigned to his fate. There was a collective gasp at the snap of his neck, soon followed by more hooting and taunting and stamping of feet. The crowd was getting overly excited. A woman screamed and fainted. Mary thought it might be the man's wife. Women and children gathered around her. His young daughter jumped up, shouting at the crowd to stop; this was her father they were booing. Mary looked away and clenched her hands tighter. She had to get through four more hangings on this day.

The constable stopped the next man. This delay was agonizing—would there be a reprieve? What was happening? Several of the authorities consulted with the hangman; they grinned at each other as the noose was adjusted and tested and adjusted some more. Finally, the captain raised his hand to have the next rebel, James Pugh, brought forward. Mary had not met him, but knew he was related to Herman Husband. The rope was put around his neck, and he told the crowd that he was prepared to meet his God. He started to speak of the Regulator's grievances, but the barrel was kicked out mid-sentence. Mary consciously exhaled; she had not realized she was holding her breath until her chest began to hurt. James Pugh's life was over way too quickly.

Another delay, another consultation. The officials seemed to enjoy dragging out the suspense, wielding some small power over the weeping women whose husbands and brothers had been condemned. The fourth man was brought to the gallows. He sagged a bit, but was able to approach his death on his own feet. His name was announced, "Captain Robert Messer of the so-called Colonial Militia." He was able to muster a bit of dignity but couldn't find words to speak before the hangman's noose ended his life.

A Quaker was next in line. Isaac was standing on the other side of the clearing with a group of men from their meeting. The guards didn't let him get close, but he tried to stay visible so that the man could draw spiritual support from his presence. Mary wished Isaac were standing beside her. She needed spiritual support too. She needed his comfort.

The man walked up valiantly and took his place. The guards knew he was a Quaker, one who should have been loyal to the crown. One of them ripped the broad-brimmed hat from his head and stomped it into the dirt. The condemned man tried to pray and to appear strong for his family. Mary was appalled; they didn't give him the dignity of pronouncing his name and allowing him his last words before the noose was put around his neck. The snap of his body when the bucket was kicked from his feet shattered the air. Several of the women from the meeting fainted, and many began to sob uncontrollably. Mary's own courage was failing her. She started to sag; she wanted to sit down and never get up. She clasped her hands tightly and tried to stay strong.

Finally, the last man, the one who had to watch his fellow prisoners die before him, was dragged to his death. His wife was weeping openly, not far from where Mary stood. Mary thought she should go to her, be a comfort to her, but she was unable to get her feet to move. She would have to live with this regret, but her own grief weighed heavily on her. Blinded by her tears. Mary missed the man's name, if they had even bothered to announce it.

The spectacle was over. A faint cheer arose from the townspeople who had opposed the rebellion, but the extent of the slaughter had been crushing even for them. Most of the crowd was silent as they gathered up their picnic cloths and collected their children.

Mary reluctantly gave one last long look at the executed men—her neighbors, her friends—strung up side by side on the wooden structure. She was loath to leave them alone, just dangling there, but she and Isaac needed to get home before dark to tend to the animals. Someone else would have to see to their broken bodies. She ached fiercely to hug her grandchildren. She wanted to believe that everything would be all right, though she knew it would be a long time before it was.

Mary waited on the sidelines for Isaac to join her. She usually felt that public displays of affection were unseemly, but she gratefully took her husband's arm when offered. She wasn't sure she had the strength to walk the long miles to their home north of town. She wished that they had taken the wagon, but in the morning light it had seemed right to leave it at home.

For the first hour, Mary and Isaac didn't say a word to each other. No words could have expressed the horror of what they witnessed. Nothing in their Quaker upbringings had prepared them for the spectacle. When Mary broke the silence, she asked, "What now? How do we go on from here?"

Isaac reached out to hold her hand. He shook his head. "I don't know. I just don't know. We must pray, listen for God's guidance, be there for our community. Be strong."

He looked at his beloved wife and had no words to still her tears. He ached to see her in such distress but knew they both would be crying for a long time.

Mary put her other hand on Isaac's arm to stop him. "Twenty years ago, we came here with such hopes. Why did we leave Pennsylvania for this God-forsaken place?"

Isaac put his arms around her, heedless of the other Friends heading away from town toward their community. "Mary, God did not forsake this place. Thee has been happy here, in thy ministry and service to our meeting and our neighbors. Our children have land of their own to build homes for their families. Our grandchildren are thriving in the Carolina sunshine. We're blessed, despite the cruelties inflicted by Edmund Fanning and his minions."

. . .

INSTEAD OF GOING DIRECTLY HOME, Isaac and Mary went to the meetinghouse, seeking solace, and found that other Friends were already there. She looked around the sparsely attended room. Missing were those men who had been killed or wounded in the battle. The men who had been disowned by the meeting because they joined the Regulators, and their families were not there either; they felt abandoned by their community and no longer welcome. And Mary deeply missed all the families who had followed James Maddock down to Wrightsboro in Georgia. Oh, it was a sad, somber occasion, and Mary was heartsick.

How shall we ever go on? she prayed until she could pray no more.

When she and Isaac resumed trudging toward home, Mary's steps felt heavier and heavier, and it took all her strength to complete the last miles. At last, they arrived. Isaac went to the barn to take care of the animals, while Mary stoked the fire under the pot of soup that had kept warm over the coals. There was much work to be done, but she decided to lie down for a few minutes. She was overwhelmed by her fatigue, not from the trek home, but from holding herself together while men from her town were slaughtered for standing up against the unfair treatment. Even her strong Quaker faith did not seem to be enough to help her push through.

Where did we fail?

Chapter Fifteen

The next morning, Mary awoke before anyone else was up and dressed quickly. Isaac, hearing her, raised up on his elbow. "What's thee doing awake so early this morn? The sun isn't yet up."

"I need to go to the meetinghouse. I need to pray, to get my heart clear after yesterday's tragedy and the bloody war before it."

He began to get up. "I can go with thee."

"Nay, my love. This I need to do alone."

"Let me at least saddle thy horse, or hook up thy wagon."

"Isaac, I intend to walk to the meetinghouse. I appreciate thy offer, but I need time by myself. Please understand."

"I do, Mary. I do understand. And I love thee."

She had a long time to think as she walked. She knew that Quakers didn't believe that a person needed a fancy church to listen to God. Their meetinghouse was not sacred space. She could be sitting in any place to hear God's message and to worship—she had done so many, many times. But Friends had now worshiped in that simple log structure for more than ten years. The very boards seemed to exude a special serenity, and there she felt closer to the Spirit than anywhere else. Today, the long walk was justified.

It was early dawn when she arrived, and the meeting-house was dim. Mary chose not to sit in her usual place on the facing bench. She sat in the women's section with her back to the door so she wouldn't be tempted by the beauty of the coming sunrise or by anyone who wandered in. She began to pray in silent supplication, pouring out her distress to God.

"Dear God, I should be listening for thy still, small voice, but my heart is so, so heavy. Thee sees everything and knows of my grieving, but I need thy help to bring healing to my community. How can I find forgiveness for those who have caused such suffering? The loss of my friends and neighbors, the unbearable cruelty of the officials who sought vengeance through the hangings, the devastation wrought upon families and farms—all for what? For money for the governor? The militia men are thy children as well! They are neighbors, brothers. How can they be so cruel and vindictive? I beg thee to give comfort to the mothers, fathers, and children who lost their loved ones in this sense-less war. Heal the hearts of the men who inflicted such horror and guide them to compassion and reconciliation. Instill in their hearts the wisdom to choose dialogue over destruction. Let love prevail over hatred and, in your mercy, bring an end to this senseless suffering."

She was heartbroken and trembling. The stillness surrounded her and, in turn, upheld her. Eventually her mind quieted, and she began to open her heart, listening for God's guidance and for God's love.

. . .

After a couple of hours, Mary began to awaken from her deep contemplation. She became aware of rustling movements and a quiet cough. An old man sneezed loudly, and the noise brought her to alertness. She looked around the room. More than a dozen Friends had come, joining her in this spontaneous meeting for worship. And in the corner sat her dear husband. Mary rose and went over to him, with both tears and a question in her eyes.

Isaac stood to meet her. He spoke quietly. "Mary, my love, I thought thee might be exhausted from thy long walk and thy deep worship. I brought the wagon to take thee home, if thee would like a ride. If thee would like to walk, I understand."

"Oh, Isaac, thee is the most wonderful husband. Of course, I'd like to ride with thee. I'm at peace, at least for now."

In Tenth Month, in the late afternoon, Mary wandered over to where Isaac was on his knees, mending a broken wagon axle, and sat down on the grassy verge. The weather was mild for a late fall day, and the sun felt good. She took off her bonnet, rolled up her sleeves, and settled back against the barn. Even though Isaac was more than fifty years old, Mary still enjoyed watching him work—the sun glinting off the coppery hairs on his tanned forearms, his shirt wet with sweat and plastered to his back, his head bowed in concentration on his task. She remembered how exciting it was to watch him in the early days of their courtship and was pleased to notice that he could still send a little flurry to her heart.

Isaac stood up and grinned. "Mary, is thee here to admire my manly physique or does thee have another reason to be sitting there so prettily?

Mary fluttered her hand at him. "Isaac, I fear thee has a very high opinion of thyself." She smiled. "I was remembering our courtship days, when thee was young and strong, and thy hair was brown and thick."

She paused to let him preen a bit until they were both laughing at his antics. "My love," she said, "I need thy advice. I've spent hours in worship and discussion with Jane Emlen. She's asking that the meeting approve a certificate stating her clearness to be wed."

Isaac glanced at her as he went back to his task. "But?"

"Jane is a widow, and Jacob, her husband, has been dead only four months. He died after suffering for weeks from injuries he received fighting with the Regulators at Alamance. She nursed him faithfully but was not able to bring him back to health."

Mary took a deep breath and continued. "The yearly meeting insists that we conform to our discipline, which says a widow should not contemplate marriage until her spouse has been gone more than a year. Isaac, Jane has two small sons—rather unruly boys, I should say, and in need of a strong man's hand. The man she wishes to wed has five young children who need a mother, since their own died in childbirth last year."

"So, this would be a marriage of convenience for them both?"

"Aye, partly. But I sense a sincere affection growing between them. I think they'll find love together, and, to be certain, the children have need of two loving parents."

"Mary, does this have to be a problem? I doubt thee needs me to give thee guidance. Has thee asked our Lord to lead thee in this decision?"

"Of course. And God answered that we should disobey our normal practice and approve their marriage. But, thee knows, I have long had concerns about the restrictions on marriage in our discipline. Am I honestly listening to God for guidance or am I hearing what I want to hear?"

Isaac nodded and wisely continued to mend the axle in silence. He had learned over the years that Mary needed to talk about her concerns, but she didn't want him to solve them for her.

"Oh," Mary said, "and Jane also would like a certificate of transfer to Deep River Meeting, near where her future spouse has a farm. This is easier to decide. Even before her husband died, their farm was struggling. The animals were confiscated by the militia, the fields are rocky and hard. She can't do it alone. Jacob was disowned by the meeting when he joined with the Regulators. Jane hasn't attended meeting since his disownment was read, but she's still a member, and she wants to be a member at her new husband's meeting. The meeting should not have a problem approving this transfer."

Mary sat back. In a few minutes, tears began to flow. "Isaac, my heart is so heavy. Jane isn't the only one whose life has been upended. Our people are suffering. After that horrible, tragic hanging, William Tryon's men set out across the countryside, burning even more farms and the homes of men they thought were part of the Regulators. They senselessly slaughtered animals and trampled crops. Our neighbors will spend most of the summer trying to recover from the destruction visited upon them. And many never will!"

Isaac put down his tools, stood and wiped his hands on his pants. He reached over to help Mary stand up and wrapped his arms around her. He let her cry, and when her tears began to subside, he said, "My dearest, we shall continue to help our neighbors. I'm grateful that our farm was not destroyed, even though the authorities viewed me as an ally of Herman Husband. Though the roving bands of militia men did destroy some of our outlying fields, we can readily recover."

Mary and Isaac stood for a long time, feeling the comfort of each other's arms. Mary heard a rustling on the side of the barn and a voice murmur, "Oh, sorry. Never mind." And the intruder scooted back from whence he had come.

"Who was that?"

"Ah, just one of our boys, embarrassed to see his aging parents in such a shameful display in public, of all things!"

Mary giggled and held her husband tighter. Soon they were both laughing. Finally, Mary pulled away and picked up her bonnet.

As she started to walk toward the house, Isaac called to her, smiling broadly. "Mary, let them wed."

THE REBELLION HAD BURNED itself out. After the hangings, Governor Tryon left North Carolina for a new position in the colony of New York. Edmund Fanning followed Tryon as his personal secretary. A new governor, Josiah Martin, was appointed by Parliament; he had a reputation for honesty, and Isaac and Mary were pleased that he was Irish. They had high hopes for their new governor. The most corrupt of the government officials were replaced. Taxes were still too high, but maybe the worst of the corruption had been rooted out.

Within a few months, the farmers and tradesmen were back at work. Mary and Isaac hoped life in the Eno Valley was returning to normal. Their fields were producing well. Isaac found new markets for his produce and put aside some money to help his children set up their own farms as they married and settled down.

·   ·   ·

Only a small number of Friends in the Piedmont had slaves to help with mills or assist with aged persons in their home. But even in the Western Quarter, emancipation for enslaved Africans remained the leading topic of discussion among Friends. The North Carolina General Assembly stepped in to make it difficult for Quakers to manumit their slaves, passing a law that Negroes could only be set free for meritorious service as judged by the county court.

Elizabeth, with all the righteous anger of a fourteen-year-old, demanded of her parents, "Da, tell me. How will the courts define 'meritorious service'? If a slave cares faithfully her whole life for an aged woman, is that not meritorious? Laboring in a mill all day when they have to care for their own family, is that not meritorious? Or does only fighting in war on the side of the militia count? And, I doubt fighting on the side of the Regulators would have been considered meritorious, as if any fighting could ever be?"

Isaac tried to say something, but she continued, her tirade heating up. "Thee said that London Yearly Meeting wrote an epistle about the abomination of importing slaves from Africa. This has to apply to the colonies too! Why are Carolina Friends so slow in recognizing this? Are we not part of England? Why aren't we doing more, Da, why? This is important! These Africans are people, just like we are. Why is it right to buy and sell them like cattle, just because of the color of their skin? What right does our colony have to make such unjust laws?"

"Aye, Elizabeth, I agree with thee. Slavery is unjust. The laws protecting the slave owners are unjust. We are doing—"

Elizabeth interrupted, "Thee is *not* doing enough! Can't Friends listen to God faster? Surely our Lord doesn't want these people to continue to suffer. Oh, I'm so frustrated by our Society dragging our feet! Ma, can't the women's meeting demand that we do more? *Thee* is the leader. Thee can *force* them to change."

Mary shook her head sadly. "My dear daughter, I can't demand that our meeting take a stand. We worship together and try to hear God's will. We can only move as we find the unity to do so. We can only move at God's pace."

"God's pace! Ha! Ma, God cares for all his children, even African children. Are we letting our own feelings dictate God's pace? Are we truly listening?"

"Enough, Elizabeth," Isaac commanded. "Thee is over-wrought, and thy anger is leading thee to say things thee wouldn't say if thee took time to consider thy words."

"But, Ma, Da ..."

"Enough, Elizabeth, enough!" Mary scolded. "Thee may come to the next meeting for business to observe. Observe only, does thee understand? Thee's not yet old enough to take part in discerning God's word."

"Mother..."

"Nay, Elizabeth. I have spoken. Ask God to help thee temper thy anger. Thy time will come when thee can do more. Now, go, finish thy chores."

Mary and Isaac watched Elizabeth stomp off. Isaac said, "Dearest, our daughter isn't yet done with her concerns or her anger."

"Aye, she's young and sure of what's right and what's wrong. But she is correct—Friends are moving too slowly in freeing their slaves, but they must work within the unjust laws. Unfortunately, that's out of our control." She sighed. "Our principles demand that our allegiance is only to God, but our government demands otherwise."

In Tenth Month, the yearly meeting again met in Perquimans. No one from Eno Meeting attended, so the next month, Isaac and Mary traveled to Cane Creek Meeting to hear from William Stanley, a Friend from New Garden who had attended as representative from Western Quarterly. He reported that the meeting had focused almost entirely on the concern for enslaved people in the colony, and had approved a new query against the iniquitous practice of importing Africans to be sold as slaves.

Isaac spoke up. "Friend William, there are few slaves in the Piedmont. While I recognize how important it is that anyone who does own such men and women care for them and guide them up in the ways of goodness, this is of little import to our own lives. What said the yearly meeting about the difficulties we've been suffering because of the past corruption in the local government and the attacks that occurred against our friends and neighbors? Our lands and livelihoods were taken. William Tryon sought to punish us for rebelling, even those of us who weren't participants in the violence. And the Regulators condemned us, too, because we didn't fight. The battle was bloody, and many were killed or wounded. Many of the members of Eno Meeting have moved to Georgia because of Tryon's unreasonable demands. Does the yearly meeting care about us?"

"Ah, Isaac Jackson, we didn't address the physical sufferings thee has witnessed and endured. Our concern is for the spiritual life of our members, not our physical wellbeing. We did affirm our desire to continue to be granted exemption from military service for members in good standing, and we appointed a committee to meet with the new governor, Josiah Martin, asserting our loyalty to the British government."

Mary jumped from her seat. "William Stanley, that sounds as if thee and the yearly meeting care only for our *political* wellbeing. Our people are *suffering*. Many of the women, our friends and neighbors, have been widowed and lost their farms and homes. Family members, especially Quaker families, are moving to Georgia or even west to the Kentucky country. Are the Friends in the east so removed from the rest of us that they ignore us completely?"

William shook his head sadly, "Aye, Mary Jackson, thee's right. We're ignored by the leaders of the yearly meeting, who see their own concerns and interests paramount. I must confess to thee—a few of us represented the western meetings, to be sure, but we're from New Garden and Deep River Meetings, many miles from here. We were not aware of the depth of suffering thy community had endured. We received news of the Rebellion, but it seemed of minor import."

Isaac put his hand on Mary's arm and murmured, "Please, my love, this isn't the place to display thy anger. William Stanley and the others from the western meetings joined as they were able in the business of the yearly meeting. We must assume that they were faithful to the leadings of the Spirit in their dealings."

Mary sat back down. She whispered, "Isaac, thee has chastised me when I hoped for support. I will be silent this time, but the yearly meeting must recognize that not all Friends in our colony are on the coast. Our needs and concerns may be different, but we are seeking God's guidance in our meetings just the same as they are."

Chapter Sixteen

1774

Following the rebellion, Mary needed all her spiritual strength to help her Quaker meeting survive. The membership was greatly reduced. Too many Friends had left the region, moving to Georgia or farther west. Their community was now surrounded by lands sold to non-Quakers, including several who established plantations that used slave labor. Many of the men who had participated with the Regulators had been disowned by their meetings; they believed they did the right thing in standing up to the officials and chose not to be reinstated. Their wives and children felt unwelcome and stopped attending in support of their menfolk.

No strong leader had been found to replace Joseph Maddock following his departure. Friends, both men and women, turned to Mary to guide them. She worked diligently to lead those who remained. Yearly meeting urged them to focus on adherence to the discipline of the Society, and Mary encouraged Friends to be diligent in attending meeting for worship and attending to the business of the meeting. She visited with widows and young mothers. She advised the few young couples asking to be married in the meeting and ensured that their courtships and their weddings were conducted in good order. She engaged Isaac in laboring with several young men who spent unprofitable time in the taverns and gambling rooms that were springing up as Hillsborough grew and prospered.

A young man from Baltimore arrived to teach the children after Rebecca departed for her own marriage. There were fewer families but giving their children a good education was important, and the sound of children in the small schoolhouse brought joy to the Friends.

THREE YEARS AFTER THE REBELLION, the meeting community tried to ignore the drumbeats of a growing revolution that were beginning to reach the Piedmont. The British Parliament, desperate for money and more control over the colonists, passed new laws imposing taxes on British goods, especially on the importation of tea. In early 1774, Friends received news about the protest in the Massachusetts colony, in which colonists, angry at the imposition of "taxation without representation," dumped hundreds of chests of imported tea into the harbor.

Many North Carolinians agreed to boycott trade with Britain, to stand united against the oppression occurring in Boston. Farmers in the colony sent bushels of corn and other commodities north to the Massachusetts Patriots to aid them in standing up to their oppressors. The Jacksons, like many of the Quakers, did not actively participate in the boycott, but they did set aside some of their crops for northern Friends. The Eno Friends felt it necessary to remain neutral in order to be true to their peaceable principles.

A few years earlier, the yearly meeting had appointed a committee to visit the governor who seemed open to hearing their concerns. The Friends had asserted their continuing loyalty, and received reassurance that they would be indulged in the free exercise of their religion, including relief from participation in the military.

The yearly meeting continued to labor with Friends who needed assistance in freeing their slaves. Now, they also sent an epistle to the meetings in the Carolinas, with advice to stay clear of joining in or supporting the uprising against the British.

It was impossible for Mary and Isaac to ignore the political machinations, which continued to dominate the discourse in Hillsborough. On market days, a man was usually standing on a corner reading the news aloud. Preachers shouting about sin and damnation used scriptures to attack the political and social evils of the day. People took sides, and there were frequent arguments, and even fist fights between those who considered themselves Patriots and those who were loyal to the Crown. Mary tried to convince the Friends in her meeting that they should remain a people apart, but it was oh, so difficult.

The threat of war was becoming a real possibility and seemed more likely as the anger between the two sides grew. Eno Friends, particularly the women, expressed their fear about having to live through another bloody rebellion. After three years they were only now beginning to recover from the destruction caused when the Regulators confronted the British. How would they be able to survive if vast armies looted their farms, and their shells and ammunition destroyed their lands? How could they endure losing husbands and sons, neighbors and friends, to the relentless violence of war?

. . .

One soft spring afternoon, Mary sat in the sun, mending the seat of one of her son's breeches. She loved feeling the heat on her face while she worked. For a while she was able to let go of the fear and anger arising in the meeting. May came over, sat beside her, and picked up a needle and thread as her mother handed her a shirt from the mending pile. There was always work to be done with such a large family.

"Ma, does thee remember Patience White, from Piney Woods Meeting? She came to talk with us at last year's annual gathering."

Mary nodded. She set her sewing in her lap and looked at her daughter. She had an idea of what was coming, as she and Isaac had been talking around it.

"Friend Patience and I have corresponded. She has been cleared by her meeting to minister among the Cherokee Indians in western North Carolina. She wants me to accompany her."

"May, thee's twenty-four and of an age when thee should be taking a husband. Has thee considered what this will mean? If thee spends a few years with Patience, thee may never marry and raise a family. Thee will be a spinster. Shouldn't thee wed first and then, when thee's the age Patience is now, thee will be free to travel with the support of thy husband."

"I have been praying about this for many months. Patience believes I have a calling to be a minister of the gospel. I, too, am convinced I'm called to travel in the ministry. I'm not ready to preach on my own, but traveling as Patience's companion is a first step. It will allow me to see if I'm really fit for this work."

Mother and daughter sat in companionable silence for a long while. Mary picked up the breeches again and unhurriedly went back to her sewing. Her daughter leaned back, too anxious to continue her work.

Finally, Mary looked at her. "May, I'll bring this up at the next women's meeting. They'll appoint a committee of elders to sit with thee and examine thy calling. I won't sit on this committee. If they feel that thee is clear to travel with Patience White, and will give thee a certificate that says thee has the approval of the meeting to minister to the Cherokees, then thy father and I'll approve thy going and will help thee with connections and funds." Mary sighed. "I'll be sad to lose thy companionship and thy help here at home. But if it's God's will, we won't stand in the way."

May threw her arms around her mother's neck. "Thank thee, Ma, thank thee! I'll write to Patience and tell her what thee requires of me."

Mary looked lovingly at her daughter. How she wished she also was being called to travel among the Cherokee, preaching the gospel and praying with them. That had been a dream of hers since meeting Mary Peisley, the Irish woman who had visited in the early days of the Eno Meeting. But it was not her calling. She truly was happy that her daughter might be fulfilling this dream in her stead.

A small committee of the women from the meeting met several times with May. A few of them knew Patience White from yearly meeting and were reassured that May would be in experienced and godly hands. They approved her request and provided a certificate in support of her ministry. Soon afterwards, Mary and Isaac said goodbye to their daughter and watched her ride down the lane, standing with their arms around each other until the women were out of sight.

Chapter Seventeen

The talk of coming war did not cease. In Fifth Month of 1775, Patriots in Mecklenburg declared all the laws of Parliament to be void, and called for the end of British rule in North Carolina. Josiah Martin, the colonial governor, fled from his palace to seek protection at Fort Johnston on Cape Fear. He escaped again just before the Whigs, the Americans in support of independence, seized the fort and burned it to the ground. The war against the British had come to North Carolina.

Mary and Isaac were aware of the skirmishes and battles being fought mostly in the northern colonies. Fortunately, the revolution had not yet reached the Piedmont. Leading Quakers continued to try to reconcile the differences between the colonists and the government in North Carolina. After a difficult gathering, the yearly meeting sent an Epistle of Advices to the local meetings, respecting the difficulties of the present times and restating that Friends should not participate in any uprising against the government.

Mary received a copy of the epistle. "Isaac," she said as she read it, "this epistle says what I've been trying to tell

Friends. It's not our work to participate in setting up or putting down kings and government. We must stay faithful to our principles. As I have been saying, we must remain a people apart."

Mary worried. *How could they stand firm in their principles when there were so few of them, and the talk to take sides was so relentless?* She knew God wouldn't abandon them, but she felt so alone in the work she was called to do.

Isaac was appointed to go with a group of representatives, this time to Philadelphia to seek the advice of the more experienced Quakers. Mary went with him, wanting to bring back to Eno Friends a message from the women of Philadelphia meetings. And she looked forward to seeing her sister Katherine for the first time in so many years.

The journey took almost a month of hard travel by horseback. She and Isaac stopped along the way to visit people they knew. They were especially welcomed by Friends living in isolated villages, who hungered to hear their words of ministry and support. Although Mary was not traveling as a gospel minister, as Catherine Phillips and Mary Peisley had been when they came to Eno, the women she visited begged her to worship with them, and her ministry was well-received. She still cringed in remembering her dismay when Catherine criticized the Eno Friends, so she went out of her way to be supportive and loving.

In Philadelphia, Mary had a long visit with Katherine. "Dear sister," she urged, "please, for thy own safety, move south with us. This city isn't safe for Loyalists like thee and thy husband."

Katherine raised her hand to stay her. "Mary, I understand thy concern. Philadelphia is at the center of the conflict. The war is coming close, too close. When the Patriots signed their Declaration of Independence in the State House, we talked long and hard about leaving the colony. But this is our home. My husband's family came to Pennsylvania many years ago with William Penn. He wants to stay on his land, the land of his ancestors. He wants to try to uphold the peaceable vision that Friend William described when he established the colony. We need to stay here."

"Katherine, can thee at least come until the impending war is over? The British troops are well trained and well provisioned. The Patriots can only stand up against them for so long. Thee would only have to be away for a year or two."

Katherine shook her head. "I don't agree that any war would end quickly. My husband says I should hear the Patriots talk in the taverns, and I do hear them openly in the streets. They'll fight as long as they have to. They're determined to break free of British control. We don't advertise that we are Loyalists, but they know. They know. We *are* Quakers, that is obvious. They tell us that even Quakers have a stake in the war. Even Quakers will benefit from the democracy they are touting. Many of our neighbors are angry with us for not joining with the Patriots."

"But, my dear Katherine, how does thee fare in such an atmosphere?"

"We keep our heads down and try to go about our work peacefully. But it's hard. So very hard. Please, let's talk of lighter things. I fear this may be the last time I see thee. We're growing old, and the distance from Pennsylvania to the Eno is so long. I desire that when thee goes back to North Carolina, we have only happy memories of our time together."

Isaac and Mary decided not to linger after his meeting was complete. The war had already reached parts of the Pennsylvania colony. Who knew how long it would be until North Carolina was forced to join the fight? They needed to get to their own home and family, before the hostilities made travel impossible.

Friends in North Carolina soon realized that the Regulator Rebellion was just the start of the opposition to British control in the North Carolina colony. The yearly meeting invited representatives from all meetings in the Carolinas and Georgia to come together to consider what actions Quakers should take in light of the inevitable violence and eventual war. Mary planned to attend with her husband, but when her daughter Elizabeth became ill with a fever, she elected to stay home.

Isaac took the long journey to Perquimans County on the eastern coast. He was accompanied by representatives from Cane Creek, New Garden, and several of the other western meetings.

The clerk, Francis Nixon, opened the meeting with a long period of prayer and worship. He read an epistle from Friends in Philadelphia who reported that the leaders were trying to remain neutral in the face of increasing confrontations between the colonists and the British authorities. The letter raised the concern that young Quaker men could be conscripted into the British Army. They warned Friends in North Carolina to take a stand now in support of the Friends historical testimony against participating in violence.

Isaac asked to be recognized. He stood, hat in hand, head bowed. "Friends, the violence has already come to our colony. We came to the Piedmont twenty-five years ago, bringing hopes of a peaceable kingdom as envisioned by William Penn. The British officials in our county were particularly corrupt, depriving farmers and merchants of their lands, livestock, crops, and goods—and money. Earnest attempts at reconciliation were in vain. The authorities held the power, and our friends and neighbors wanted retribution. Nay, they deserved restitution, but they wanted retribution. There was a bloody battle. Lives were lost. Even worse, the governor's men hanged some of the leaders and destroyed the homes and barns of others. We lost friends and neighbors in the melee. Some Friends joined in and were disowned from their meetings. I'm ashamed that I went along with the mob against the government, at least until it turned violent. I didn't do enough to help Friend Herman Husband negotiate a truce. Perhaps we could've done more to prevent this new call to arms. Haven't we suffered enough? Haven't we?"

He wanted to say more, but he was spent. He sat, his head in his hands, overcome with the emotion of reliving events that had occurred just years ago, much too close to home. His words were followed by a long, deep silence.

Thomas Matthews of Cane Creek Meeting rose next and confirmed the destruction that resulted from the conflict in his county. "I have young sons," he added. "My wife and I are raising them in the discipline of our Society. They say they are committed pacifists, but they are still so tender in years. I fear that if the colonies do go to war against Britain, my boys will be conscripted into the army or imprisoned by the governor's men. We must take a firm stand against war, but we must also receive assurances that our boys won't be forced into the fight."

While the men were discussing and praying under Francis Nixon's leadership, the women met similarly in their own meeting. The clerk, a Friend from an eastern meeting, asked, "Where is Friend Mary Jackson? We need her wise counsel in this matter."

Deborah Stubbs rose. "I have a letter from Mary. She sends her regrets and exhorts us to be strong in our convictions that non-violence is the only response in these times. As Mary would tell thee, we in Eno Meeting have been through too much violence with colonists against the British militia. It was Mary who helped us stand firm. She reminded us that we are British citizens and don't seek to sever relations with our mother country."

The women began their discernment prayerfully and earnestly. While they appreciated Mary's wisdom through Deborah's words, without Mary being present to guide them, they began to squabble. The clerk tried futilely to settle the women back into worship.

"Friends," she announced. "Let's quiet ourselves for a few minutes and then break for the day. We're all tired and hungry."

The men and women continued to meet separately over several days. At times, one of the women carried a message to the men's meeting, telling of their progress toward a statement of their sense and judgment on the issue. And the men, likewise kept the women informed.

At the end, the men's and women's meetings agreed that a delegation from the yearly meeting should meet with the royal governor, Josiah Martin, to express their concerns. The yearly meeting had prepared a message of loyalty to British rule and, more importantly, had reaffirmed their denial of all wars and insurrections.

Isaac returned to Hillsborough and reported to the Eno Quakers that he had been appointed to the committee to visit Governor Martin, and had met with him in New Bern before returning home.

"Friends," he explained, "we told Josiah Martin the

basis of our testimony, what our founder George Fox had said to Oliver Cromwell, that 'We do utterly deny all outward wars and strife and fighting with outward weapons, for any end or under any pretense whatsoever. And this is our testimony to the whole world.' And we begged Governor Martin to continue the policy of exempting Quaker men from military service, in order that we may be true to our conscientious objection to war and continue as faithful subjects to the crown. We further provided assurances that we'll avoid any involvement in disputes between the colonists and the British government. The governor was most receptive to our entreaties, although he made no promises."

The Eno Friends had many questions, which Isaac and Deborah Stubbs did their best to answer fully and thoughtfully.

IN SEVENTH MONTH, the adoption of the Declaration of Independence was announced in newspapers in all of the colonies, and copies soon reached the settlers in the Piedmont. The members of Eno Meeting gathered at the Jacksons' home to read the words, and to try to understand what it meant in stating that the colonies had severed their official connections to Great Britain. They had heard rumors that British ships were en route to North Carolina's coast. Hillsborough area residents recognized that this action was a potential threat inland, and many had already joined the militia to defend their homes. The Patriots, however, had sweetened the pot by offering land west of the mountains after the war for volunteers who joined with men from the northern colonies for at least two years. This was especially appealing to those families whose livelihoods had been taken for taxes or who were yet to recover from the droughts. Even Quakers were tempted by the chance to start over. The promise of the war for independence was that there would be a free country open to all and governed by the colonists themselves.

The North Carolina Provincial Congress met in Hillsborough that year. This move made the conflict an immediate concern for the Eno Friends. They were aware that Great Britain was tightening its control of the colonies—how could they not be? Some of the new laws and regulations imposed by Britain seemed almost designed to provoke the Patriots, who were convinced that British rule endangered their freedom and their livelihoods. After many contentious meetings and discussions, the Friends in Eno Meeting affirmed their loyalty to the Crown. They had preferred to remain neutral, but that became almost impossible when the provincial capital was moved to Hillsborough. The Eno Friends, identifying as British subjects, had no intention of joining the colonists in their uprising. They were tired of the fighting and wanted to live peaceably on their land.

As the war came closer to Hillsborough, the Quakers, including the Jacksons, were labeled as Loyalists, traitors to the new country's bid for independence. The locals who defined themselves as Patriots began to harass the Quakers, who refused to join the fight; they began an information campaign to punish the holdouts. The Provincial Congress then levied taxes on the Quakers that were three and four times what was assessed to the colonists ready to fight. In the Patriots' estimation, the Friends would benefit from independence and so should share in the cost.

Isaac returned from Hillsborough one market day with most of the crops that he had taken to sell. No one wanted to buy Quaker goods. Soon thereafter, their crops and livestock, even the horses they needed for transportation and working the fields, were commandeered by one side or the other in the hostilities. Many of the Friends were afraid to go to town, of dealing with hostile merchants and traders, or even of making their case before the magistrates. Some Friends moved away. A few abandoned their professed ties to Britain and joined with the Patriots. Even the Eno Friends who continued looking to the meeting for support and encouragement were arguing among themselves. Tensions were high. Mary accepted that Friends were motivated by fear and anger, though she struggled to maintain discipline, especially in meetings for business. In First Day and midweek worship, many of the messages were political and reflected the discussions being carried on in the streets.

Later that year the government began enforcing military conscription. Friends reminded Governor Martin about their testimony against participating in war but with little success. In 1776, the yearly meeting declared, "Thus we may with Christian firmness withstand and refuse to submit to the arbitrary injunctions and ordinances of men who assume to themselves the power of compelling others ... to join in carrying on war and of prescribing modes of determining our religious principles."

The yearly meeting also sent messages reminding Friends not to take an oath or affirm allegiance to either side of the warring factions.

THOMAS APPROACHED Mary one afternoon as she worked in the yard. "Ma, may I speak with thee? I have not yet talked with Da, but I'm asking thy blessing." He took a deep breath to steel himself. "I'm led to join the army of the Patriots to fight against the British."

Mary was shocked. "What is thee saying? We—our

family—we are British subjects! We owe our land and our livelihood to the Crown."

"Ma, I'm not a Loyalist like thee and father. I was born in the New World, here by the Eno. This is my land, *my* home, not Ireland or England." He shook his head. "No, I have no loyalty to the king or the parliament across the ocean. Independence is the right way forward for our new country. We must prevail. And I must be a part of it."

Mary looked at her son sadly. "Thomas, thee has been reared in the ways of the Society of Friends. Thee has been raised a pacifist. George Fox warned us against bearing arms, and even Jesus in the Gospel said, 'Blessed are the peacemakers' and 'Turn thy swords into plowshares.' This is how we have taught thee. If thee does this, thee will be disowned by the meeting. Is that what thee wishes? To be expelled from thy family and friends?"

Thomas took out a letter he'd received from a cousin in Philadelphia. In it, he showed her that some Friends believed this was the fight for the soul of the nation. When they were disowned for not upholding the peace testimony, they formed a new society and called themselves Free Quakers, adhering to all the other tenets of the Society of Friends.

"I'm not alone in wanting to join the army," he said. "I'm willing to take this stand and suffer the consequences. War is coming to North Carolina, and I must—and will—do my part."

Mary sat with her son, barely able to hold back the tears. "Thee must talk with thy father. And with the elders at our meeting."

"I know, Ma. I'll do as thee says."

Thomas met with the elders but was not persuaded to reject the call to arms. Mary sat with tears in her eyes at the

Eno Meeting as a letter was read revoking Thomas's membership and acknowledged by the members.

Thomas soon began mustering with the local Patriots in their militia, and by the time British troops were marching toward Hillsborough, he was ready to go to battle against the land of his ancestors. He was not the only young man in Eno Meeting who chose that path, much to the dismay of their parents and the elders of the meeting.

Chapter Eighteen

1777

One fall afternoon, Mary and Isaac sat quietly on their bench by the Eno. Mary had received a letter from her beloved sister. Katherine reported that the Quakers in the Pennsylvania legislature had been forcibly removed from office. Quakers had been involved in governing the colony since it was established, but no longer. The Friends had refused to authorize spending for the revolution from the colony treasury and, even more damning in the eyes of many, they refused to swear loyalty to the Patriots. The Quakers attempted to remain out of the increasing violence, only to be harassed as harboring Loyalist sentiments. Their protestations of neutrality were brushed aside. Katherine wrote that the Patriot government now in charge had denied the Quaker leaders a hearing and had them exiled to a farm in western Virginia.

Mary looked up from reading the letter aloud. "Isaac, the Quaker leaders were sent as a punishment to exile in Winchester. They'll be among Hopewell Friends. Oh, what a blessing! They will be well cared for in their exile."

Isaac said, "I agree with thee. We must write to our kin at Hopewell and offer our assistance. I'm sure that some shillings would be useful with these new mouths to feed."

Silently, he got up and walked close to the river. "Mary, my love, I'm sad for the state of our former colony. William Penn started it with such a big dream, of a peaceable kingdom in the new world. I fear that the men who have taken over the government and banished these Friends have a very different vision for Pennsylvania. I hope the Friends are able to remain out of the fray if the colonists do join the war with the British, but I fear they won't be able to."

"Isaac, what'll we do if war comes to us? After the damage done to our Quaker community during the battles between the Regulators and the British, I don't know how Eno Meeting can endure. So many of our friends and neighbors moved to escape the violence and the corruption. How many more will be tempted to flee west or to Georgia? Joseph Maddock has been tempting more of our meeting members to join him. Will more take him up on his invitation? How can this meeting survive any more removals?"

Isaac walked over to his wife and held her. She rested her head on his chest and wept softly. She hiccoughed several times and whispered, "My love, I'm utterly tired of trying to hold Eno Meeting together. I don't think I have it in me to continue as an elder in the women's meeting. Why won't God release me from this burden that has been laid on me?"

"Mary, we'll do what has to be done. We decided to stay when Friends were leaving for Georgia. We won't leave our home now. Even if Eno Meeting were to fail, God will not forsake us. But thee needs to stay strong. Thee is their leader, whether thee desires it or not."

"Isaac, I'm worn. I've served the women's meeting as clerk for over twenty years. Oh, some others have occasionally stepped up, but mostly they think that sitting at the clerk's table makes them important. They want the title, but not the ministry. They are willing to sit with young couples who wish to marry, but aren't called to the spiritual work of leading this community. They don't see the many hours I spend laboring with families in the meeting, dealing with the yearly meeting, holding them all together during the recent tough times. Some of the strongest women have gone to Georgia. The ones left are barely willing to even attend meeting for worship, much less participate in the business of the meeting."

Isaac started to say something, but stopped when he saw the defeat in Mary's eyes.

"My love," she said, "I'm no longer the carefree, joyful woman thee married. I'm old, gray, and cranky." She held up her hand. "Stop, Isaac. I know thee'll say thee loves me as I am, but I don't know *who* I am anymore. I have no more to give."

They stood in quiet contemplation for a long while. Finally, Isaac turned to her and took her hand. "Mary, I do so love thee, and yes, thee's still as beautiful as the day I wed thee, maybe even more. My love for thee grows each day. I don't know who will step up to relieve thee of the burden that God has laid on thee. Perhaps thy ministry of leadership is drawing to an end. Perhaps thee will be called to give even more. I just don't know.

"I do know that thee needs a break from thy responsibilities," he went on. "Let's travel to Wrightsboro for a visit to Edward and his wife in that colony. We have not seen our son for more than three years, and we have yet to meet our new grandson. Thee does find joy and renewal in our grandchildren. Thee can put away thy cares and let worries about Eno Friends rest for a while."

"Oh, I do so miss Edward." Mary's voice was sad. "Our first son and now so far away. It will be many days journey, and I don't see how we can get away. There is so much to do on the farm and around the house."

Isaac looked at her in surprise. "Mary, Elizabeth, our baby, is already nineteen years old, and she has taken on more and more adult responsibilities while thee has been tending to the needs of the meeting. Thomas and Isaac are older than she. We can ask my brothers to look in on them, and Hannah isn't so far away. I believe the change of scenery will help thee become clearer in whatever work God is calling thee, whether to continue to lead the Eno women or in some other ministry."

"Oh, Isaac, what a wise idea. I don't know if it will happen, but just the thought brings me great pleasure. It'll be good for us to get away for a long while, just the two of us, as when we were first wed."

"Mary, we will make it happen" Isaac assured her. "We'll go to Georgia and see our son and dandle our new baby grandson. We can see our old friends who left Hillsborough and bring back their news. Even that will be a welcome joy to our neighbors. Remember, our Lord promised us 'When thou passest through deep waters, I'll be with thee.'"

Isaac made most of the plans for traveling, trying to relieve Mary of any added work. He contacted the neighbors about their plans and arranged with his sons for the care of the animals and farm. Elizabeth agreed that she was able to do the cooking and cleaning. She smiled. "And I'll keep my older brothers on the straight and narrow path." Her brothers were young adults, Elizabeth knew, but sometimes she thought they acted like children.

"Agreed," her father said. "Although I'm not appointing thee as the boss of thy brothers. They, too, recognize that thy mother is weary and needs to let go of her responsibilities for a while. I'll warn them that they should behave as though we were here while thy mother and I are away, to get all their work done every day, and to help thee with thy household chores." He hugged his daughter. "Thy mother will be able to relax for a month or two knowing our home is in thy capable hands."

The road from the Jacksons' home was well-traveled in some of the places, but there were still sections where the path was not so clear, and there were many rivers and streams to cross. They decided to take their time, visiting Friends along the way and stopping for refreshment near pretty creeks and meadows. They arrived in Wrightsboro in a little more than three weeks.

Mary was thrilled to meet her grandchildren and to get to know her daughter-in-law, whom she had met only a few times before Edward's wedding. She spent hours cuddling with the baby and laughing at the other children at play. Isaac was right—she did so love these children. She guessed this would be the last time she would be able to visit them in Georgia, so she intentionally stored up memories for when she was sitting quietly at home, mending or just enjoying the view from her bench by the Eno. Some of the older children drew pictures for her, and even the toddler put her scribbles on a scrap of paper.

While Isaac visited and talked with the men he knew from Eno, Mary spent long hours in consultation with the women who had moved with Joseph Maddock's group. She told them of her distress and asked them to help her find clarity. Could she lay down the burden of leadership or was

God asking her to do more? They listened deeply to her concerns and held her in prayer. By the end of her visit, Mary was clear that she would continue as she had been, and would consciously try to nurture leadership in the next generation of Eno women. She was at peace.

After their visit to Wrightsboro had lasted several months, both Isaac and Mary were ready to return home. She knew she would miss her family and friends but they had many warm memories to carry home and to share with Eno Friends.

The Wrightsboro Friends loaded their cart with food for the journey. Isaac and Mary gathered a large packet of letters to take back to the families who remained in North Carolina. The women of the meeting had made Mary a scrap quilt as a gift, which delighted her. Each of them had made blocks which they had signed with their name or initials. Some were beautifully stitched; some were crudely made with coarse fabric. But all were made with love. A few of the blocks had brief references to passages from scripture or words of encouragement. The center block, in a pale blue fabric, included a paraphrased passage from Luke 12:48: "To whomsoever has committed much, of her they will ask the more." As Mary gently smoothed her finger over the finely worked stitchery, she knew the centerpiece was especially chosen to encourage her in her ministry. She would treasure this forever, and it would remind her daily of her commitment to the Quakers who left Eno and to those who remained.

Isaac and Mary didn't dally on the trip home, as the growing, constant threat of war hung over them. On their return to Eno, they learned that the British General Charles Cornwallis had marched to Hillsborough with all his troops, but fortunately, the Patriots didn't engage them in battle. Mary and Isaac breathed a sigh of relief at the news that his troops then left for South Carolina. The respite at Edward's home had been so good for her, and now she was anxious to resume her care for the Eno Meeting community.

IN EARLY FALL Mary received a letter from May, who was working in the west with Patience White. She eagerly rushed to the barn to read it to Isaac. Opening it, she read, "Dear Ma and Da, Do not worry. Patience and I are safe."

Mary paused; her heart seemed to skip. Her beloved daughter had been in danger, and she was unaware. She looked at Isaac with fear in her eyes. He put down his tools and walked to stand beside her. "Go on," he said. "Read the rest of the letter. She is alive and safe or she couldn't have written."

Mary began again, reading the dreaded words. "Patience and I are safe. This past summer, a Patriot general, Griffith Rutherford, waged a campaign against the Cherokees in the western part of our colony. A small group of Moravians were at work east of us and heard that he was coming with his troops to attack the natives. They helped us escape, and we're now staying with them in their community in Salem."

Mary lowered the paper. "Oh, Isaac, we must go to her. We must bring her home." He hugged her and pointed back to the letter. He was overcome himself and unable to speak.

May's letter continued, "We heard that the army devastated a large portion of Indian country and slaughtered many of the natives. I am heartsick. We have been living and working with these people for many months. They are kind, loving people who only want to be left alone to raise their families. We wanted to wait until it was safe to return. Patience and I wished to reassure ourselves that our Cherokee friends had survived the attack, but they were no longer in the area. We heard that many, even women and children, were slaughtered. We have no idea where they have gone. All we hear is that the Cherokee leaders signed a treaty which ceded to the whites all lands east of the Blue Ridge Mountains. Oh, Ma, Pa, we have stolen even more land from the natives! We have become sinfully greedy! And I say 'we' because even though we didn't participate in their exile, we're also to blame because we got our home on the Eno River because white settlers pushed the Indians off their land. How could God let this happen? How could God see us as anything but sinners?"

There was a tear stain at the bottom, smearing May's signature. Mary and Isaac stood in silence, holding each other. Both had tears flowing down their cheeks.

Mary looked at her husband. "Isaac, we must send word that she must return home. She *must*. Our daughter is hurting. She says she's safe. She may be physically safe, but she is spiritually broken. Isaac, go to her, please."

"Mary, my love, our daughter is a grown woman. She and Patience White must make their own decisions. We'll encourage her to meet with Friends in New Garden to test their leading to continue. Perhaps, they will go farther west to again minister to the Cherokee when the threat of violence abates. Perhaps they will seek another direction for their ministry. I will go, of course, if May sends word that she wishes to come home. We can but hold her in our hearts."

Chapter Nineteen

1780

After General Cornwallis moved his troops south, there was no other military action in North Carolina for almost four years. British authority was ended in the colony. Although the progress of the war elsewhere still dominated the news, Friends found it easier to be faithful in upholding their pacifist principles.

That is, until the legislature increased its demands for supplies for the army. Property seizures followed. The Quakers held to an ideal of staying neutral, but they were accused of being traitors because they wouldn't participate in supporting the war. The colonial government first doubled, then tripled, then quadrupled taxes on Quakers as a result of their non-participation. Justice demanded that Quakers who were "sharing the benefits" of the war should bear a proportionate part of the cost. The Western Quarterly Meeting issued an advice to local meetings, to maintain their "peaceable Testimony by an Honest refusal to Act or Willingly (comply) with any Requisitions or Demands made by men in Supporting or Carrying on wars, or the shedding of blood."

At a First Day meeting, with all the Friends gathered in prayer, Mary stood and said, "The first Friends accepted persecution for professing their faith. Can we do any less? We must not compromise our religious convictions. And we must accept the consequences. We may have to sacrifice our money and our property. We won't sacrifice our sons and brothers. We won't sacrifice our souls. We won't sacrifice our commitment to the path of peace given to us by Christ Jesus."

She called on the women to stand together, to provide food and shelter for those families who suffered most for their consciences.

THE WAR eventually came closer to the Eno Friends. In 1781, General Cornwallis and a large army marched across the western Piedmont. He and his men briefly occupied the town of Hillsborough and used this as an opportunity to recruit Loyalists to their cause. In March, they headed toward Guilford County. There, the Patriot army under the command of General Nathanael Greene was able to defeat the British troops, who suffered great losses. Greene's troops were able to drive Cornwallis and his men into Virginia.

The third colonial governor, Thomas Burke, was installed at the state capital, which was now located in Hillsborough. Unlike his predecessor, Burke encouraged the militia and their resistance to the British and Tory forces. On a foggy fall morning on the twelfth of Ninth Month, the Loyalist army, led by David Fanning, was able to enter the town undetected and quickly overpowered the local militia. Fanning's men secured the town and captured over two hundred prisoners, including Governor Burke. Several former Quakers were among the imprisoned. The raiding army ransacked the government offices and looted the supplies. Many of the men got into the liquor stored in cellars and drunkenly loaded up the wagons with their booty. By noon, British troops left Hillsborough, heading back to Wilmington.

When he heard what had happened, the Patriot General John Butler immediately rode with his men to the ford on Cane Creek, near the mill owned by the Quaker Thomas Lindley. They ambushed the British attackers to rescue the prisoners, and killed several of the leaders.

After the battle at Thomas Lindley's Mill, the members of the Spring Meeting on the lower Cane Creek put out a call for aid. There were hundreds of wounded men from both sides, many using the local meetinghouse as a makeshift hospital. Mary and Isaac loaded up the wagon with herbs and salves, cloths to use as bandages, blankets, and other supplies. Elizabeth, now married, was living at home while her husband was in the Kentucky County looking for land to claim for their home. She went with her parents to help, as did her brothers Isaac and John. Mary's brother-in-law agreed to look after their livestock, since he didn't feel able to travel at the time. Along the way, they stopped at the homes of their neighbors, asking for contributions of supplies and for others to accompany them.

When they arrived at the Lindley mill, they looked at the chaos. Wounded men were lying on the ground all around the meetinghouse grounds. Boys were rushing back and forth with pails of water, and others were carrying buckets of old bandages to be washed in the creek. Girls were doing their best to comfort the groaning men and assist the few surgeons who were providing medical care.

Isaac and his sons went to work unloading their wagons while Mary and Elizabeth grabbed bandages and blankets to join the women in caring for the wounded. The men then went to assist in digging graves for the dead. So many had died that they were forced to bury them in mass graves with no coffins. Isaac noticed that an open grave already had fourteen bodies that he could see, and this was only one of the many graves.

The work went on for several days before all of the wounded were stabilized and the dead buried. The members of Spring Meeting invited everyone to join them in a meeting for worship and settled into silence, exhausted from the work and the grief. Several of the men and women offered heartfelt prayers consigning the dead to God's mercy and begging for relief for the suffering survivors. One elder of the meeting spoke at length about the Quaker testimony that Christians should not engage in violence, but added that they had a responsibility to help heal the results.

The Jacksons stayed in the area for a few extra days to help clean up the debris from the makeshift hospital. Mary tended to the men who were too wounded to move. Finally, they climbed into their wagons and headed home.

Chapter Twenty

1781

The war was coming to an end. After Cornwallis was defeated at New Garden, he marched his troops to Yorktown in the Virginia colony. There, he finally surrendered. The British appealed to the Americans for peace.

Despite the reports of continued skirmishes, Mary renewed her desire to travel in the ministry. She always hearkened back to that early visit from Catherine Philips and Mary Peisley. On a mild fall day, she and Isaac strolled down to the bench by the river, their special place where they felt God's presence deeply. Mary was melancholy, so Isaac sat beside her in companionable silence.

When Mary spoke, she said, "Isaac, I wanted to do so much more with my life. I wanted to travel in the ministry like our visitors from overseas. I would have liked to be a preacher in our faith. My life has been of little import."

"Sweet Mary. That is thy pride speaking. Thee has borne me eight fine children who have grown to adulthood. Thee was a tower of strength in the Eno Meeting through

the most difficult times and held us together as our membership declined, and the meeting stayed strong. God called
thee to this work, and thee answered the call."

"Aye, my husband, 'tis true. But our children no longer
need me. I'm feeling my years. I'm tired and worn, but thee
is a blessing to me."

"No more so than thee is to me," Isaac said.

Mary knew she had put her efforts into growing the
local meeting, from its early days through the building of
the meetinghouse and school. She and Isaac had worked
tirelessly to dissuade their neighbors from participating in
the Regulator Rebellion. They tried to remain loyal to Great
Britain prior to the American Revolution. Even as the Eno
Meeting had dwindled in numbers, the Jacksons and their
extended family struggled to maintain a Quaker presence in
Hillsborough.

Despite Mary's wish to take up the work of a traveling
ministry, her health began to fail. She was forced to stay
close to home, and Isaac grew worried. A few months later,
he sent word to their children and their families to come
home if they were able. He spent long days by Mary's
bedside, holding her hand and softly telling her stories
recalling their life together. Hannah came to help. She
brought her father bowls of soup and freshly baked bread.
She encouraged him to keep up his strength, but he was
only able to take a few bites.

"Oh, Mary, my love," he said, "thee has been a blessing
in my life and a boon companion. Thee is my strength and
my support; thee is my very life. How will I go on without
thee by my side?"

Hannah sat beside him, holding his hand and her mother's hand. "Da, Ma is in great pain. She's suffering, though
she tries not to let thee see; she loves thee so. God is calling
her home. Ma's work on earth is done. Say thy goodbye and

release her from the bonds of earth. I'll be here for thee, and thee will be able to go on."

Isaac did as his daughter said, and together they watched as Mary's spirit left her earthly body. He turned to Hannah and held her, weeping inconsolably. He could not imagine his life without his one true love and helpmeet. When he was able to speak, he looked at his daughter. "Hannah, my precious dear, our lives won't be the same without her."

"Da, we will carry on her work and her legacy, even though she's no longer among us. We'll be strong for her, and she will watch over us from her place in heaven."

Isaac pushed on for several more years, but his heart was not in it. He died quietly, surrounded by his children and grandchildren. Mary and Isaac Jackson were buried together in the Eno Meeting burying ground.

The meeting continued, but without Mary Jackson's strong leadership, they were never as vibrant as they once were. Eno Meeting joined with Spring Meeting and eventually folded in 1843, and the meeting school was turned over to the town.

Historical Note

This is a work of fiction based loosely on the life of Mary Jackson, who lived for most of the 1700s, and uses the limited information I could find about the original Quaker community in Hillsborough, North Carolina. Contrary to standard Quaker practice, Eno Friends Meeting did not keep records, and no journals or letters have been found from the early days of the community. The founding of Eno Meeting and its subsequent decline are documented occasionally in the minutes of Cane Creek Meeting and other nearby meetings, as is the Eno Meeting's dereliction in keeping records. Mary Clare Engstrom[1] provided all the data she was able to find about these people, but, of necessity, her information is drastically incomplete.

Most of the historical events are described as accurately as possible, although I shifted a few dates and locations for the sake of the story. I did take liberty with the journey from Pennsylvania to North Carolina. The journey south went over trading paths worn by Native Americans and, in some places, the Friends had to carve openings through deep woods. In reality, these trails were often too narrow for wagons. Women and young children usually rode horses, and the men and older boys walked the entire way. I gave them a wagon because it better fit the story I wished to tell.

I tried to use common eighteenth-century first names combined with the actual family names of Eno settlers. Joseph Maddock and Deborah Stubb were actual people, and I tried to portray their actions to the extent known. Most of the other people are fictional, even though the names may be actual names in the region. This includes, for example, Sarah Chamness, Rachel Maddock, Richard Mendenhall, and Patience White.

I simplified the growth of Eno Meeting. Theirs was a complicated process, having first to seek permission from Cane Creek Meeting to hold First Day and mid-week meetings for worship, then being granted status as a Preparative Meeting whose business was overseen by the Cane Creek Friends. Eventually the settlers were designated as a meeting, allowing them control of their own business meetings, but their status was precarious, and they were often reduced back to preparative status at the request of Cane Creek Meeting or the Western Quarter.

Quaker men and women held separate meetings for conducting the business of the community. The women's meeting was responsible for overseeing marriages, family relations, education of children, discipline, care for widows and orphans, and support of women who had a spiritual calling. Mary Jackson was appointed to be the first overseer for the women of Eno Friends, and this is recorded in the minutes of Cane Creek Meeting. She had a reputation as a gifted minister and leader, but little else is known about her. She became the clerk when Eno formally became a meeting. The clerk was primarily responsible for the administrative functions of the meeting and for guiding the discernment in their meetings for business. Because Quaker meetings did not have pastors or paid ministers, the clerk was expected to work with other women to provide pastoral and spiritual care for the Friends in her meeting.

I describe Isaac as a significant person in the work of the yearly meeting, the larger body of Quakers in North Carolina. However, his name never appears in the minutes as a representative nor appointed to committees. I needed to place him there to help portray the work of the larger body of Quakers during this period. I also referred to Mary's influence among the women at yearly meeting, but this is only an assumption as the minutes of the women's meeting have been lost.

In 1781, Mary Jackson was recorded in the Cane Creek minutes as being an approved and recognized minister of the gospel. While there are many Mary Jacksons, I'm choosing to believe that it was Isaac and Mary's daughter Mary Jackson, called May in this book, who was recognized as a minister and became a well-known and powerful Quaker preacher in the Carolinas.

In most genealogical records, but not all, Isaac is identified as having been born in 1717. Mary was born in 1711, 1713, or 1720, depending on the source. One source said their marriage happened in 1730, which would have been unlikely given that most sources agree that Isaac was born in 1717. I chose to use 1720 as the year of Mary's birth and 1740 for their wedding.

I was unable to definitively identify her family. There are many Isaac Jacksons, Mary Jacksons, and even several marriages of an Isaac and a Mary Jackson in the historical records. Those were popular names in the larger Jackson clan. I found genealogical records stating that Mary and Isaac had three adult male children when they moved to North Carolina in 1750, which does not fit with their presumed marriage in 1740. I also found reference to Mary having one child, three children, seven children, and eight children. I chose to use the eight children identified on the website *mykindred.com, record F2301*, mostly because it fit best in the stories I wanted to tell. I wish I could have been more successful in precisely identifying Isaac's and Mary's genealogy. I apologize if I'm wrong.

The Regulator Rebellion is little known outside North Carolina, but some historians consider it a precursor to the American Revolution. The Quaker involvement in the Rebellion, including Herman Husband's role, is well-documented and is known to be a major factor in the decline of Eno Meeting. Two very good references are by Carole Troxler[2] and Marjoleine Kars[3]. I took liberties with the episode outside the courthouse when Herman Husband arrived to present their demands. I combined several historical events to keep the focus on Mary's story. Husband was an interesting and complicated person and worthy of a more complete story in his own right. One good source is by Bruce Stewart.[4]

In the chapters on the Regulator Rebellion, Herman Husband, Simon Dixon, and the named government officials were real persons, although the specific actions depicted in this story are fictionalized. Twelve men were sentenced to be hanged for their roles in the Rebellion; six were pardoned the night before. The other six Regulators were hanged in Hillsborough on June 6, 1771. Four have been identified—Benjamin Merrill, Capt. Robert Messer, Robert Matear, and James Pugh—and are named on the site's historical plaque. The names of the other two are not identified in the government's records, and they are lost to history. Pugh, the only Quaker named, was the brother of Herman Husband's first wife. I chose for the sake of my story to identify one of the unnamed men as Quaker. Who knows? He might have been.

So, I used the historical information I could find and

extrapolated from eighteenth-century Quaker writings to imagine messages given in worship and the text of their minutes. Most of the other characters, their thoughts, conversations, messages, personalities, etc., and of course, all the all the interactions between Mary and the other characters are purely from my imagination.

1. Engstrom, Mary Claire. "Early Quakers in the Eno River Valley ca. 1750-1847." Durham, NC: The Association for the Preservation of the Eno River Valley: *Eno*, Volume 7, Number 2, 1-74.
2. Troxler, Carole Watterson. *Farming Dissenters: The Regulator Movement in Piedmont North Carolina*. Raleigh: North Carolina Department of Cultural Resources, Office of Archives and History, 2011.
3. Kars, Marjoleine. *Breaking Loose Together: The Regulator Rebellion in Pre-Revolutionary North Carolina*, Chapel Hill and London: The University Of North Carolina Press, 2002.
4. Stewart, Bruce E. *Redemption from Tyranny: Herman Husband's American Revolution*. Charlottesville: University of Virginia Press, 2000.

References

The Holy Bible, King James Version. Cambridge Edition: 1769; *King James Bible Online*, 2023. www.kingjamesbibleonline.org.

Baker, Pearl. *The Story of Wrightsboro 1768-1964.* Thomson, GA: Wrightsboro Restoration Foundation, 1980, 4th printing.

Dowless, Don. "Preserving the Quaker Way: Guidance of Quaker Social Life by the Monthly Meetings in Colonial North Carolina." Greensboro, NC: *The Southern Friend*, Volume XI, Number 2, Autumn, 1989, 1–16.

Engstrom, Mary Claire. "Early Quakers in the Eno River Valley ca. 1750–1847." Durham, NC: The Association for the Preservation of the Eno River Valley: *Eno*, Volume 7, Number 2, 1–74.

Hinshaw, Seth B. *The Carolina Quaker Experience 1665–1985: An Interpretation.* North Carolina Yearly Meeting, North Carolina Friends Historical Society, 1984.

Kars, Marjoleine. *Breaking Loose Together: The Regulator Rebellion in Pre-Revolutionary North Carolina*, Chapel Hill and London: The University Of North Carolina Press, 2002.

Magnuson, Tom. "The Roads Made the Town: The Approaches to Hillsborough in Pre-Modern Times." Durham, NC: The Association for the Preservation of the Eno River Valley: *Eno*, Volume 2, Number 2, July, 1999, 1–12.

Phillips, Catherine. *Memoirs of the Life of Catherine Phillips to Which are Added Some of Her Epistles.* London: Printed and sold by James Phillips and Son, 1797.

Stewart, Bruce E. *Redemption from Tyranny: Herman Husband's American Revolution.* Charlottesville: University of Virginia Press, 2000.

Troxler, Carole Watterson. *Farming Dissenters: The Regulator Movement in Piedmont North Carolina.* Raleigh: North Carolina Department of Cultural Resources, Office of Archives and History, 2011.

Weeks, Stephen. *Southern Quakers and Slavery: A Study in Institutional History.* NY: Bergman Brothers, 1968. [originally Baltimore: Johns Hopkins Press, 1896]

Wood, Peter H. *"When the Roll is Called Up Yonder": Black History of Hillsborough, North Carolina.* Hillsborough, NC: The Burwell School, 2005.

Author Note

When my husband and I moved to Hillsborough, North Carolina, we discovered that the property we bought was on land originally granted by Lord Granville to a Quaker community from Pennsylvania. (These British grants were made after the original indigenous tribes – the Occaneechi and Eno Indians – had been pushed further north.) After reading the writings of Mary Claire Engstrom and visiting the Quaker archives at Guilford College, we learned that no meeting records, diaries, or letters had been found from the once-thriving, eighteenth-century Eno Friends Meeting.

From the minutes of the "Mother of Meetings," Cane Creek Meeting, we learned that Mary Jackson was appointed an overseer of Eno Meeting (in modern terms, she would have been named "clerk" of the women's meeting.) I have served as clerk of my own Quaker meeting during difficult, but definitely not turbulent, times, and I envisioned what it would be like to lead the women of the meeting as they set up their farms, cared for their families, established worship, built a school and meeting house, and tried to survive as a community through drought, conflict, and war. How would Mary Jackson hold the meeting together when outside forces impacted their pacifist community? What spiritual and personal resources and relationships did she turn to in times of crisis and concern? Who was Mary Jackson as a real person?

I am grateful to the many friends who helped me along the way. Gwen Gosney Erickson, the curator at the Friends Historical Collection at Guilford College, provided valuable guidance, references, and wonderful connections. Mark Chilton gave me his typed transcription of the handwritten records of Cane Creek women's meeting for business. Courtney Smith, the Exhibits and Programs Coordinator at the Orange County Historical Museum, was a continuing source of encouragement and support. My early readers, Debra Frantz, Rausie Hobson, John David Ferrer, and Marcia Winters were diligent in helping me get the story and tone right. Paula Stahel, an outstanding editor from Breath and Shadows Productions, guided me during the revision process; her suggestions and insights were an invaluable contribution to my manuscript. Lia Fairchild carefully proofread the final text. Clearly, any errors and sloppy writing are mine and mine alone. I am so very grateful to Melissa Bourbon, an author and book designer from Hillsborough, who designed the captivating illustration and created the perfect cover for my novel. And then, she did an excellent job of laying out the book and preparing it for publication.

Most importantly, my husband, David Haines, was a terrific sounding board, a source of continuous encouragement, an early (and later) reader, and an excellent researcher. One of his biggest contributions to this book, and to eighteenth-century North Carolina Quaker research, was to transcribe hundreds of pages of eighteenth-century handwritten manuscript minutes from North Carolina Yearly Meeting, Western Quarterly, and the Standing

Committee of the Yearly Meeting. He also transcribed the
1755 Discipline of the North Carolina Yearly Meeting, and
the 1704 Discipline of Philadelphia Yearly Meeting on
which North Carolina based its Discipline. He developed a
skill in reading the early eighteenth-century penmanship, so
I could easily read the typescripts for the tidbits I needed.
The transcriptions are now available at the Friends Historical Collection at Guilford College.

About the Author

Nancy Learned Haines decided in ninth grade to become an engineer, to use her love of math in practical applications. She received a master's degree in industrial engineering and worked for almost seventeen years as an engineer before she decided that she didn't have to continue in a career choice made while she was barely in high school.

Her husband, David, had been collecting books by and about Quakers for many years and had introduced her to the lure of used bookstores. So, when she "retired" as an engineer, she became a bookseller. Her bookstore, Vintage Books, offered general used books and wonderful antiquarian books in a renovated barn in Massachusetts, with a specialty in used and rare Quaker books and manuscripts; at that time, Vintage Quaker Books was the largest source of out-of-print Quaker books in the world. Nancy closed the shop after twenty-five years in business.

In 2000, they acquired a collection of letters written between a pacifist who went to France with the Quakers during World War I and his activist girlfriend at home in Cambridge, Massachusetts. This collection is the basis for Nancy's first book, *We Answered With Love: Pacifist Service in World War I*. She also wrote a children's book, *Approved! A Story About Quaker Meeting for Business*, which introduces children to the Quaker process of communal decision-making. Currently, all her projects have something to do with Quakers.

Nancy and David now live in Hillsborough, North

Carolina, on land granted to Quakers on the ancestral grounds of the Occaneechi and Eno Tribes of Native Americans along the Eno River. Their property was originally deeded to the Quaker Fincher family. Discovering that tidbit piqued their interest in learning more about the Friends who settled along the Eno River.

The original Eno Friends Meeting was laid down in 1843. All that remains now is the Friends cemetery, which is on private land. Nancy is a member of the new Eno Friends Meeting in Hillsborough, which was established in 2013.

For more information, visit her website—https://nancy-haines.wordpress.com.